Blue Blood

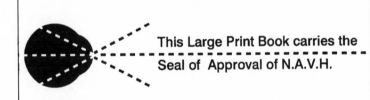

This Large Print Book carries the
Seal of Approval of N.A.V.H.

Blue Blood

A Debutante Dropout Mystery

Susan McBride

Published in 2004 by arrangement with Avon Books, an imprint of HarperCollins Publishers, Inc.

Wheeler Large Print Softcover.

The text of this Large Print edition is unabridged.
Other aspects of the book may vary from the original edition.

Set in 16 pt. Plantin by Christina S. Huff.

Printed in the United States on permanent paper.

Library of Congress Cataloging-in-Publication Data

McBride, Susan, 1964–
    Blue blood : a debutante dropout mystery / Susan McBride.
      p. cm.
    ISBN 1-58724-811-5 (lg. print : sc : alk. paper)
    1. Women detectives — Texas — Dallas — Fiction.
2. Restaurateurs — Crimes against — Fiction. 3. Undercover operations — Fiction. 4. Dallas (Tex.) — Fiction.
5. Restaurants — Fiction. 6. Debutantes — Fiction. 7. Large type books. I. Title.
PS3563.C33363B55 2004
813'.54—dc22   2004057179

This book is dedicated to everyone who has ever felt like an outsider.

As the Founder/CEO of NAVH, the only national health agency solely devoted to those who, although not totally blind, have an eye disease which could lead to serious visual impairment, I am pleased to recognize Thorndike Press★ as one of the leading publishers in the large print field.

Founded in 1954 in San Francisco to prepare large print textbooks for partially seeing children, NAVH became the pioneer and standard setting agency in the preparation of large type.

Today, those publishers who meet our standards carry the prestigious "Seal of Approval" indicating high quality large print. We are delighted that Thorndike Press is one of the publishers whose titles meet these standards. We are also pleased to recognize the significant contribution Thorndike Press is making in this important and growing field.

Lorraine H. Marchi, L.H.D.
Founder/CEO
NAVH

★ Thorndike Press encompasses the following imprints: Thorndike, Wheeler, Walker and Large Print Press.

Acknowledgments

As always, I'm indebted to my mother, Pat McBride, for her support through thick and thin, and to my dad, Jim McBride, for cheering each small success.

Having an agent like Victoria Sanders and an editor like Sarah Durand is akin to winning the lottery! My thanks to both for seeing something special in this book.

My sincere appreciation to the wonderful Alice Peck, whose brilliant insights made the story shine.

I am lucky to have the hardest working Web Diva in the biz, Janell Schiffbauer, who designed SusanMcBride.com and has kept it running like a well-oiled wheel for the past few years.

And, finally, much love to my amazing family and friends for their faith in me and for making every day of my life such a blast! You all rock.

"It's not your blue blood,
your pedigree or your college degree.
It's what you do with your life that counts."

— Millard Fuller, Founder,
Habitat for Humanity

Prologue

 Unlucky.

That's what she was.

Molly O'Brien pulled her T-shirt down over her head, not bothering to tuck the hem into her jeans. She squinted at her watch, barely illuminated by the faint stream of light flowing in from the hall, and she groaned when she realized it was well past midnight. God, how she wished she'd weaseled out of helping Bud Hartman close the place! He was creepy enough in broad daylight. If that didn't bite, now she also owed the babysitter overtime.

She grabbed her purse from its hook, slammed her locker and turned around.

Bud stood in the doorway, watching.

"Christ," she breathed, her heartbeat thumping overloudly. *How long had he been there?* She swallowed and willed herself to sound far calmer than she felt. "You almost gave me a heart attack."

His lips curved like a Halloween pumpkin. "You girls are too damned jumpy."

"Hard not to be with you sneaking around."

"Hell, it's my joint. I can do what I want. Or *who* I want."

His eyes gleamed from the shadows, and a chill shot up her spine. She tightened her hand on her purse.

"Well, I'm taking off, okay? The money from the register's in the bank bag on your desk. I've gotta get home to pay the babysitter. I'm already an hour late."

But he didn't move. His body filled the doorway, blocking her path.

Molly's only alternative was to squeeze past him. He put an arm across the threshold, but she bit her lip and ducked beneath. She kept going up the hallway, into the kitchen and toward the rear exit, which loomed dead ahead.

"What's your hurry, O'Brien?" he growled from behind her and caught her shoulder, jerking her back. He spun her around and forced her against the stainless-steel countertop. The cold metal jabbed hard into her spine, and she grimaced.

"Hey, cut it out!"

"Then stop playin' so hard to get."

She felt the hot hiss of his breath on her face as his body pinned hers beneath him. He was six-two to her five-six, and he outweighed her by at least a hundred pounds. He had her trapped, and he knew it.

"You're hurting me, Bud."

But he didn't seem to care.

His brown eyes bore into hers and the stretch

of his brow beneath the slicked-back hair glistened with sweat. "What's the problem, huh?" He smelled of beer and testosterone, and bile rose in her throat. "You were nice to me once."

"Temporary insanity," she said.

He grinned.

Her mouth dry, Molly wet her lips and tried again. "I've got a six-year-old boy, remember? I'm a mother, not one of your bimbos. I can't screw around with my life, not anymore."

For a moment, he hesitated, and his hold on her loosened the slightest bit. A bubble of hope swelled in her chest.

And burst.

His head came down fast and hard, his mouth smothering hers. His tongue rammed past her teeth, choking her.

You disgusting piece of. . . .

With her free hand, she reached behind her, frantically looking for something, anything, to get her out of this. Her fingertips ran into a wooden block and then upward into slender handles.

She slipped a knife from its slot and blindly swung it as Bud came up for air.

He howled and released her.

Molly dropped the knife and sprinted to the exit door.

Flinging herself into her Ford pickup, she took off in a squeal of tires, never glancing back.

Chapter 1

 Music played in the background, a soft tinkling of piano keys that filtered into the yellow-walled dining room at the Palm, a swanky restaurant with white linen tablecloths, pricey lobster and steak, and an even more expensive clientele that Mother had selected for what she'd told me was a "girls' night out."

Ha.

I could swear the tune that teased my ears was "Mack the Knife," a fitting soundtrack for the murderous thoughts running through my head, though I could hardly hear the notes over the careful rise of her voice.

"Did I tell you, Andrea, that Trey has a Ph.D. in philosophy from Southern Methodist?" Cissy drawled above the hum of surrounding conversation, laying a smile so thick on Haskell E. Maxwell III that he blushed and nearly fogged up his Coke-bottle lenses.

"Hmmm," I turned away from Mr. Maxwell entirely to plant a glare on my mother that could've set her fashionably styled blond hair on fire. "Come to think of it, I don't believe you told me anything at all about Trey."

She fluttered her eyes, playing innocent. Badly. "Oh, didn't I? Just an oversight, darling, I swear."

I swore as well. At her, under my breath.

Her "oversight" had started with a lie about dinner this evening — "Oh, it'll be fun, Andrea, just us girls at the Palm, what do you say?" — never letting on for a moment that — surprise! — our reservation would include a *ménage à* Trey, as it were. A blind date for *moi*. My prospective match, not surprisingly, was the son of a bosom buddy of Mother's. He was nearly forty, rather gawky (I'm being kind), and never married, which might be a chronic problem for him if what I'd seen so far was any indication.

"He's a musician, you know."

"Oh?" I arched an eyebrow at Trey, studying the long face, drooping hair, and geeky specs with black rims. Did he secretly wield a Fender Stratocaster for a rock band when he wasn't off philosophizing? For a moment, he almost seemed interesting.

Until Mother answered, just a tad too brightly, "He happens to be a brilliant pipe organist."

My eyebrow fell, along with any spark of intrigue that had flared at the idea of Haskell III as a closet Rolling Stone.

"It's a difficult instrument, Andrea, sweetie, one that requires years of study. Trey is nothing if not dedicated, and that's such a rare quality in men of your generation." She put the hard sell on me, like a Mary Kay cosmetics lady just a lipstick shy of a pink Cadillac. "Did I tell you he played the most breathtaking rendition of 'Ave Maria' at Highland Park Presby last Christmas?"

Cissy clasped a beautifully manicured hand to her silk-covered heart at the memory, drawing my eye to the triple strand of pearls at her throat so that I found myself wondering how tightly I'd have to pull them to cut off her oxygen.

"Please, Mrs. Kendricks, you're embarrassing me," Trey feebly protested, and I wondered how a man who'd grown up on a Texas cattle ranch the size of Rhode Island could be so meek and pale. Someone obviously hadn't eaten his Wheaties.

"A doctor of philosophy who plays the pipe organ. How . . . unusual." I glanced at the bespectacled buttoned-down fellow across the table without a drop of my mother's enthusiasm, all the while thinking that a Ph.D. in basket weaving might have been handier. But, then again, Trey had a trust fund that could pay off the federal deficit, so employment probably wasn't his biggest concern.

"And he's a member of Mensa, if that isn't enough."

"Oh, it's enough already," I murmured and felt the pointed toe of a Prada pump poke me in the shin.

Cissy Blevins Kendricks strikes again.

How like her to fix me up with a guy who thought he was smarter than everyone else, played the organ (which doesn't sound like a good thing any way you put it), and who could quote Plato ad nauseam.

Perfect.

He fit right in with all the others she tried to foist on me when I least expected it. Last month it was an investment banker who wore a black eye patch but "had an impeccable nose for IPOs" and collected Lladro figurines. The month before, it was the heir to an ostrich farm whose long neck, receding hairline, beaked schnozz, and supersized Adam's apple lent him a striking resemblance to his feathered beasts. Though I was the one who'd wanted to bury my head in the sand.

I wished my mother could just let me be. It's not as if I were an old maid or anything, at least from my perspective. I was still on the sunny side of thirty and not desperate enough to settle for money instead of love. For Mother, good bloodlines superseded matters of the heart. Any son of Ross Perot would do, even if that meant her grandchildren would have Dumbo ears and a squeaky drawl that made nails on a chalkboard sound pleasant in comparison.

Trying to change her mind was a hopeless cause. Sort of like investing in Enron while they were making packing material out of financial reports.

Part of me wondered why I hadn't stayed in Chicago instead of coming home again, though I'd felt so guilty for leaving Mother alone and going off to art school after Daddy died that I'd nearly succumbed way back then and remained in Dallas to attend SMU. Cissy had her diamond-studded arrow badge ready to pin on me, expecting I'd go through sorority rush and pledge Pi Phi, as she did. But my father had always insisted I follow my dreams, and so I'd undermined all of Mother's plans and forged ahead with my own, as much for myself as for Daddy.

Still, it hadn't taken Mother long after my art school graduation to lure me back where I belonged. Though I'd certainly adored Chicago, with its mix of sophistication and Midwest sturdiness, I'd missed Texas more, down to the scuffed toes of my Tony Lama boots. Must've been my DNA. Having both Blevins and Kendricks in my family tree made for some pretty deep roots. Though, sometimes, like now, I had grave concerns about what I'd gotten myself into.

I picked at my hearts of palm salad as Cissy made small talk with Trey, asking about his family's recent trip to their mock chateau in Telluride, though I knew she'd already gotten a blow-by-blow from Trey's mother, Millicent Maxwell (after whom Bar Bush supposedly named the book-writing presidential pooch).

And I pondered how the hell I was going to

make it through several more courses without screaming and tearing my hair out at the roots. So I gazed at the crowd of faces on the yellow wall above, depictions of the Palm's famous patrons, scowling when I spotted my mother's image.

"Trey, darling," Mother purred, "why don't you tell Andrea about the time you played the pipe organ for the pope?"

I wasn't fast enough to escape to the ladies' room.

"All right." He cleared his throat and opened his mouth so I could see the hunk of chive stuck between his front teeth. "It was four years ago, no, five, excuse me, when I made a pilgrimage to Turkey to find the answer to my quest for the meaning of life," Mr. Maxwell Number Three started up, Mother egging him on with gentle coos and keeping me in line with nudges under the table until I was sure my shin was black and blue.

". . . it was in Istanbul when I ran into a priest with one leg who'd lost his church organist to a tragic rug-weaving accident. . . ."

I didn't even pretend to listen. Instead, I scoured the Palm's extensive wine list, wishing I'd ordered something stronger than Perrier with lemon.

Wondering how I'd ever fallen for another of Mother's schemes.

Thinking that, if they didn't bring me a plain old hamburger as I'd requested instead of the filet mignon my mother had indicated to the waiter behind her hand, I'd order every damned dessert on the menu and rot out the teeth she'd spent so much money to straighten and whiten when I was growing up.

Though Mother owed me a lot more than chocolate mousse.

And she would pay for it.

Dearly.

The phone rang, shattering my dreams, which had something to do with a purple-haired woman and a handsome televangelist saying, "Praise the Lord" a lot and trying to pry money from my hands in order to save starving children in Nepal.

It rang again, and I peeled open an eye just wide enough to read the glowing arms of my alarm clock.

Five-thirty.

I groaned and rolled over, thinking this was just part of the nightmare that had started with the set-up at the Palm and had ended with a headache requiring Excedrin P.M. and watching late, late night TV until I'd fallen asleep. Which accounted for the dream about the televangelist and his wigged sidekick.

Maybe it was Cissy, calling to spoil the start of the day since she'd managed to do such a bang-up job ruining the previous evening by forcing me to endure the company of a philosophical Mensa pipe organist during one of the longest dinners of my life. Besides, she was the only one I knew who'd dial me up before the sun had risen. Tormenting her only child was more fundamental to her than sleep.

When the phone rang twice more, I fumbled for the receiver before my voice mail could pick up. "Okay, okay, I'm up already," I groaned.

"Andrea?"

The voice that said my name wasn't my mother's smooth drawl. It seemed familiar somehow, though I couldn't quite place it, not at the crack of dawn when my normally sharp senses were still snoozing.

"Andrea Kendricks?"

"Yes?"

"Oh, God, it's me, Molly O'Brien."

"Molly?"

"You've got to help me, Andy, please."

Fear shook her every word, and I was suddenly wide-awake. Last time I'd seen Molly, we'd shared a place at Columbia College in Chicago, before she'd dropped out and run off to Paris with a Hemingway wannabe sporting a long black ponytail and a nose ring.

"I'm in trouble, real trouble. They came to my apartment this morning and got me out of bed and I had to leave David with my landlady. . . ."

"Hey, slow down." She was talking so fast I could hardly understand what she was saying. I sat up, reached for the lamp, and switched it on. Blinking at the flood of brightness, I felt around for my glasses and knocked a paperback off the night table.

"Take a deep breath and start over," I told her.

"I'm at the police station," she blurted out.

At that point, I was the one who needed to take a deep breath. "Which one?"

"Far North Dallas," she cried like someone whose house was on fire. "They said Bud's dead and that I killed him."

The terror in her voice shot through me faster than a cup of caffeine.

I didn't stop to ask who Bud was. I kicked off the covers and swung my legs over the side of the bed, telling her as confidently as I could, "Just hold on. I'll be right there."

Then I hung up and called Mother.

Chapter 2

I had met Molly as a freshman in high school.

She had been on scholarship at Hockaday, and I was there because my mother had been a Hockaday girl and couldn't imagine I'd go anywhere else, least of all — God forbid — to public school. Molly had been quiet, pretty with her dark hair, fair skin, and more shape than any teenager deserved, but a loner because of her lack of social standing. I, on the other hand, had enough good background to go around, what with being half Blevins and half Kendricks, two of Dallas's oldest families, if anything about Dallas can truly be called "old." But I was no more popular than she.

Gawky and flat where others were graceful and curved, I made up for my lack of poise and T&A with an overflow of creativity. To my mother's chagrin, I didn't try out for field hockey, golf, or tennis. Instead, I experimented with brushstrokes and ink strokes, like a modern-day Mary Cassatt. I volunteered to paint murals over graffiti-covered walls in the city, and gleefully slaved over graphics and layout for the yearbook and school paper. While I was so-so with watercolors and oils, I was daVinci with freehand drawings. I once overheard a teacher tell another that I was "a patchwork purse in a sea of Guccis," which may have been devastating to my self-esteem had I not taken it as a compliment.

Molly and I sat next to each other in art class, which bonded us more permanently than Elmer's craft glue. She wanted to be a fashion designer and whipped up the wildest pint-sized outfits that she'd display on Barbie dolls, hoping to work her way up to real people. Before she'd entered Hockaday, she'd lived with a foster family on the outskirts of the Park Cities. I was the only child of Cissy and Stanley Kendricks of Beverly Drive in Highland Park. She taught me what it was like to grow up with nothing, and I showed her what it meant to be raised from the pages of the Neiman Marcus catalog. We both envied the other somehow, which sealed our friendship tighter than spit or blood.

Long before graduation, we'd made a pact to attend Columbia College, a small art school in downtown Chicago. Despite Cissy's threats to disown me if I didn't attend a Texas university and rush her beloved Pi Phi, I followed my heart and moved to the shores of Lake Michigan. I settled in quickly, despite the weather and the tiny off-campus apartment Molly and I rented. My course load was heavy on graphic arts and basic computer, while Molly studied fashion. Somewhere along the way, she met Sebastian, with his nose ring and ponytail. He'd filled her head with talk of Hemingway's Paris and reminded her that the greatest couturiers hailed from the land of Gitanes and Gauloises (aka, the brands of stinky cigs he'd pretentiously smoked). Little more than halfway through our studies, she packed up, bid me "adieu," and flew the coop.

Though I got a few postcards from her initially, after six months, I didn't hear a peep. She never returned to Chicago, and I concentrated on my own life, without her in it. A handful of years later, after guilt and homesickness drove me home, I heard from the friend of a friend that Molly had resurfaced in Big D, alone and with a child in tow. Word had it she was serving cocktails in order to support them both. I'd thought of looking her up, but was so busy starting my web design business — and enduring Mother's schemes to marry me off — that I never even cracked the Yellow Pages to track her down. We hadn't spoken in almost a decade.

Until this.

I phoned the private line — the "pink phone," as I'd always called it — and woke my mother in two rings.

She lived there alone with a handful of staff. Sixteen rooms and guest quarters, but she couldn't bear to sell the place. I'd been raised in that house. Daddy had died there. And Mother said it was too full of memories to let go.

I could hear the rustle of sheets as she breathed a soft, "Hello?"

"It's me," I said.

"Andrea, for heaven's sake." I could picture her pushing the pink silk shade off her eyes and into the blond puff of hair. "My first good night's sleep in . . . God, I don't know how long . . . and you've just ruined it."

"Good morning, Mother." I was pulling on my jeans as I spoke, the receiver caught between my jaw and shoulder. "I need your help," I told her, echoing Molly's own words.

"At this hour? Whatever for?"

"A friend's been accused of murder."

"Stop teasing, Andrea."

"It's Molly O'Brien."

I heard her sharp intake of breath. "The Hockaday scholarship girl? The one who had a child out of wedlock?"

My mother was nothing if not quick. "She needs a lawyer, a criminal lawyer, so could you call the firm and see if they can send someone over to the Far North Dallas substation to get her out?"

"Why couldn't you have listened to me, darling? Have you ever heard of a Pi Phi getting arrested?"

"Oh, please, not again." It was like a broken record. "It's too early for a lecture."

She sighed. "I'll see what I can do."

"Thank you," I said to show her that the Little Miss Manners classes she'd enrolled me in when I was five had not been for naught.

I got off the phone and finished zipping my jeans. I drew my nightshirt over my head, knocking my glasses askew in the process. Found a bra in my top dresser drawer and unearthed a paint-flecked sweatshirt from the closet.

After slipping my feet into a pair of driving moccasins, I headed for the bathroom, lingering just long enough to squint at my predawn self in the mirror. At least my skin hadn't broken out overnight, though my shoulder-length hair was seriously flattened on one side. Since no amount of brushing could fluff it up, I settled for a ponytail. I pushed my glasses onto my crown and splashed cold water on my face, drying off with a thick terry towel.

A fast gargle with Listerine, then I went in search of my purse, which had a way of getting lost despite the fact that there were few places for it to hide in my nine-hundred-square-foot condominium. It was a far cry from Mother's house on Beverly Drive, but I felt comfortable here. I was only five feet five and a hundred twenty pounds. I didn't need a lot of room. Besides, I'd been waited on hand and foot since I was born, and I rather liked taking care of myself, even if it meant my spoons were stainless steel instead of silver.

Outside, the stars still clung to the sky like thumbtacks, the moon close to full. It was colder than I'd anticipated, and I nearly went back for a coat.

A cat darted out from beneath a nearby car as I approached my Jeep Wrangler, but otherwise all was still.

The two-storied townhouses and condos that surrounded mine crouched in staggered shadows against the navy backdrop. Most of the windows were dark. Yellow bug lights gleamed on every porch.

I drove off in a sputter of engine, making it to the Far North Dallas substation in a record seven minutes.

My cell phone rang as I pulled into the parking lot, thick with blue and white Ford Tauruses and Crown Victorias. I angled the Jeep into a space, cut the motor, and picked up.

"Andrea?"

"Mother," I sighed, unable to keep the relief from my voice. "You did get a hold of someone at the firm?" The woman could throw a catered affair for five hundred in the blink of an eye. I had to believe she could summon a lawyer on short notice.

"I called J.D. directly," she informed me, sounding pleased with herself despite the circumstances. J.D. was J. D. Abramawitz of Abramawitz, Reynolds, Goldberg, and Hunt — aka, ARGH — one of the top law firms in Texas.

"He said he'd send a man to the police station to meet you. Though, God knows, I don't understand why you feel the need to bail out that scholarship girl."

"She used to be my best friend."

"If only you'd spend time at the Junior League. . . ."

"I've got to go."

I put away the phone and locked the Jeep even though it was parked in a lot full of cop cars. These days, nothing was guaranteed.

I had only been to the police station once before when I'd had my car broken into and my stereo ripped off. It wasn't anything like what you saw on television. Not the Far North Dallas substation, anyhow. The area was relatively crime-free, or at least as close as you could get these days, and seemingly worlds apart from neighborhoods to the south, east, and west, where daily drug busts and homicides made the nightly news with frightening regularity.

Chairs lined one wall, but all were empty. Above them hung posters with safety tips. UNLOAD YOUR FIREARM BEFORE CLEANING, one warned, and another, DON'T SHARE NEEDLES. Whatever happened to the good old days of LOOK BOTH WAYS BEFORE YOU CROSS THE STREET?

My mocs made noisy slaps on the linoleum as I approached the crop-haired desk clerk, interrupting her perusal of *People* magazine.

I could see movement through the glass doors

to my right, the back of a woman's dark head, and I wondered if that was Molly. There didn't seem to be much else going on this early in the morning.

"Can I help you?"

I tried to look poised and in control, not like a thirty-year-old web designer whose clients were mostly penniless nonprofits. "I'm here to see Molly O'Brien," I said, hoping I sounded authoritative. "She was brought in about an hour ago."

"Ah, the waitress who offed her boss," she said, perking up.

"*Allegedly* offed her boss," I quickly corrected, realizing now who Bud was. But that was about all I knew.

"You her lawyer?" she asked and gave me the once-over, wrinkling her nose so that I was tempted to give the sleeve of my sweatshirt a sniff. It had a nice smudge of cobalt blue on the front from some recent work in oils, but was otherwise clean.

"I'm a relative," I told her. "Has she been formally charged?"

"She's still being questioned."

"Can I see her?"

She hesitated, squinting at me before giving a nod, apparently deciding I was harmless enough. Then she pushed a clipboard at me. "Sign in."

When I had, she slipped me a plastic visitor's badge.

"Through the doors there." She pointed a nail-bitten finger.

"Thanks," I said, but she'd already gone back to her *People*.

I clipped the badge to my sweatshirt, then pressed my purse against my belly, which was making awful noises. Whether from hunger or anxiety, I wasn't sure.

I hesitated at the doors, peering through them at the three people in a room crammed with desks. A female with a gray pageboy and a barrel-chested male fixed their attention on the woman whose back was to me. I could discern more than dark hair now: slim shoulders slightly slumped, hands gesticulating and then falling unseen into her lap.

The door buzzed as I pushed it open. It dropped closed behind me with a click.

"Molly?" I said.

Voices quieted at my entrance.

The detectives looked up.

The dark-haired woman turned around.

The face was not quite as I remembered. Even pale and drained, there was less flesh to the cheeks. The baby fat was gone, replaced by well-defined cheeks and jawbone. She had grown into features that had always been pretty and now bordered on knockout.

I swallowed, feeling suddenly gawky and thirteen again in my ponytail and sweatshirt.

"Andy?"

Green eyes brightened as recognition dawned,

and the tight line of lips fell open to release a squeal of pleasure. A flush colored bloodless features.

"You're here!"

Her chair scratched the floor as she flew out of it and toward me. She flung her arms around me and held on so tightly I nearly lost my breath.

"Thank you," she said, again and again.

But I hadn't done anything yet. Merely shown up. Maybe, to her, that was enough.

"Are you okay?" I asked when I managed to pry her to an arm's length away. I studied her closely; saw the telltale puffiness around her eyes.

"I'm holding up." She bit her lip and fresh tears welled at her lashes.

"The lawyer's on his way over. It's all arranged." I rubbed her arms, oddly protective of this woman whom I hadn't seen in years. She sorely needed a friend now, just as she had back at Hockaday. As had I. "Don't say another word till he arrives."

She nodded.

"It'll be all right," I said instinctively and patted her hand, wondering how many times she'd heard the same fairy tale before only to have it proved a lie.

I heard the noise of a clearing throat, and I looked up and over Molly's shoulder. The gray-haired cop and her broad-bellied sidekick stood and watched us. Both had their arms crossed. Neither appeared as overjoyed as Molly to see me. "You shouldn't be here, ma'am."

"But I'm family," I announced to them, deciding that "her long-lost friend, the artist" was pretty lame. "And you are?"

The detective with the pageboy stepped closer. "Detective Lydia Taylor." She flicked a hand toward the Pillsbury Doughboy. "My partner, John Lord."

Lord and Taylor?

I nearly made a joke about frequenting their shoe department, but figured it wasn't wise since they were armed.

"Nice to meet you," popped out of my mouth instead. Habit.

"Charmed, I'm sure," Detective Taylor drawled, not appearing that in the least. "I hate to interrupt your little reunion, but Ms. O'Brien was about to give us a statement."

"If you don't mind" — I summoned the nerve to cut her off — "I think she'll just hold off saying anything else until she has counsel present."

The detectives exchanged glances, and I waited for one or the other to say something, but neither did. I was rather proud of myself. Heck, I didn't read Erle Stanley Gardner for nothing.

"And if it's all right with you, could I have a minute alone with my, uh, sister?" I asked, directing my plea at Taylor, who seemed to be in the driver's seat. Her partner hadn't yet uttered more than a grunt. "Please?"

With a sigh, she gestured toward an empty desk well within earshot. Once Molly and I had seated ourselves, I leaned close to her and whispered, "Tell me everything." I wanted to know exactly what I'd gotten myself into.

First, she made me promise to take care of her boy, and I swore that I would. She gave me directions to her place and made sure I wrote them down. Then she snapped a tissue from a box on the desk and began to shred it. "I don't know where to start."

I thought of the Game of Life and how often she and I had played it on the rug in my room at the house on Beverly when Mother had let her spend the night. Then I quietly urged her, "Start at Go."

She stopped fiddling with the tissue, drew in a deep breath, and met my eyes. "I stayed late to help him close."

"Bud," I said, and she nodded.

"Bud Hartman," she clarified, her voice so low I strained to hear. "He owns Jugs." A flush spread upward from her collar, and I realized why. The place was well known in North Dallas, what with all the controversy it stirred up. I'd always thought of it as a hangout for macho men who believed they were better than their counterparts who hit the strip clubs.

"He's a pig," she ground out, then hastily added, "I mean, he was a pig."

32

"Did he harass you?"

"You could say that." She rolled her eyes toward the ceiling. "Bud hit on anything that moved. He was like an octopus, you know? All arms. You had to be quick on your feet, or look out." Her mouth quivered and her chin dropped. She stared down at her shoes. "Guess I didn't dance fast enough this time."

I saw the tear that splattered on the linoleum near her sneaker, and I knew I'd better forge ahead before she completely choked up. "Tell me what happened after everyone else left the restaurant. Do you usually close up with Bud?"

"No, it wasn't my turn, but Julie said she was feeling sick during the shift and took off early."

"Julie?"

"Julie Costello. She used to be a cheerleader for the Cowboys, but got busted for fraternizing with the players. She and Bud had a thing going, though he wasn't what I'd call faithful. I doubt she was either."

Molly paused, chewed her lip, then continued slowly.

"I put the cash from the day's take into the bank bag, just like we're supposed to, and I left it on Bud's desk. He liked to make out the deposit slip himself, so I didn't total it up except in my head. There must've been four or five thousand, at least. All those protestors just seem to make the place more popular." She toyed with the tissue. "Like I said, I took the bag to his office and set it on the desk, then I went to the

33

lockers to change. He'd shut off most of the lights, so it was pretty dark. I didn't know where he was until I'd finished dressing and turned to go. He was there, Andy. Watching me."

Her pupils widened like a cat's, and I noted the twitch of muscles at her jaw. "All I wanted was to get home to my kid, but apparently he had other plans." The slim hands clenched the Kleenex so hard her knuckles blanched. "He came after me, Andy. I was scared shitless." She swallowed, and her neck quivered. "He had me pinned against the kitchen counter, and he started kissing me." She stared off somewhere past my shoulder, seeing things that I couldn't. "I got hold of a knife." Her voice got lower, softer, quicker. "I lashed out at him."

"Did you cut him?" I asked, reaching for her hands and holding them. They were trembling.

"Maybe . . . yes." She closed her eyes and shuddered. "I must have, I guess. I'm not sure about anything anymore. I ran out of there so fast. I heard him call after me, so I figured he was pissed as hell. But he was alive."

"You didn't kill him?"

She didn't hesitate. "No."

The door banged open, and I raised my head to catch a lanky young man shooting into the room.

He stopped and pushed his preppy glasses up the narrow bridge of his nose. "I'm Brian Malone," he announced, slightly breathless and flushed. He smoothed a palm over tousled brown hair and shifted his briefcase to his left hand, approaching the detectives with his right hand extended.

When neither Lord nor Taylor met him halfway, he dropped his arm to his side and began to work at the buttons on a rumpled blue blazer. He didn't look old enough to buy beer without getting carded. Okay, I'm exaggerating, but he was too fresh-faced to be more than twenty-nine, thirty tops.

"I'm from Abramawitz, Reynolds, Goldberg, and Hunt," he said and squared his shoulders with Napoleonic flair.

The detectives appeared bored rather than impressed.

So he stammered, "I'm here to represent, uh" — he pulled a folded slip of paper from his coat pocket and squinted — "Polly O'Brien."

Molly stared at me with round eyes.

I tried to keep my mouth from falling open.

This was the shark that J.D. had sent to get Molly off the hook for murder?

Chapter 3

I stood helplessly as the detectives led Molly away.

They were taking her down to the basement to book her for murder. She peered tearfully over her shoulder before she disappeared from my sight. A tremor shot through me. Goose bumps rippled over my skin.

I turned on Brian Malone and hissed, "Don't just stand there. *Do* something!"

"There's nothing I can do."

I wanted to challenge the statement, to curse his law firm for putting him on the case instead of an older man, someone who appeared to have actually spent some time in a courtroom, much less a police station, but I pressed my lips into a tight line and said nothing. No doubt his credentials were impeccable, or he wouldn't be driving the carpool at ARGH, much less handling criminal trials.

"They've got cause to charge her with murder," he told me, giving his glasses a little shove. "Unfortunately, from the sound of things, they've got enough on your friend to lock her up and throw away the key."

"It's all circumstantial."

"No, it's not."

I tapped my foot on the floor, wishing I could cover my ears with my hands, not wanting to hear another word.

"They have a witness who saw her run out of the restaurant at close to one o'clock this morning. The shopping center security guard watched her exit the back door, hop into her truck, and take off like Mario Andretti." Malone ticked off each point on his fingertips. "He got her license plate, which is what led them to her so quickly. Did you know she has a prior conviction for writing bad checks?" He didn't wait for an answer. "They got a warrant to search her apartment, and turned up a white T-shirt and a pair of sneakers with traces of blood. And they have the knife from Bud's back, which is covered with her prints."

"Enough," I stopped him and let out a held breath, feeling like a balloon with a slow leak. It didn't look good for my old friend. That was abundantly clear. It didn't hit me until then how deep in trouble Molly was. I'd imagined before that it was all a mistake, a fluke that could be cleared up with the right words, the right kind of persuasion.

But that wasn't going to happen.

A man named Bud Hartman was dead, and all the evidence pointed to Molly.

I felt a light touch on my arm and found

Malone's eyes on me, the pity so plain in them I had to glance away.

"Maybe you don't know her as well as you thought you did," he suggested. "Your mother told J.D. that she was someone you'd befriended in high school. That you'd lost touch years ago. Maybe she isn't the same person you used to know."

I shook my head and shrugged off his hand, denying his words with a vehement "No." More vehement because I had wondered the same thing myself and didn't want to believe it. I couldn't believe it. Maybe I didn't know everything about Molly, but I knew enough to be sure she was no killer.

"She didn't do it," I said and met Malone's gaze, seeing my own bespectacled eyes reflected in his glasses. "Molly told me what happened, that Bud forced himself on her and she fended him off. She might have cut him with the knife, but he was alive when she left. She heard him shouting."

"So she says."

"She didn't stab him to death."

"It may have been self-defense." He rubbed his chin. "She's a very pretty lady. If the guy got rough with her, it makes sense. It's a common enough scenario. Juries usually take pity on the woman and sentences aren't so stiff."

"She's innocent, for Pete's sake!"

"I'm only being realistic."

"Pessimistic is more like it." My hands curled

to fists, and it was all I could do not to swing at him.

A half-smile took shape on his mouth. "You're amazingly loyal, Ms. Kendricks. And different than I expected."

"Oh?"

"I know your mother," he explained, tugging on his earlobe. "She has quite a reputation at the firm. I thought you'd be more like her."

"A demanding diva, you mean?" I filled in the blanks. "Dressed to the nines? As you can see, I rarely wear haute couture." I swept a hand over my paint-smudged sweatshirt and blue jeans, an outfit that Cissy wouldn't be caught dead in.

"Your words, not mine." He smiled fully now, not embarrassed in the least, which made me believe he might have more backbone than I'd suspected.

"Fair enough."

"Listen, Ms. Kendricks. . . ."

"Andy," I said instinctively, and I felt my anger draining away as quickly as it had surged.

"Andy," he repeated, nodding. "It doesn't look good, but I'll see what I can do for Ms. O'Brien. I promise."

He appeared so earnest and well meaning. Somehow I knew he was doing the best job he could.

I glanced toward the door through which they'd taken Molly, and I felt wiped out. My head was heavy, my mind unable to focus. Perhaps someone would shake me, and I'd wake up to find this was all a bad dream.

The fatigue must've shown in my face because Malone said gently, "You might as well go home. There's nothing you can do here."

I didn't even look at my watch, but figured it wasn't yet seven. I'd promised to go over to Molly's apartment complex and get David from the landlady. It would give me something to do, something to keep me from feeling completely useless.

"I'll stick around until they take her to Lew Sterrett, then I'll head downtown myself and handle her bond hearing. Though I don't think they'll let her go. She has no family in town, no one except her son. There's nothing to say she won't flee."

"Whatever she needs, I'm good for it," I told him. "Do you have to use a bail bondsman? Where do you find them anyway? Are they listed in the phone book, like plumbers and florists?" I was babbling, and I might have gone on forever had Malone not placed a hand on my shoulder.

"I'll call you if the judge grants her bail, okay? But don't bet on that."

I started to protest, then shut up. I couldn't argue with him. If I were in Molly's place, I might take David and run as far as I could without a second thought.

"You have to trust me, Andy."

I nodded, wondering if that would be enough.

Chapter 4

The sun had risen to flesh out the deep purple of dawn, tinting the air a soft blue and shell pink.

I got caught up in traffic on Belt Line, each green light way too short, the lines of cars far too long. I turned on the radio to KRLD but only half-listened to news updates and weather reports. My mind was on Molly and how she'd come back into my life ten years after running out of it. And I wondered if I were going to lose her again as abruptly.

I thought of what Malone had said, that the evidence against Molly appeared airtight. I didn't know much about the law except what I saw on TV, and I found myself imagining the worst: Molly being found guilty of murder and sentenced to spend the rest of her days behind bars, separated from a son who would be forced to grow up without his mother. Would David be placed in a foster home like Molly? Would he feel abandoned, too? Would he turn out to be a criminal, his face featured on *America's Most Wanted*, his mug shot tacked up in every post office from Dallas to Duluth?

Stop it, Andy, I chastised. This wasn't helping. Molly needed support. She needed someone who believed in her innocence. And right now, I was all she had.

A horn honked behind me, and I realized the light had turned green. In my rearview mirror, I saw a guy in a black Seville scowl.

I plunged ahead, shifting gears, watching as the Cadillac maneuvered around me, changing lanes as if it owned the road.

Caddies were as omnipresent in Texas as cockroaches. As oversized, too.

My father had driven one, and I'd always cringed when I had to get in it. The Cataract, I'd called it, because of the tinted windows that made me feel as if I had a glaze over my eyes. I never liked that car, feeling as if I were trapped inside an ostentatious cage where I couldn't touch sticky fingers to leather seats or put muddy shoes on the carpet. I had envied kids whose mothers had hauled them around in station wagons. I'd wished I were one of them, sitting in the rear seat gazing at the car behind, making faces and pressing noses to the glass, eating greasy McDonald's French fries without fear of leaving stains on the upholstery.

I shifted in my seat, gripping the steering wheel tightly, uncomfortable suddenly as old sensations seeped up to the surface.

Had I been an ungrateful child? Unappreciative of the things my parents had given me? Shiny new bikes, closets full of designer-label clothing, more dolls than I could ever play with, expensive birthday parties attended by gobs of children they'd handpicked, as my close friends had been few.

When all it took to make me happy was an easel with a blank canvas and a set of basic oils, or a big sheet of butcher's paper and finger paints the colors of the rainbow. I had never been good at pretending to be someone I was not.

I can still picture my mother with her hands on her hips, tiny frown lines wrinkling her slender brow. "Daddy said you didn't want to play tennis at the club this afternoon because the light was perfect for painting the gazebo? Now, Andrea, I adore the idea of your work someday hanging in the Louvre, but young girls need to exercise regularly or they end up spending their summers in fat camp. You don't want that, do you?"

I hadn't even tried to explain, not back then.

At one point, I wondered if I'd been adopted. I'd even dared to pose the question to Mother.

"How could you ask such a thing?" she'd cried, taking my charcoal-smeared, nail-bitten hands into her perfectly manicured ones. "I was in labor with you for twelve hours while your father passed out cigars in the hospital lobby. It was too late for an epidural, and I didn't take so much as an aspirin. I have never been in such pain in my life. And if that isn't proof enough that you sprang from my loins, my dear, I don't know what is."

I couldn't tell her the truth, that I wasn't at ease in her world, where who I was inside didn't seem to matter as much as what I looked like or the size I wore. Being pretty had always seemed so important.

Which is why Molly and I had gotten along.

She had never understood pretension. Her world had been a harsh one, rough where mine was glossy. Neither of us had felt like we belonged.

At times, I still didn't.

The light shifted to red, and I slowed the Jeep to a stop behind a Camry. The sunlight poked into my eyes, and I drew down the visor, turning to look the other way.

I found my gaze drawn to a shopping center near the tollway.

To Jugs.

High above the asphalt at the Villa Mesa Plaza — a fancy name for a plain old strip mall — an enormous sign depicted a pair of moonshine jugs shot from above, giving the undeniable impression of very round female breasts. Several squad cars were parked below the soaring billboard. A van with the Channel 8 logo rolled into view and then another from Channel 5. I bet it wouldn't be long before the other television and radio stations joined them.

A horn honked, and I jumped, quickly fixing my attention on the road ahead of me. I sent the Jeep lurching forward.

Ironically, Molly's apartment wasn't but a couple miles from where I lived, located on Montfort past a dozen other complexes that looked nearly identical. The names were similar as well: Montfort Oaks, Montfort Landing, Montfort Acres. They all passed in a blur.

Finally I reached Montfort Lakes.

I pulled into a street book-ended by brick walls and trimmed shrubs. A few pickup trucks and compact cars lingered beneath skeletal carports. The four-storied buildings surrounded a very small manmade lake.

I homed in on Molly's unit without difficulty and pulled into an empty parking space.

She'd told me her apartment manager lived on the ground floor, and I checked the piece of paper on which I'd scrawled the number. Then I locked up the Jeep, crossed the pavement to #121, and knocked on the door.

I heard a click before it opened as wide as a chain would allow. A brown eye peered at me from above an unsmiling mouth. "Yes?" Even the voice was suspicious.

"Maria Rameriz?"

"Do I know you?"

"I'm Andrea Kendricks." So what? Her silence seemed to shout. "I'm an old friend of Molly O'Brien's. I saw her this morning," I proceeded carefully, just in case six-year-old David was anywhere around.

"Ah, yes, Andy," she said after a slight pause. "Molly told me you were once like *su hermana.*

Her sister." A hand waved at me from the crevice. "Just a minute."

The door shut and reopened minus the chain. I could see all of her now, from the fuzzy pink toes of her slippers to the pilled chenille robe knotted tightly at her middle to the brown hair pinned up in sponge rollers. "Come in, please." She stepped back to let me in.

I waited until she'd locked us in, then followed her up a hallway with off-white walls into a brightly lit living room with furnishings that would have made my mother wince in horror. Dark woods and lots of orange and brown that screamed, "1970s." But the place was spotless, and I didn't hesitate when she offered me a seat on the plaid sofa. She perched on an arm, a slippered foot dangling, and looked me over.

"David's sleeping," she said. "It was rough for him, the police coming for his mama and dragging her away. He doesn't understand."

"What did you tell him?"

"The boy is smart. He knows something's going on. Something bad." The light in her dark eyes flickered. "All I would say is that the police made a mistake and think his mama did something she didn't do. I promised him it would be fixed soon, and his mama will be home again."

I only wished it were that easy.

"She has a lawyer," I told Maria. "He's from the best firm in the city. If anyone can clear this up, he can," I added, wanting to believe it as I said it. What I yearned for was the aggressive style of the rhyming Johnny Cochran or the down-home confidence of Gerry Spence. I tried hard to blot the image of the clean-scrubbed Brian Malone from my mind.

Maria nodded. "How is Molly?"

"Scared."

Her fleshy face tightened, the slashes of dark brow low over her eyes. "*Díga me la verdad.* Tell me the truth. Does it look real bad for her?"

I fiddled with my purse strap, remembering Molly's tearful eyes, the terror in her face as they'd taken her downstairs for booking. I finally rallied the courage to meet Maria's unflinching stare.

"The police have evidence they believe points to Molly, and right now they're not looking for anyone else," I admitted. "The man who was killed, her boss. . . ."

"Bud," she spat, mouth wrinkling. "Molly told me all about him, that he was a *cucaracha.*"

Unfortunately, he was a very dead cockroach, I thought, pushing my glasses up the bridge of my nose.

Maria watched me closely.

"They've charged her with murder," I said and my own voice sounded foreign to my ears. Soft and afraid. "Malone . . . her lawyer . . . he doesn't think they'll let her out on bail because she has no family in town. They'll be scared she'll take David and run."

"*Madre de Dios,*" Maria sputtered and crossed herself. She started rocking, back and forth.

"David," she breathed, a hand at her breast. "What will happen to him? They're not going to make me turn him over to strangers?"

"No," I quickly answered and sat up straighter. "Molly asked me to take care of him, and I will. I'll make sure he doesn't go to a foster home," I told her, though I wondered how I would keep my promise. What would I do with a little boy? There wasn't much room in my tiny condo for anyone but me.

"He's quiet," she said. "A good child."

But a kid just the same, I thought, with the need to run and jump and play. The last time I'd done any babysitting, I'd been a teenager, and I hadn't even liked the gig much back then. I didn't even own a cat, for Pete's sake.

An idea popped into my head. One that wouldn't win me a Nobel Peace Prize, but it would solve the problem at hand.

"He's not in school now, is he?" It was mid-May, so there was a good chance classes were over, even if he were enrolled somewhere. "No one will miss him if he's away for a bit?" I asked, figuring that, unless Molly had him signed up for a summer day care program, it would go unnoticed by teachers or truant officers if he took a little cross-town trip.

"No, *no escuela ahora*. Molly's got him in the mornings and then he either stays here at night while she works or she has a girl from the next building sit with him."

Great. So I cranked up Plan A.

"Can you wake him?" I asked. It was now past seven o'clock, and I wanted to get him settled as soon as possible.

Maria nodded and rose, smoothing squared fingers over her robe. She seemed more relaxed, perhaps even relieved that I'd be taking David with me, even though I could see how much she cared for him and Molly.

"*Un momento,*" she said and shuffled out of the room.

I got up and slipped my purse over my shoulder, checking out the framed photographs on the walls. The nearest to eye level featured a pair of girls in plaid skirts and knee socks, uniforms not unlike the one I'd worn at Hockaday. Maria's daughters? I wondered. Probably grown now with children of their own. Other pictures showed families, women with Maria's olive skin and strong features standing alongside men who held babies in their arms.

Crossing the room, I went to the patio doors and pushed aside the curtains. Dead leaves floated upon the murky water of an in-ground swimming pool.

Behind me came the rustle of footsteps and hushed voices.

I turned to see Maria prodding a small boy forward. The laces of his sneakers had come untied.

"Hey, David." I squatted low so we were eye to eye.

He shrank back into Maria, his head squashing her belly. He looked so like his mother, I realized: the same heart-shaped face, the thick-lashed eyes and good bones. He'd doubtless drive the girls crazy before he could drive.

I held out my hand. "I'm Andy," I said. "I'm a very old friend of your mommy's. We went to school together."

He tipped his face to Maria, who gave him a gentle shove. "It's okay," she told him. "Andy's a nice lady."

Shyly, he lifted his hand to shake mine. His "hi" was barely audible.

"Good to meet you." I took the small fingers in mine and gave a gentle squeeze before letting go.

"I have his things," Maria told me, indicating a faded green knapsack on the floor. "I got them from the apartment after" — she caught herself, gaze shifting to David — "after Molly had to leave. He has his pajamas and a tooth-brush. Some clean underwear, shirts and socks."

"He'll be fine," I assured her. "If he needs anything, we'll just buy it." I nearly flinched at my own words: my mother's motto all my life.

"You ready?" I asked him.

He stared at me, wide-eyed, for a long moment, and I thought I saw his bottom lip quiver. Then he puffed his chest out and whispered, "Ready."

"We'll have fun," I told him, hoping I wasn't lying through my teeth. "It'll be an adventure, you'll see. And then your mommy will be back before you know it."

The boy tucked his thumbs into the straps of his knapsack and nodded. I patted the top of his head. His tousled hair felt like down.

While Maria hugged him goodbye, I slipped a business card from my purse and set it on the nearest table. "Here's my cell and home phone if you need me," I told her. Then I picked up David's knapsack and headed for the door, waiting there for him.

David whimpered a bit and dragged his feet when I led him outside to the Jeep. As I buckled him in the front seat, I thought about where we were headed and wondered what Mother would say when I dropped him off at the house on Beverly Drive.

Chapter 5

 Sandy answered the door. She looked both pleased and surprised to see me.

"Andrea, sweetie," she said in her honey-smooth drawl, the stern frown she wore to scare off solicitors morphing into a smile.

She drew me into her sturdy embrace, muffling my own greeting in the cushiony folds of her breasts. She wore a blue cardigan over a white silk blouse and tan trousers, and she smelled of roses. My mother had hired Sandy Beck as a housekeeper some thirty-odd years ago, and she'd become so indispensable that she'd evolved into Mother's social secretary — her best friend, if truth be told — and my fairy godmother.

"What brings you here so early in the morning?" she asked, and then her broad mouth fell open as I drew apart from David. Until that moment, he'd been hiding behind me.

"For heaven's sake," she breathed, the folds of skin lifting above her bright eyes. She touched a hand to her neat gray hair, a sure sign she'd been thrown for a loop. "Now, sweet pea, I'd know if he was yours," she said, recovering quickly. "You couldn't hide a thing like that any more than you could keep a secret."

I smiled at her teasing. "No, he's not mine."

Sandy tugged her cardigan closed. The morning air was cool despite the sun. "Don't tell me you've taken to babysitting."

"He's Molly O'Brien's," I told her, catching the change in her expression. No doubt she'd already gotten an earful from Mother.

"I see," she replied, though her quizzical expression told me she awaited further explanation.

"I promised Molly I'd look out for him until . . . well, until she can come home."

"You'd like him to stay with us?" she asked pointedly, and I blushed.

"Do you mind?"

Sandy put her hand on my arm. "If it means so much to you, Andy, then it's no trouble at all."

I covered her fingers with mine. "Thank you," I said. "It does."

I'd embarrassed her. Her cheeks reddened. I let go of her hand, and she fiddled with her collar.

She cleared her throat, leaning nearer to ask me, "Will she be there long?" With the unsaid word being "jail."

I sighed, feeling the helplessness creep in again, knowing I would have to do more for Molly than keep David safe. Wondering exactly what that might be and where to start. "I hope not."

I shifted my eyes from Sandy's face with its comforting wrinkles to David. He was ignoring the two of us entirely as he cautiously approached one of the pair of whitewashed terra cotta lions standing sentry on either side of the front door. He'd looked entranced ever since I'd pulled the Jeep off tree-lined Beverly into the circular drive in front of Mother's. I always thought of it as her house, never mine, perhaps because the Highland Park estate had always reflected her tastes, from the vaulted ceilings and gold-leafed moldings to the cast-stone fireplaces, marble baths, and Chinese silk rugs. It was like a palace in a fairy tale with Mother its queen and me a visiting commoner.

I hoped the boy would feel comfortable in a setting so different from what he was used to. If I knew Sandy, she'd make sure of that. For Mother's sake, I prayed he would behave as he had on the drive over. Though I sensed he was not the kind of child who broke things or ran around screaming and smearing jelly on the walls.

"You want to head inside, David?" I said, and he turned to me, as if only then remembering I was there. His cheeks glowed pink. His knapsack clung turtle-like to his back; on his slight frame, it looked heavy. I waved at the door Sandy held wide for him. "C'mon," I prodded. "Let's go."

He walked toward me, eyes downcast, and I

set my hand atop the soft nest of his hair, guiding him beneath the arched doorway and into the marble foyer.

I knew he was terrified, what with his mother being taken away in the early morning hours by the police and no one telling him exactly what was happening. But, for all his shyness, he hadn't cried or pouted. In fact, he'd hardly said a word except to ask a question now and then. Molly had been quiet, too, back in school. The kind of girl who had so much going on behind her eyes, but rarely spoke unless spoken to.

"Why don't you let me take David to the kitchen for some breakfast," Sandy offered as we paused near the foot of the curved staircase. "And you can go up and visit Cissy."

Before I'd answered, she put her hands on her knees and bent forward, nose-to-nose with David. He backed against me, and I placed my hands on his shoulders to still him.

"How does that sound, young man?" she said directly to him. "You haven't eaten breakfast yet, have you?"

"Nope." He shook his head, then looked up as if to get my approval.

"Go on," I told him. "Sandy'll take good care of you. And wait till you taste her pancakes. Um-um good."

I worked the knapsack from his arms, and he wriggled out of the straps. Sandy took his hand, speaking over her shoulder, "Cissy's having tea and toast in her sitting room."

I listened as their footsteps dwindled, the click of Sandy's pumps and the shuffle of David's sneakers.

Then I put a hand on the carved railing and took a deep breath.

For some reason, I felt a little like I was paying audience to the queen when I visited Mother. Cissy Blevins Kendricks had always been a formidable person, still was even as she neared sixty, and she had always intimidated me, even if she hadn't meant to do it. She had a way of making me feel small and rumpled and awkward without saying a word. I didn't blame her for it, and I didn't hate her, either, though I'm sure some psychiatrists would find me dysfunctional for being so accepting. She was who she was, and I would never be that. Knowing exactly where I stood made it easier for me to be with her. And, I figured, for her to be with me.

I started up the stairs, following the pattern of the Oriental runners. The house seemed so still in the early morning, the soft moan of the wood beneath the patterned wool sounded loud to my ears, though the way my heart hammered noisily in my head it was a wonder I could hear anything at all.

I briefly poked my head into Daddy's old study. Mother hadn't touched it in years, except to have the maid do an occasional light dusting. If I closed my eyes and breathed deeply, I could detect the vague aroma of his Cuban cigars, which he'd smoked religiously before his first heart attack. After that, he'd had to quit. "Come hell or your mother," as he liked to say. He had framed two of my "masterpieces" and hung them on either side of a favorite landscape by John Singer Sargent. "Can you imagine that Degas dismissed Sargent's work entirely?" he'd remarked to me once when he'd caught me closely admiring the texture of the brushstrokes. "Shows that you can't listen to anyone else when it comes to your destiny, Andy. You have to listen to your heart."

I smiled even now as I remembered. Daddy always knew just the right thing to say.

Mother was a different story.

Before I crossed the threshold to her sitting room, I steeled myself. Surely Cissy would try to convince me to let Brian Malone take care of Molly, maybe even hand over David to the Department of Children and Family Services (or whatever it was called), and I couldn't do it. I only hoped she'd understand why, even if she didn't agree.

Just as Sandy had said, there she sat, propped up on the roll-armed Queen Anne settee, bifocals perched on the tip of her nose as she sipped tea from a Limoges cup and read the morning news.

As I took a step inside, a floorboard creaked beneath me.

Mother's chin lifted. She peered over her spectacles. "Well, well, well," she said and put aside the paper.

I was hardly in the mood for one of her "I told you so" speeches, but I knew I was going to get one regardless.

"So she's really in the slammer?"

I laughed at her choice of words, and my nerves settled down. Mother had a knack for breaking the ice. "You watch too many old movies."

"Who did she kill?"

I groaned as I sank into a damask-covered wing-chair. "She didn't kill anyone," I said quite plainly, not returning her curious stare but glancing around me at the watered silk on the walls and the gilt-framed Impressionist paintings that Mother and Daddy had bought in Europe years before. They had inspired me as a child and even now I could hardly take my eyes off them.

"The police arrested her for sport, I suppose."

I turned my head, scowling at her. "Mother."

Her hair was brushed high off her forehead, but she wore no makeup yet, and I could see the grooves of concern etched in her brow. "Darling, I do realize you mean well, but," she paused dramatically and shook her head. "You're asking for trouble, getting yourself involved in something that's none of your concern."

"But it *is* my concern," I insisted and managed to keep my voice from rising like Minnie Mouse, something I'd learned to do with much practice. I didn't want her to accuse me of being shrill, not now when I needed her help. She was the one who could pull the strings in Dallas society, not I. She was responsible for getting Molly an attorney in the wee hours of morning, even if it did happen to be Malone.

I set my forearms on my knees and leaned forward. "Okay, I realize you don't think much of Molly" — I paused at the telling arch of her eyebrows — "but I honestly believe she had nothing to do with murdering Bud Hartman. She might not be a blue blood, but she's a decent person with responsibilities and a son to take care of." I grinned nervously. "You should see him. He's a doll."

Mother's face tightened up in an "I can go you one better" expression. "I've seen him already."

I blinked, wondering how she'd managed that. A crystal ball?

Her mouth curved smugly, and she gestured toward the heavily draped window to her left. "My sitting room overlooks the front drive, or have you forgotten?"

I had.

"How long do you intend for us to keep him here?"

"Um," I said, ever articulate, and nervously pushed at my glasses. "Just until Molly's out of jail." I tried not to wince.

"And how long will that be? Twenty years to life?" She crossed her arms to punctuate her sarcasm.

I ignored it and replied in my best positive-speak, "Soon, I hope. Brian Malone will handle her bond hearing. He'll get her out on bail, I'm sure." I sounded far more confident than I felt, especially after Malone's assurances that Molly wasn't going anywhere.

She cocked her head and settled her hands gracefully in the lap of her pale pink caftan. "Do you know what you're doing, Andrea? Getting entangled in the troubles of a woman you haven't seen in years, one who's been accused of murder?"

I started to say something in my own defense as well as Molly's, but I couldn't go through with it.

She was right. I had no idea what I'd gotten myself into or how to get out.

"If you were married, you wouldn't feel the need to seek out lost causes, like all those stray pets you used to bring home when you were little," she said, the molasses sweetness of her drawl nearly masking the zing of the arrow shot point-blank into my chest. "You shouldn't have been so rude to Trey Maxwell last night," she reprimanded when I merely stared at her, open-mouthed, unable to think of a comeback that would be equally stunning. "I doubt he'll be calling you anytime soon after the way you be-haved."

Trey Maxwell?

Talk about a lost cause.

I turned away for a moment, unable to look at her, afraid I'd start laughing hysterically.

"And to think you refused the invitation I finagled for you to appear in the Pi Phi charity style show." Mother clicked tongue against teeth and picked up the paper again, opening it with a crisp snap. "Oh, yes, I can certainly understand how playing social worker is so much more appealing than modeling Donna Karan in the ballroom at the Anatole."

I dropped my head into my hands and softly moaned.

Chapter 6

 I went back to my condo and took a long hot shower. The water soothed me, and I stood under the spray for longer than usual, letting it loosen up the knots in my back and shoulders. But it did nothing to wash away the knots in my stomach.

The phone rang as I toweled off, and I raced to the bedroom to pick it up.

"Hello?"

"Ms. Kend . . . Andy?"

Brian Malone. The uncertain stammer could belong to no one else.

"The bond hearing," I said before he had the chance. My damp hair dripped down my neck, chilling me. "Did the judge grant bail?"

His sigh told me the answer well before he uttered, "No, I'm sorry. I tried everything, but Judge Harmon felt she was a risk for flight."

"Damn." This whole thing sucked. It wasn't fair to little David or poor Molly.

"There'll be a hearing next week. I'll move to dismiss, of course, but the motion will be denied. I hate to say it, but your friend gave them enough evidence to make the rope that'll hang her."

I gripped the receiver tightly. "Hey, you're supposed to be on her side."

"I'm just being honest."

"Then we have to poke holes in their theory, we have to dig up something the cops didn't see. . . ."

"Whoa, Andy, whoa," he cut me off. "You can't interfere with a police investigation."

"What investigation? Sounds like they think they've got the case sewed up already, so they're not even trying to find the real killer."

"But you can't sniff out clues."

"How hard could it be?"

"You're a web designer, not a private eye," he scoffed. "You can't run around playing Columbo."

Maybe he was right. I couldn't exactly flash a badge and ask questions. But there had to be other ways to find out what had really happened last night and who was responsible for Bud's death. If only I could get to the root of things, go back to where it all began.

"Andy? You still there?" Malone squawked, already sounding panicked. "Aw, geez, you're not cooking up something stupid, are you? Your mother said you weren't good at taking instructions."

"Did she mention I didn't play well with others, too?"

"You can't do this."

Those words only fanned my fire.

A crazy idea had already taken hold of me, and nothing he said was going to stop me from trying to get Molly out of this mess.

"I'll be in touch when I have hard evidence for you, Malone," I told him, feeling better suddenly. Not so helpless after all.

"Andy, nooo. . . ."

I disconnected, cutting off his plea.

The phone rang again almost instantly, but I let it go, humming aloud as I headed back to the bathroom to dry my hair, thinking that my mother was wrong. This particular cause wasn't lost, not by a long shot.

I had a client to see that afternoon, a woman named Anna McLaughlin who owned an antiques shop at Knox-Henderson. Normally, I didn't make house calls for web projects, but Anna insisted on my personal touch. I charged her by the hour, so it was no skin off my nose. Mother had been buying pieces from Anna for years and had used the power of her purse strings to drum up the business for me when I'd first hung out my shingle. Not that I'd asked for her help, but that had never stopped her from doing exactly as she pleased. I much preferred to do jobs for nonprofits — the latest being a site to display the artwork of kids with cancer for a local charity — but I figured it didn't hurt to do a favor for Mother on occasion. I never knew when I'd need some-

thing from her. Like getting Molly an attorney.

Once a month, I made the trip to Anna's store
to show her some updates for her web pages on
the computer in her back room. Then I'd shoot
some digital photos of new merchandise she
wanted to peddle, adding the pictures, descrip-
tions, and prices to her online inventory. It
never took more than an hour, two tops, and I
didn't mind going there besides. Anna was always keen to show off her latest treasures from
her trips to France or England (or to the
Preston Hollow estate sales, if truth be told).
I'm sure she assumed I'd tell my mother what
goodies I'd seen and that "darling Cissy" would
high-tail it over to Anna's Antiques in her cham-
pagne-hued Lexus, whip out her Platinum
American Express, and clean out the place.

I dressed carefully in black jeans and Tee with
a silver chain around my hips. I put in my contacts and swiped my mouth with pale pink lipstick, which made me feel, if not look, more
thirty than thirteen.

I picked up the funky "Alice" bag in the crazy
black-striped Wurlitzer print that I'd ordered
from mavery designs.com as a treat for finishing
a recent project. I loved that Megan Avery used
fabrics with colorful patterns dreamed up by
artists. I had several of her bags, in different
styles, and they suited me far better than the
latest from Europe.

My car keys in hand, I headed for the door,

catching sight of the blinking red light on my Caller ID. Without even scrolling through the memory, I knew it was Brian Malone. I dialed in my number and code to listen to what he had to say. As I'd suspected, it was another plea for me not to do anything rash that might jeopardize the case.

Right, I thought, locking the door on my way out.

As far as I could tell, Malone had no case.

The sun was high and bright and hot. It felt at least ninety degrees. And it was only May. By June, all Dallasites who took a step out of their air conditioning could empathize with poor Humpty Dumpty when his innards hit the pavement.

Just as soon as the motor turned over, I cranked up the cold air in the Jeep and drove east to Central Expressway, taking it south to the Knox-Henderson exit.

Anna's shop was on the first floor of a tangled two-storied building with a whitewashed exterior and lots of windows.

A bell jangled overhead as I entered, and the scent of old upholstery, new varnish, and Anna's overpowering White Diamonds hit my lungs.

I wove through a tight path between gorgeous gilded consoles and chairs that were clearly French, a Chippendale dining set with heavy ball and claw feet, a Victorian bed with a carved six-foot headboard, and polished mahogany china cabinets and chests of drawers. Above me, chandeliers with Austrian crystals glittered amidst Art Deco fixtures with odd shapes and jewel tones. Silver tea sets and delicate pieces of Nippon and Lalique tantalized from shelves and tabletops. Beneath my comfy black espadrilles, faded Persian rugs made each step a whisper.

"Andrea? Andrea, is that you? Right on time, as always."

Anna emerged from the rear of the shop in a gust of perfume. A bright green silk sheath hugged her ample body. She'd tied a colorful scarf around her neck (to hide her chins, so Mother liked to say). Her still-pretty face was painted in the Texas tradition of too much is never enough, and her shiny blond hair was upswept in an immobile 'do that had probably cost the world an additional hole in the ozone (another Texas tradition).

"How's my favorite web diva?" she cooed and hugged me to her bosom.

"I'm okay," I got out, nearly breathless from her clinch.

She stepped back and clasped be-ringed hands together, an "I know better" look on her face. "Your mother phoned me a little while ago," she admitted. "Cissy told me all about that girl in prison."

I should have known. Mother could get out a story faster than CNN. And she didn't even have a satellite feed.

"I don't want to talk about that, Anna, if you don't mind."

"Sure, honey," she said, but looked disappointed.

I two-stepped around her and followed the narrow path toward the rear office. I'd barely set my things down on the desk and switched on the computer when Anna appeared, studying me from above the flat screen monitor.

"May I ask you something, Andrea?"

I finished typing the password onto the screen and hit the enter key. Then I shrugged and glanced up at her. "Shoot."

She caught her hands beneath her breasts and cocked her head like a chicken. "Why does a nice girl like you . . . a well-endowed girl with no need to work" — I nearly cringed at the obvious reference to my trust fund, not my boobs — "why do you live the way you do when you could be part of the crème de la crème of Dallas society? Cissy told me you refused to debut when you were eighteen. She said it near to killed her."

So Mother was still getting pity with that one, I mused, frowning. My father had his fatal heart attack just months before my deb ball at the Fairmont and, somehow, without him there to make the situation bearable, I didn't see the point of going through with the charade. Not even for Cissy.

"And she told me that a friend of yours from Hockaday who'd chaired last year's Fur Ball was just engaged to one of the Hunts. 'It could have been Andrea,' she said to me. Her very words."

I wanted to tell her that Mother would've married me off to Ted Bundy if he'd had the right pedigree, but instead I sighed softly. I'd been through this enough times to know how to deal with it.

Folding my hands atop the desk, I looked up at her, meeting her curious eyes with my steady gaze.

"I like my life just the way it is, Anna, but thank you for your concern." I knew my face was probably as deep a red as the ruby glass Anna's store had on display, but I still managed to be polite. "I'm happy the way I am, despite what Cissy would like her chums to believe. I don't have any regrets whatsoever. And isn't that what's important? Living for yourself and not for other people?"

Anna's face crumpled slightly. There was no way for her to reply but to say, "Yes, of course, dear."

It seemed to work with all of Mother's friends, though, like the rest of them, Anna seemed befuddled. No doubt behind my back — and Cissy's — they discussed what an odd bird I was, probably wondered what was wrong with me.

Sometimes it was tricky being so different from the "village" that had raised me. It would have been so much easier if I'd fit neatly into the

69

world in which I'd been born instead of fighting it every step of the way.

"Now, Anna, would you like to see the new designs I've come up with before I update your site? Then we'll do the photographs of your new inventory, and I'll put them up. . . ."

The bell on the front door jangled, and her bored expression vanished, as she put her party face back on. "Do whatever needs doing, hon. I'm sure I'll love it."

"Okay."

I didn't realize until she'd left that I'd been holding my breath. I laced my fingers together, cracked my knuckles, and got down to business.

Within an hour, I had updated some of the text and graphics on her home page, then spent a good twenty minutes maneuvering carefully through the shop with my digital camera in hand, taking pictures of the pieces Anna pointed out between her intense discussions with this customer or that. When I felt like I'd accomplished enough to justify my coming over, I picked up my bag from Anna's office, palmed my key ring, and ducked my head into the store.

Anna was tending to an expensively dressed blonde with a Louis Vuitton bag the size of a suitcase.

She wiggled her fingers at me as I made my escape, but I didn't slow down until I'd reached the Jeep.

No wonder Molly O'Brien had never felt accepted at Hockaday, I thought as I climbed inside. It was hard enough to actually belong and still not fit. To be an outsider without papers and pedigrees must have been truly painful. It made me thankful that we'd found each other back then.

Maybe Molly and I were more alike than we were different.

I smiled at that, knowing Mother would catch the vapors if she heard me utter such blasphemy. As far as she was concerned, Molly O'Brien would forever be "that scholarship girl." Not worthy of a deb ball, not worthy of a "good" marriage, not worthy of a house in the right zip code or a Mercedes SUV in which to carpool the kids. Not worthy of a friendship with a Blevins-Kendricks.

My cotton T-shirt stuck to my back, and I turned up the air conditioning. I checked behind me in the rearview mirror as I shot onto the highway and headed for downtown.

I was going to Lew Sterrett.

I had a plan, and I needed Molly's help.

Chapter 7

 I sat across the Plexiglas barrier and stared at her.

She'd tied back her dark hair in a ponytail, emphasizing the high angles of her cheekbones, the slashes of her eyebrows dark against pale skin, though I can't say the orange jumpsuit did much for her complexion. Smudges ringed her eyes, and the whites were red-veined. She looked like a woman on the verge of losing everything, and her expression reflected her despair.

"How are you?" I asked, but she shook her head and picked up the black receiver to her right. I followed suit and wrinkled my nose at the odor of congealed bad breath on the plastic.

"Hi," she said softly.

"Are you okay?"

"I've been in worse places. You should've seen some of the dives where Seb and I lived in Paris," she said and gave a halfhearted grin, but there was fear on her face. "I'll survive this, too."

"I would've put up the money to get you

out," I told her, and she pressed her mouth into a thin line. "I can't believe the judge denied bail."

"Guess he was afraid I'd pack up my kid and disappear," she murmured. "And he was right, Andy. I would have run. I would've done whatever it took to stay with my baby." She bent toward the Plexiglas. "How is he?" she asked, her grim features suddenly anxious. "He's never been away from me for more than a few days."

"He's doing fine," I said and smiled to prove it. "He's staying at Mother's in Highland Park."

"No kidding?"

I held up my hand. "Scout's honor. I dropped him off this morning. Last I saw him, Sandy was herding him into the kitchen for some pancakes."

"Oh, God." She chuckled. "I can't imagine Cissy Kendricks babysitting my son. I thought she ate children for breakfast."

"Only if she's out of marmalade."

"I hope he doesn't get too used to Buckingham Palace."

That's what she'd called it when we were in school. The first time Molly had ever visited the house on Beverly Drive, she'd been afraid to touch anything. Just to show her it was okay, I'd picked up one of Mother's crystal ashtrays and pretended to juggle it, only to toss it so high I missed the catch and sent it shattering at my feet. Cissy had assumed Molly had broken it

73

and that I'd covered up for her by taking the blame.

"I'll tell Sandy not to spoil him too much," I promised.

"Sandy's a good lady."

"The best."

The brightness faded from her eyes. Her chin quivered. "I blew it, didn't I? If I'd had any sense, I would've stayed in Chicago and finished school instead of leaving everything I'd worked so hard for to be with Seb." She didn't look at me when she continued. "He totally freaked when I told him I was pregnant. He wasn't ready to be anybody's daddy." She pressed her lips together so hard they disappeared into a thin white line. Then she lifted her eyes again. "But I'm glad I made the choice I did. Because it gave me David."

So it was true. The poetic Sebastian was David's father. Or at least the sperm donor. I couldn't imagine how hard that decision had been on Molly. Keep her baby or lose the man she loved. If I'd had Sebastian in the room with me, I'd have wrung his scrawny neck.

I wanted to ask her more, but figured she'd tell me in her own time. Catching up while she sat on the other side of the Plexiglas probably wasn't the best place for that. I held my curiosity in check, for now.

"I was so stupid back then, such a damn romantic fool." She puffed her cheeks and blew the air out. "If I'd had any sense, I would've kept in touch with you, Andy. But, once I was back and had David to look out for, I was so busy trying to stay afloat that I let everything else slide. I did learn you were back from Chicago, and I meant to connect with you, but" — she shrugged — "something always came up."

I was as responsible for letting our friendship go by the wayside as she was, but I didn't want to argue. Instead, I told her, "You don't have to apologize."

She poked a finger at me, tapping the barrier between us. "You're the same person you always were, you know? I figured maybe you'd changed in the years I was gone, but you didn't. I still can't believe you came to my rescue, getting me a lawyer and taking care of my son, without asking anything of me. Andrea Kendricks. Patron Saint of Lost Causes." Tears glistened on her lashes, and my heart ached.

I wanted to reach for her hand, but the glass stopped my fingers. "Hey, that's what friends are for."

"Except for you, I wouldn't know."

The metal door behind her swung open, and Molly visibly tensed. Her shoulders squared, and her chin went up. A prison matron in blue blouse and pants led a jumpsuited woman into the room.

Molly exhaled, slumping down in her chair. Her skin turned ashen. "I thought they were taking me back already."

I leaned nearer the clear partition as if I could

whisper to her without anyone overhearing. If I was going to put my scheme into action, I needed her help. And there wasn't any time to waste. "Can you answer some questions for me, Molly? About the restaurant and the people you worked with?"

She wrinkled her forehead. "Like what?"

"Did Bud have a partner, for one? Or was he sole proprietor?"

"I heard he had a silent partner, but I don't know who."

"Did he keep his own books?"

"I guess so."

I was on a roll. "And what about his relationship with that ex-cheerleader, Julie Costello? Was she the jealous type? Were there any other waitresses he was boinking? And do you know if he gambled or if he owed money . . . ?"

"Hold on a minute," Molly stopped me, her voice low and suspicious. "What are you up to?" She was clearly worried. "Don't get yourself involved in this mess any more than you are right now."

"I just want to be prepared."

"For what?"

Without further ado, I blurted out: "I thought I'd apply for your job."

There, I'd said it.

Molly blinked. "What?"

I shifted in the plastic chair, saying aloud what I'd been dreaming up in my head. "Well, they've got to be short a waitress, right? And I'll bet they don't stay closed any longer than it takes the police to blow through the place. They'll probably be open again by morning."

"Oh, Andy."

"It's the only way," I insisted, having tried to come up with another solution and finding no alternatives. "The police have set their sights on you, Molly. They're out to convict you of murder," I reminded her, though I doubt she'd forgotten. "They figure you did it, so they're not wasting any time looking for another suspect. They're busy piling up evidence against you for the prosecution to hammer you with. Once this gets to court, there's no turning back. This is the best chance we've got. . . ."

"All right, all right, you had me with 'convict.' " She leaned against the ledge on her side of the window, shoulders concave, head bowed, seeming suddenly smaller and more vulnerable. She transferred the receiver from her right ear to her left. "As much as I want to tell you to go home and forget about this, I can't. There's no way in hell I want to take the rap for something I didn't do."

I felt victorious despite the flutter in my belly. It was all I could do not to rub my hands together. "Now about those questions," I said into the receiver and started over, finding more to ask each time Molly responded to one.

When she'd told me all she knew about the general operations, I got down to the trickier stuff. "So how does a girl go about getting hired

77

at a place like Jugs? Do I wear a G-string or spandex?"

A tiny smile played on her lips. "Jeans and a T-shirt should do just fine."

"Tight?"

"Right."

"Should I shovel on the eyeliner and lipstick?"

She laughed. "What do you think?"

"Hair up or down?"

"The bigger, the better."

"Maybe I should invest in a Wonderbra," I suggested, glancing down at my barely there chest.

"The bigger, the better," she said again.

We both started to giggle, but the levity didn't last.

The matron came up behind her, hands on her hips. "Time's up," she must've said, though I could only see her mouth move and hear the vague crackle of her voice through the line.

"I gotta go," Molly whispered, adding, "Tell David I love him," before she quickly hung up.

She looked like a skinny kid in oversized orange pajamas, I thought as I watched her being led through the door and away.

It hit me hard that this was for real, and I suddenly felt sick to my stomach. This wasn't the Game of Life that she and I used to play. It wasn't even Monopoly.

Her future was at stake. The whole rest of her flipping life, no chance to "Get Out of Jail Free" with a roll of the dice.

And what about David? What would be his fate if his mother were condemned to hard time?

I got out of there as fast as I could, ignoring the air so warm and thick it nearly mugged me, trying not to notice the stink of urine that clung to every downtown building I passed on my way to the seven-dollar-an-hour Car Park.

Funny how easy it is to take things for granted when you have no fear of losing them.

Chapter 8

The offices of Abramawitz, Reynolds, Goldberg, and Hunt were located on the tenth floor of a modern high-rise a couple blocks from Lew Sterrett.

I decided it couldn't hurt to drop in on Brian Malone and see what information he'd managed to dig up so far. Maybe he'd seen the final version of the police report or heard something from the medical examiner's office.

My espadrilles shuffled over pink marble tiles as I crossed the foyer toward the elevators. A crowd of business-suited men and women waited quietly beside me until a light blinked above one of the four sets of doors. A gentle ping sounded as the doors slid open to disgorge a horde of people who looked not unlike the ones who pressed inside the mirrored space alongside me.

"Ten, please," I said, because I'd been pushed into the far corner and couldn't have reached the buttons unless I'd had the wingspan of Shaquille O'Neal.

A few cleared their throats, but no one said a

word as we rose upward. The blend of colognes and perfumes in the cramped space made me dizzy so I breathed through my mouth instead of my nose.

The elevator stopped on practically every floor, and I felt more than a tad claustrophobic by the time it reached level ten.

A glossy plaque on a pair of glass doors identified the offices of Abramawitz, Reynolds, Goldberg, and Hunt, and I slipped in and headed toward a kidney-shaped reception desk in a lobby that was dimly lit with mauve walls, leather sofas, and area rugs. I heard the faint strains of a Mozart piano concerto being piped into the room.

The woman behind the desk wore a headset over the pale blond of her hair, and I listened to her put half a dozen callers on hold before she looked up with a white-toothed smile, asking, "May I help you, ma'am?" Something about being called "ma'am" always needled me. Made me feel as if they were talking to my mother. I nearly glanced over my shoulder, expecting to find Cissy standing there.

"I'd like to see Brian Malone, please."

"Name?"

"Andrea Kendricks."

She scrunched up her tiny nose and peered at the computer screen, her fingers tapping on the keyboard, and then she glanced at me again, this time without the toothpaste-perfect smile. "You're not listed on his schedule, ma'am. Perhaps I can make you an appointment for next week?"

"It's important that I. . . ."

"One moment, please," she interrupted and raised a pink-tipped finger as the telephone buzzed for her attention. "Abramawitz, Reynolds, Goldberg, and Hunt, one moment, please," she rattled off in staccato quick succession. She put the line on hold and looked up again. "If you want to see one of our attorneys, you'll need an appointment, ma'am."

"Andy?"

Turning at the sound of his voice, I sighed with relief at the sight of Malone standing in the mouth of the hallway, a cup of coffee in his hand. "I was just taking a break, and I thought I saw you out there."

"Yep, it's me all right." I gave the receptionist a little smirk as I left the front desk and walked toward him. "You have a few minutes?" I asked.

"I can spare about ten. I'm proofing a brief for one of the senior partners before a meeting with a client."

"Thanks."

I followed him out of the mauve lobby and through a maze of hallways with wood panels and wildlife prints that reminded me of a series my dentist had on the wall across from the spit sink.

I peered into the offices we passed, noting shelves floor-to-ceiling with books, patterned area rugs, and big dark desks behind which sat a succession of mostly white male occupants.

So much for diversity.

"Here we are," Malone said, stopping outside a door at the end of the maze. His nearest neighbor, I noted, was an enormous copy machine currently spewing out collated papers at about a page per second.

He ushered me inside and gestured at a barrel-backed chair opposite his paper-cluttered desk. I had a feeling the firm's interior decorator had bypassed his office entirely. Or maybe that was an incentive for making partner.

There were no windows, but the room was well lit, and someone had deposited a large closet plant in the corner so there was living green amidst the grim palette of deep blues and browns. Brown shelves, brown floor, faded blue dhurrie, brown chairs, brown desk, navy drapes. I glanced at Malone and wondered if he'd color-coordinated his attire of brown suit and blue striped tie.

He set his Styrofoam cup down atop a stack of manila folders and leaned back in his big chair, setting his hands in his lap. "Now, what can I do for you?"

Though I realized he had to be about my age, he appeared so boyish with his tousled hair and clean-shaven jaw. His eyes were clear and wide behind his glasses. A part of me wished he were older and grayer, but he had an earnestness about him that I found appealing.

"This isn't a social call, is it?"

I held my purse on my knees and fiddled with the strap. "I just came from the county jail," I confessed, and he didn't seem surprised. "I can't believe they've got her locked up already. I mean, I know the wheels of justice are swift, but this is ridiculous."

"I'm working as fast as I can."

"Well, go faster, Malone. We can't let this thing go to trial or the prosecution's going to railroad her. I can see it happening as we speak."

His chair squeaked as he bent forward over his desk. "Listen to me, Andy. Nobody ever knows how a jury's going to react to a case before it's presented. Not even the consultants who help pick them."

"But it looks bad, even you said so."

He shrugged, and his long fingers encircled his coffee cup. "It'll depend on who they believe. Molly or the cops."

"Great," I groused, knowing who always came out on top in Texas. The cops were the good guys here, not like in L.A. where they so often seemed to wear the black hats. "Have you seen a copy of the final police report yet? How about the autopsy findings?"

"Preliminaries only," he said and fished through some of the papers on his desk. He apparently found what he was looking for. "What do you want to know?"

So many questions came to mind that I wasn't

sure which to ask first. "How about the time of death?"

Malone skimmed the pages. "Estimated TOD is somewhere between midnight and three A.M. Rigor mortis had just started setting in, and the body temp had cooled by a couple of degrees."

I felt a flash of hope. "So Bud Hartman could have been alive when Molly left like she told us. He could have been killed an hour later . . . maybe even two."

"But the security guard saw her fleeing the scene just before one A.M. Guy's name is Fred Hicks. He's been working for Lone Star Security for almost a year. They have a contract with the Villa Mesa Plaza. In his statement, he said that he wrote down Molly's plate number on instinct, but everything else seemed quiet so he went about his regular duties and finished his rounds. He was distracted for a while by a problem at the Zuma Beach Club, across the parking lot from Jugs."

"Zuma Beach?" I repeated, easily imagining what the distraction might have been. The bar was popular with the college crowd. Some girls I knew from Hockaday who'd attended SMU or Texas Christian used to hang out there regularly on Saturday nights long after graduation. They'd called it the "meat market" back then, and I didn't figure things had changed much over time. "Did some drunken frat boys cause a scene?"

Malone nodded. "Bingo. Hickman had to break up a fight between a couple kids who were blotto, then he called them both cabs. It was nearly three when he went back to Jugs and saw Hartman's car still there. Apparently, that happened occasionally, but he did get curious enough to go over and that's when he found the rear door unlocked. When he went inside, Hartman was lying face down on the floor with an eight-inch chef's knife protruding from his back."

I wasn't about to give up. "That leaves almost two whole hours for someone else to have stabbed him. The killer could've come and gone while Hicks was taking care of those yahoos at Zuma." I caught my second wind. "My God, Malone, anyone could've gotten into Jugs if the back door was open and no alarm was set. From what I've heard so far, Hartman was a real ass. He probably had enemies up the wazoo. Maybe a jealous boyfriend or husband came after him and took the opportunity to teach him a lesson he'd never forget."

Malone patiently waited until I'd finished, then told me, "The cooks who worked the last shift at Jugs that night said they'd sanitized all the cooking utensils before going home. Molly's prints were the only ones on the handle of the murder weapon."

"The killer could've worn gloves."

Malone sighed.

"Maybe this was premeditated," I suggested,

hating that he was so ready to give up because a shopping center security guard and a few fingerprints pointed in Molly's direction. Besides, everyone knew how unreliable eyewitnesses were. All you had to do was watch a rerun of *Law & Order.*

I pointed this out to him, adding, "Someone could have hidden in a closet, waiting for everyone to leave. Only Hartman went after Molly, and she picked up the knife to scare him off."

Malone's brows arched.

"Okay, so she nicked him a little, but she didn't do the deed. What she did was leave enough evidence to make the cops believe she's guilty. Now she's accused, and the real murderer is walking around, scot-free."

My heart pounded in my chest, and I realized I'd come halfway out of my seat. My purse had fallen to the floor, and I scooped it up and settled back into my chair, primly crossing my ankles.

Malone watched me, his head tilted to the right, his eyes narrowed, and I felt warm despite the air conditioning.

"You think I'm nuts, don't you?" I dared to ask, though I could guess his response by the disbelief on his face.

He smoothed a hand down his tie and cleared his throat. "No, Andy, of course I don't think you're nuts."

"No?"

"I just think you're tilting at windmills. Your mother said you've always been a sucker for lost causes."

"Is that so?"

"And that you had an overactive imagination."

"I see," I said through gritted teeth and flushed from ear to ear. I wondered what else Cissy had told him behind my back. Did he hear about the time I was suspended from school for a day because I'd refused to dissect a frog in biology? Did he know the size of my shoes or the score on my SATs?

Focus, Andy, I reminded myself, because anything my mother did could too easily distract me.

We'd been debating whether or not someone could have been hiding in Jugs when Bud attacked Molly.

I reconsidered the scenario I'd described, and there didn't seem to be anything "overly imaginative" about it. It was perfectly plausible to me. So I challenged him, "Will you at least admit it's not impossible?"

"Nothing's impossible this early on. Not from where I stand."

Well, that was progress, wasn't it?

"Tell me what else the preliminary autopsy report has to say about the body," I asked, changing the subject entirely. I could tell I was going to have to convince Malone a spoonful at a time. Maybe he'd been born in Missouri, the

"Show Me" state, because he obviously liked to rely on "just the facts."

Some people, huh?

"I'll give you what I can, okay?" He glanced at the papers on his desk. "There was a superficial laceration on Hartman's face. . . ."

"You see!" I jumped in. "That must've been where Molly caught him with the knife when he had her pinned against the counter in the kitchen." I smiled smugly. "She told us the truth."

He nudged at his glasses. "I'd like to believe that."

"It accounts for the blood on her shirt and shoes."

He pressed his fingertips together in a steeple, probably waiting for me to stop interrupting.

"What does it say about the money bag?" I prodded.

Malone again rifled through the papers, though this time it took him longer. "The only place it's even mentioned is in Molly's statement. She claims she put the cash and the credit card receipts from the register into the bank bag and placed it on Hartman's desk. But no such bag was found by the police." He shifted in his seat. "Look, Andy, the D.A.'s office got a copy of her credit report, and Molly's in debt up to her eyeballs. They're going to contend she stole the cash herself, maybe even killed for it."

I scooted to the edge of my chair. "Then why would she even bring it up?"

"Because they would've found out it was missing sooner or later."

"So where is it?" I asked point-blank. "Did they find it when they searched her place? Was it in her car?"

"No."

"Aha!"

But my moment of glee was short-lived.

"They'll say she hid it somewhere, planning to go back for it later."

I sniffed. "Give me a break."

"It gives her a motive, Andy."

Why did it seem like he was fighting me instead of taking up the battle cry of Molly's innocence?

"Look, Malone, she said there was at least four or five thousand in cash, though she didn't do an official tally. She told me Bud always made up the deposit slips, never the wait staff. Maybe he did that for a very good reason. Like he was being a little creative with his bookkeeping."

Malone scratched behind his ear. "You're the one who's getting a little creative here. Let's stick to the facts for now, please."

Facts schmacts.

I pressed my lips together, saying nothing, but my mind was making such a racket I was surprised he couldn't hear it. If Molly didn't take that bank bag from Bud's desk when she ran off just before one o'clock, clearly someone else had been there.

Whoever it was, I'd figure it out.

I left Malone's office and headed to the only place with any answers.

Chapter 9

The sun was sinking fast below the flat horizon as I drove north on the tollway and exited at Preston Road.

I pulled off at the sight of the Golden Arches, detouring at McDonald's just long enough to drive through and order a Filet-O-Fish and fries. I'd missed lunch, what with going down to Lew Sterrett to see Molly and stopping by ARGH, and my stomach had started a vicious rumbling that didn't stop until I washed down the last fry with a chug of cold soda.

Across the street, most of the vans from the local TV stations still camped in the parking lot at Jugs.

This was big news, I realized. Juicy scandal. The owner of a restaurant famous for its half-naked waitresses had been stabbed to death. One of those half-naked waitresses had been arrested and charged with the crime. The story would likely knock the latest Dallas Cowboys' escapades off the front page of the *Morning News*, at least for a couple days.

There was no need to think WWND (What

Would Nancy Do — as in Drew), because I had that all mapped out. Like a rubbernecker drawn to a highway accident, I was magnetically pulled across the street.

I drove over and slid the Jeep into an empty space at the Zuma Beach Club since it wouldn't open for hours yet.

Yellow crime-scene tape fluttered across the front doors of the restaurant. The enormous pair of jugs on the billboard high above seemed to stare as I approached.

Now I understood why the anti-Jugs protestors had once painted a giant pink bra over them. They were rather disconcerting.

I wondered how Molly had felt about coming here night after night, having to work for a guy like Bud Hartman who, from what I'd heard, seemed to think his waitresses were his personal possessions. Did the men who frequented the place have the same macho outlook? Had they treated her with more respect than Bud, or had Molly been responsible for fending off their advances as well with little more than a smile as her defense?

I felt steamed just thinking about it.

A blue-and-white Dallas patrol car was parked near the restaurant's front entrance, and I noticed one of the uniformed officers stationed outside the door. He kept turning back the reporters who approached him with microphones and minicams at the ready. Apparently "no" wasn't a word they'd learned at J-School.

The cop had his arms crossed over a beefy chest. His black mustache only emphasized his scowl, which deepened with my approach.

"Sorry, lady, but no one gets inside till tomorrow morning," he said before I'd even opened my mouth. "As of now, this is a secured area."

"No problem, Officer," I replied, thanking him for the information, which is all I'd really wanted.

So Jugs would reopen tomorrow. By then, they'd have Bud's blood cleaned off the floor, all the mess left behind by the crime lab technicians scrubbed away, and everything in perfect order again as if nothing had ever happened.

That suited me fine. I wasn't a big fan of blood. It was reassuring to realize the place would be tidied up when I returned to apply for Molly's position.

I skirted the camera crews and vans scattered around the four corners of Jugs like swarms of buzzing insects. But they apparently weren't the only ones attracted to the murder scene.

A minicam's bright light overexposed a reporter with mike in hand, interviewing a contingent of picketers lifting signs that read: MAP — MOTHERS AGAINST PORNOGRAPHY and STOP DEGRADING WOMEN! I got close enough to hear a youthful woman with a baby in a sling between her breasts shout that "Bud reaped what he sowed!"

Lovely sentiment.

Which got me thinking more about what Molly had said, about Bud's hitting on the waitresses and pressuring them for sexual favors. I had asked her why no one had called the EEOC or some other agency that purported to protect workers against harassment, and Molly had simply shrugged. "The money's too good, Andy. I can get three hundred each night in tips, easy. The only way I could do better would be if I took my clothes off and let a bunch of drooling dogs stuff bills into my G-string."

I didn't think putting up with an abusive boss was worth any amount of money, but then I'd never had to worry about how I was going to pay my bills or put food on the table. There was a lot I couldn't comprehend about the world Molly lived in, no matter how much I sympathized.

"It wasn't an awful place to work. The customers were pretty decent. Just a few bad apples now and then, but no more than if I'd been working at IHOP. Putting up with guys like Bud was part of the job, and I could do it if I had to," she'd explained. "For David's sake as well as mine."

It wasn't fair, I decided. But then life wasn't about justice. Some people seemed to get all the breaks and others just got broken.

I went around to the back door and spotted another blue uniform keeping people away.

A blonde accessorized with microphone and

cameraman seemed determined to get the officer to utter more than a "No comment."

"Is it true that Bud Hartman was illegally watering down the drinks he served his customers?"

The cop squinted into the minicam's light and said gruffly, "I'm trying to do my job, ma'am, so if you'd kindly step away."

"I heard he may have sexually preyed upon his female employees," the blonde tried again.

"Could you step back, please?"

"Was he a date rapist?"

The officer turned beet red. "Are you hard of hearing?"

"Was he killed in self-defense by that waitress?"

This time, our friend in blue pointed a finger in the nose of the reporter. "Unless you want to be the victim of self-defense, you've got two seconds to get that microphone out of my face."

I stood back a couple yards, enjoying the exchange, rooting for the cop and hoping the reporter didn't move. I wouldn't have minded seeing her take a pop to her collagen-enhanced pie hole. There had been times I'd wanted to punch her myself.

Unfortunately for me, the blonde with the mike did a 180-degree turn and drew a finger across her throat. "That's a wrap, Kevin," she told her cameraman, who cut the high-powered light and lowered the contraption from his shoulder. "If you've got enough footage, then we're done here."

She very nearly walked through me, but I lifted a hand in a small wave and said, "Hey, Cinda Lou."

Only then noting my presence, she stopped and stared through the descending dusk until recognition dawned. "Andy Kendricks? Is that you?"

"Last I checked."

"Well, whaddaya know."

Oh, hell, I knew plenty.

Cinda Lou Mitchell had been in my class at Hockaday. If she wasn't the most popular girl, she was runner-up. Mother had always hoped Cinda and I would strike up a close friendship, but it hadn't happened and never would. It didn't help that I could hardly stand to be around the girl for more than five minutes. Still, her mother and mine cochaired so many society soirees that I'd never completely lost touch, occasionally bumping into her at whatever dinner or dance Mother guilted me into attending every once in a blue moon. I knew Cinda had already been married three times, and each divorce had left her wealthier than the last, so that her reporting gig was basically a hobby.

"For heaven's sake," she murmured and, still clutching her microphone, set her hands on the hips of her red tailored suit. The trademark smile for which she was renowned throughout the Dallas-Fort Worth metroplex beamed so brightly I felt like a deer caught in headlights. "I haven't seen you since Cissy dragged you to last summer's charity ball to raise funds for the homeless."

"I've been busy with work," I explained, and it wasn't a total fib. "I don't have much time for a social life."

Cinda Lou tossed pale-gold curls, a knowing look in her eyes. "Well, I guess Cissy has social life enough for you both. I don't think she's missed a charity event in thirty years. Why it wasn't but two days after your daddy passed that she showed up to emcee at the Calf Fry and Rodeo for Battered Women."

Leaving me alone to bawl my eyes out, I wanted to add, but held my tongue. Mother had always been — and would forever be — a social butterfly. It's what had kept her going since Daddy died, and I didn't begrudge her it. It's who she was. Even in grief, she could air kiss with the best of them.

"So what brings you over to the Villa Mesa parking lot?" Cinda asked without further ado, peering at me as though I were hiding a deep dark secret. "Don't tell me you managed the web site for this outfit? Though I can't imagine our goody two-shoes Andy getting her hands dirty working for a guy like Bud Hartman. I heard he was a real swine despite being great-looking and" — she bent her head toward mine — "wild in bed."

I felt a blush creep into my cheeks. "No, no, I don't work for Jugs." Not yet anyway. "I'm doing a favor for Molly O'Brien."

Cinda Lou lifted finely plucked brows. "The woman they arrested for stabbing Hartman?"

"She went to school with us," I reminded her, though Cinda's expression was blank. "She was my closest friend."

"The waitress from Jugs went to Hockaday?"

"Yes."

She squinted at the purple sky, then her eyes abruptly rounded. "Oh, my God! The scholarship girl. She lived in a foster home or something. *She*'s the one who stabbed Bud Hartman?"

"Well, yes and no" — I squirmed — "but she didn't kill him."

"Geez, Andy, thanks for the tip." She yelled for her cameraman. "Kevin! Call my mother, would you? Tell her to dig up my yearbooks so we can swing by and pick 'em up on our way back to the studio."

"Cinda Lou." I tugged at her sleeve, but she was already focused on creating a new angle for her story. Thanks to my big mouth. "Keep Molly's private life out of this, please. She has a little boy. Besides, she's innocent until proven guilty, right?"

"Sure, sure, whatever."

Cinda brushed me off like lint. Her mind was already at work. I could practically see her eyes spinning.

"From Hockaday to the hoosegow," she said, punctuating each word with a stab of the mike in the air. "Catchy, don't you think?"

"Cinda Lou Mitchell," I said, slow and low, so she'd know I meant business. The Filet-O-Fish and fries churned in my stomach. "Don't do this."

"But, honey, it's my job."

"She was a classmate."

"Which makes the story more personal."

"Have some compassion," I begged her, but Cinda just laughed.

"I'm a journalist, Andy. I don't get paid to have compassion."

I didn't get the chance to respond.

A red Corvette pulled up behind Jugs with a screech of tires. A big-haired blonde jumped out of the driver's side and rushed toward the police-guarded back door.

Cinda froze. "Ohmigod, that's Julie Costello." She nearly dropped her mike, but did a quick save and shouted for Kevin to bring the camera pronto. Like a tornado, she spun off in pursuit of the ex-professional cheerleader who, if Molly's info was correct, had been the dead man's lover.

Maybe I should have left at that point, having opened my yap once too often.

But my curiosity got the better of me, and I hung around to catch the action between Cinda Lou, girl reporter, and Julie Costello, grieving girlfriend.

This could be a really big shoe, to quote Ed Sullivan.

If only I had some popcorn.

Cinda had her microphone in Julie's face as the cameraman fixed his bright light on them both. Ms. Costello certainly didn't seem to mind being the center of attention. She primped at hair teased to cotton-candy fullness and batted big eyes painted with enough makeup to rival a drag queen. She wore a cut-off JUGS T-shirt that bared her very flat midriff and accentuated grapefruit-shaped breasts. Ah, the fine art of plastic surgery.

"He was special to me, Bud was," I heard her remark as I worked my way nearer. "He liked to flirt with pretty women, sure, but he was a decent man at heart. I don't care what anyone else says about him. No one knew him as well as I did."

A single tear glinted in the spotlight's glare and slipped down her cheek.

"Speaking of flirting with pretty women, do you believe the prime suspect, Molly O'Brien, killed your boyfriend in self-defense?" Cinda asked in her best Baba Wawa imitation.

Ms. Costello turned directly to the camera and howled, "I should've stayed on my shift! I felt sick last night and left early, but if I'd toughed it out instead of letting Molly help Bud close up the place, he'd still be alive! I know he would! That bitch took something precious from me, and I hope they fry her for it."

I couldn't listen to another word. It was like watching a bad soap opera, only I knew it was all too real.

I didn't wait to say goodbye to Cinda.

Twilight darkened the sky as I drove down to Highland Park to Mother's house.

By the time I arrived, Sandy was tucking a tired David into bed in one of the guest rooms, so I dropped in on Mother. She was staring at the TV screen.

Her bifocals pushed low on her nose, she glanced at me over the rims and shook her head. "They've got constant break-in updates about the murder, Andrea. On every channel."

"Just make sure David doesn't see them, will you, please?" I leaned my back against the doorframe, needing its support.

"What if they discover the child is here and flock to my door?"

"Have Sandy scare them away just like she does the Jehovah's Witnesses."

"Andrea. . . ."

But I ducked out before she could say anything else. I headed up the hallway toward the room where David would stay until. . . .

Well, just until.

I heard his soft crying even before I'd entered. He was sitting up in bed, wrapped in Sandy's arms.

"Rest easy, sweet pea," she hushed him. "Everything will work out fine, you'll see, and your mama will come after you soon."

"P-promise?" the boy softly wailed.

"Cross my heart and hope to die, stick a needle in my eye," Sandy told him, the closest thing to a sure bet that I'd ever known.

The little boy nodded against her chest.

My heart tightened, and I closed my eyes, fighting tears of my own.

"Don't worry, David, your mama loves you," Sandy soothed him, muffling his sobs against her shoulder. "She'll be home soon."

Even I wanted desperately to believe her.

Chapter 10

 I waited to head home until after David had fallen asleep, glad for the cozy solitude of my condominium. Being at Mother's house even for a few minutes had made me feel tense from head to toe. With all that was going on, I was beginning to grind my teeth.

I changed from my wrinkled clothes into a pair of boxer shorts and a much-washed, over-sized Tee. Victoria's Secret had scratched me off their mailing list years ago, no doubt putting me in their "hopeless" file. Well, it wasn't as if I had anyone around to impress with silk teddies or lacy negligees. I didn't have to worry about how I looked, and I liked it that way.

For now.

The beige wall-to-wall carpeting flattened underfoot as I padded to the galley kitchen and fired up a Stouffer's macaroni and cheese in the microwave. With that in one hand and a glass of milk in the other, I plunked myself down in front of the boob tube and tried to relax for the first time that day.

I didn't have cable, so there weren't many

channels to choose from. I found a rerun of *Matlock* and ate with my bare feet propped up on the blanket chest that had been my mother's and her mother's before that. It was a hope chest, actually, though I think Cissy had already given up hoping I'd ever store a trousseau in it. I wasn't in the market for a husband. I was simply enjoying the freedom of living each day on my own without too many eyes peering over my shoulder.

As I finished up the last bite of mac and cheese, I looked around at my walls, thinking how different my place was from Mother's. No real antiques, save for the chest and an Eastlake bed handed down from an uncle. Whatever else I owned I'd purchased at consignment stores and flea markets. My mother thought my idea of conserving money and sticking to a budget was silly. Maybe it was my way of asserting my independence, of distancing myself from the child who had grown up with everything, but had lost what was most important of all.

My father.

I liked knowing what I had was mine. Most of the framed art consisted of charcoal etchings or acrylic work I'd done through the years. A few were original oils I'd dug up at estate sales, someone else's castoffs that suited me beautifully. The pretty 1930s dresser in my bedroom had been refinished with my own elbow grease, the black drippy varnish replaced by a warm walnut. I'd done the same with the four dining room chairs I'd bought for a steal at the Junior League rummage sale (five bucks apiece!). I felt proud just looking at them, like I'd accomplished something.

"Why does a well-endowed girl like you with no need to work live the way you do?"

Anna's query seeped into my consciousness, and I wiped the back of my hand across my milk-damp mouth, wondering if I was truly as eccentric as everyone seemed to believe.

Daddy had set up a trust fund for me when I was born. He'd wanted to make sure I could go to any college of my choosing and could become whatever kind of person I wanted to be without student loans or financial insecurity hanging over my head for eternity.

I used the money only when I simply couldn't afford not to; but most of the interest and annuities I reinvested carefully.

I wondered if all my money — hell, all my family's money — could have gotten me out of jail had I been in Molly's shoes.

I'd like to believe that justice was truly blind and could neither be bought nor sold, but I'd seen quite a few of Mother and Daddy's acquaintances pay the right lawyers and get off the hook for things like insider trading, fraud, and embezzlement. Even murder. (Okay, murder for hire.) The Great State of Texas liked to keep its rich out of the pokey so they could build more houses, drill for more oil, raise more cattle, buy more land, and sell more IPOs. The kind of things that were supposed to keep the economy rolling. I wasn't sure if the high-priced defense attorneys were really that good or if prosecutors just had a hard time convicting and sentencing well-groomed men and women dressed in Armani.

So what would happen to Molly?

She wasn't rich. I'd bet she didn't own an Armani.

Would the jury look at her and see a killer? Would they assume she was a desperate woman who'd stabbed a man in order to make off with five thousand dollars of restaurant receipts? Would the security guard's testimony and her fingerprints on the knife be all the proof they needed to put her away for life?

The mere idea that Molly might actually be convicted rankled me to the core. Heck, I was a Libra. I always wanted the world to be fair — which it rarely was — so the whole thing didn't sound right to me. It was different for the rich. Just ask good ol' O.J.

Would Molly stand a chance against those odds?

Sighing loudly, I drew my legs up and wrapped my arms around them, setting my chin on my knees.

"I ran out of there so fast. I heard him call after me, so I figured he was pissed as hell. But he was alive."

Molly hadn't stabbed Bud to death. The superficial cut on his face proved to me that she wasn't lying. It explained why her prints were on the murder weapon and accounted for the blood-spattered shirt and shoes.

I thought of the missing bank bag containing the day's receipts and tried to figure out where it might be, who might have taken it. Its disappearance made me surer than ever that someone had been at Jugs after Molly had run off. Maybe there was more than one person involved in Bud's death.

My head throbbed, and I reached up to rub my temples.

"Do you know what you're doing, my dear? Getting entangled in the troubles of a woman you haven't seen in years, one who's been accused of murder?"

I groaned.

Mother's warning returned to nag at me, and the pounding in my brain increased.

". . . now for an update on the murder of the local restaurateur. . . ."

I glanced up to see the ten o'clock news anchors for Channel 11 filling the television screen. They quickly switched to a close-up of Cinda Lou Mitchell wearing her "I'm a serious reporter" face. The tape of her interview with Julie Costello rolled and ended with a mug shot of Molly on a split screen with her senior class photo from the Hockaday yearbook.

Oh, Cinda was good about using the word "alleged," as in "alleged knife-wielding murderer," but it pissed me off just the same.

Snatching up the remote, I flipped channels only to find the story playing out on the news at every other local station.

Except for one.

A twenty-four-hour local UHF setup (Channel 3, if you had cable) featuring the Reverend Jim Bob Barker and his purple-wigged cohort who cried "Amen!" every time the man uttered a word. Just watching the two was enough to cause indigestion. No wonder I had nightmares about them.

Though the number for their prayer line running constantly across the bottom of the screen tempted me briefly.

With a jab of my finger, I shut the television off and sat in the quiet of my living room, wondering what had ever made me think I could actually help free Molly from Lew Sterrett when even the Dallas P.D. believed she'd killed a man.

"You're a good friend," I heard her voice then, soft and tremulous, and I saw the tears in her eyes when she'd said it. *"Coming to my rescue, getting me a lawyer, taking care of David."*

Yikes, what had I done?

Was I giving her false hope where there was none?

Were Malone and my mother both right? Should I have stayed out of this entirely and allowed the chips to fall where they may?

I hugged my knees harder.

My daddy had always told me to listen to my gut, to believe in myself and in whatever I did (so long as it wasn't immoral or illegal). With that in mind, I swallowed down the nasty taste of uncertainty in my mouth.

I was all Molly had.

Even if I'd wanted to listen to Mother and bail out now, I couldn't have done it.

I liked to think Molly would have done the same for me.

Chapter 11

I called Mother's first thing in the morning to check on David. I felt sorry for the kid. No doubt he was scared to death. Thrust into new surroundings, not knowing when his mom was coming back to him. Living in a sort of limbo in which no six-year-old should have to live.

Sandy answered on the kitchen extension. I heard the sizzle of bacon frying on the griddle.

"How's he doing?" I asked right off the bat. "Did he sleep through the night?"

"Not entirely."

"Oh?" A lump of anxiety rose in my throat until I heard her soft chuckle.

"Would you believe I found him snoozing in the den with Cissy?"

I nearly dropped the phone. "What?"

Sandy's drawl thickened with amusement. "They must've both had insomnia. The second half of *Gone With the Wind* was stuck in the VCR, though I doubt either of 'em made it much past the burning of Atlanta."

I grinned. Score one for Mother. "I'll be by

later on to see him, okay?"

"We're having Kentucky Fried Chicken to-night for dinner if you'd like to join us," she said, quickly adding, "David's choice."

Mother serving food from a paper bucket?

This was a once-in-a-lifetime thing, far rarer than a total eclipse of the sun.

I'd have to bring my digital camera.

"Cissy has a meeting of the Dallas Diet Club at Millicent Maxwell's so she won't be around this evening," Sandy said, as if reading my mind. The Diet Club was a group of Mother's cronies who gathered once every few weeks to play bridge and eat desserts named "Death by Choc-olate" or "Killer Crème Brûlée" whipped up by the city's best pastry chefs. It had zero to do with dieting, obviously.

Rats.

Guess there would be no glossy photos of Cissy Blevins Kendricks with her bejeweled fin-gers wrapped around a greasy drumstick on this year's Christmas cards.

"You want to talk to your mom?" Sandy asked at my silence. "She's upstairs dressing. I could give a holler."

"Just tell her I'm still working on getting Molly out of jail."

"Oh, Andy. Do be careful." Sandy sounded truly concerned.

"Aren't I always?"

"Do you really want me to answer that?"

"No comment," I said and felt like the cop

at the back door to Jugs, fending off the reporters.

After a breakfast of Pop-Tarts and juice, I showered, then stood at my closet door with a towel wrapped around my middle as I tried to narrow down what to wear for my audition to be Molly's replacement. At least it felt like an audition. I had to dress and act the part of a woman who actually wanted a job wearing hot pants and serving food to drooling men who hid copies of *Playboy* in their tool chests.

The last time I'd tested my thespian skills was during tryouts for the all-female production of *The King and I* in high school. It was my first and last attempt at acting. I hadn't won the role of Anna or the king for that matter. I ended up being "Siamese, if you please," in the chorus, thankfully drowned out by far better voices than mine.

Hopefully, I'd do better at Jugs.

At least singing wasn't required.

I finally pulled on a pair of jeans that hadn't been worn in several years because they'd shrunk in the wash — or so I'd told myself — and fit so tightly I could barely breathe when I buttoned them up. I didn't own a Wonderbra so I did the next best thing, inserting a couple of foamy shoulder pads into the cups of a sports bra.

Voila! Instant C-cups.

I tackled my hair next, blowing the dust off my set of hot rollers and putting them to work.

Then I dug out a shoebox full of Mary Kay cosmetics accumulated over a decade and probably past their expiration date, if such a thing were possible. I painted, tweaked, glossed, and blushed until there wasn't an inch of face left untouched.

When I was done, I didn't even recognize the woman in the mirror. And it was a good thing, too.

I had to remind myself over and over that I was doing this for Molly; otherwise I would never have made it out my front door. What was that line Dolly Parton used? Something like, "It takes a lot of work to look this cheap."

I *so* understood.

Molly had told me that Jugs opened for business at eleven o'clock on weekday mornings, so I made it a point to arrive at the restaurant at ten. *"Bud was always there at least two hours early to make sure everything was ready and everybody showed up,"* she'd said, and I figured that whoever was taking over would probably follow the same routine.

There were several cars in the restaurant's back lot when I pulled the Jeep into the Villa Mesa shopping center, but the blue-and-whites and media vans were mercifully absent. I spotted Julie Costello's red Corvette as soon as I rounded the corner. A shiny white Lincoln Town Car sat beside it, the dark-tinted windows reminiscent of my father's Caddy. Only, on closer inspection, the Town Car had some hail damage, visible dings marring the snowy white surface.

I drove around to a space on the other side of Jugs where I could check my makeup in the rearview mirror with some degree of privacy before I dared step out of the car. I wiped a smudge of Paradise Plum from my front teeth, feeling a little like Mata Hari in stonewashed Gap denim.

Despite the circumstances, I smiled, wondering what Mother would do if she could see me now. Faint? Drag me by the ear and wash my face off with spit? Though a stroke wasn't out of the question. I looked less like an artist than a striptease artist. But that was the point, wasn't it? I certainly wouldn't be hired to wait tables in hot pants if I showed up in my paint-stained sweats and wire rims.

"Well, here goes nothing," I said to the stranger in the rearview and gave my bra an upward push. Satisfied that my shoulder pad–enhanced bosoms were symmetrical, I opened the car door and got out.

The billboard that hovered high above again drew my attention upward. The oversized pair of jugs followed my every move like eyes, giving new meaning to the phrase, "Big Brother is watching."

The yellow police tape that had criss-crossed the front doors was gone, though a torn piece had caught on a nearby holly bush and fluttered in the breeze.

I approached the glass doors and pulled at the green metal bars, but they were tightly locked.

The best-laid plans, I mused with a sigh. But I wasn't discouraged. I knew for a fact that Julie Costello was inside. I'd get in somehow, even if I had to bang on the windows and beg entrance.

I went around back to the door where the uniformed officer with the mustache had stood guard the day before. There was no sign of him now. The door was actually ajar, the deadbolt lock turned so that it couldn't close properly. With a tug on the smudged metal handle, I was inside. The cool tickle of air conditioning raised goose bumps on my skin.

"Ready, Freddy?" I asked under my breath. Then I straightened my shoulders, sucked in my gut, stuck out my chest, and plunged forward, the door clanking shut behind me.

"Hello?" I said to the empty kitchen that sprawled before me in a maze of stainless steel countertops and grills. "Anyone home?"

The overhead fluorescents glowed a sickly yellow green, and I tiptoed around gingerly, focusing on the floor, looking for bloodstains. But all I saw were some chips in the tiles. One of the faucets dripped with the precision of a metronome, seeming to imitate my footsteps with each blip-blop, blip-blop. I kept looking over my shoulder, imagining someone following me.

The air reeked of ammonia, and I figured the cleanup crew had swept through sometime earlier. There was nothing left to remind anyone that this had ever been a crime scene. Every surface gleamed.

I shivered, the hair at my nape bristling as I recalled Molly's description of Bud pinning her against the countertop and forcing his tongue down her throat. She had felt helpless with his weight atop her. Terrified of what he'd do, she had had no choice but to grab the knife and lash out at him in order to escape.

And she had gotten away.

She had run out of the restaurant while Bud had howled and cursed. That's exactly what had happened. I was sure of it.

I looked around me at shadowed corners and closed doors. There were plenty of places to hide in the kitchen. Someone certainly could have been watching what transpired between Bud and Molly.

Watching and waiting.

My heartbeat quickened. I was giving myself the willies.

"Hello? Anyone here?"

I walked toward a swinging door and into the restaurant itself. Dozens of tables with red-and-white checked cloths stood in neat rows, chairs carefully positioned around them. A television beamed noiselessly from above the bar, and I caught a glimpse of racecars buzzing around a track.

ESPN, I realized.

Not a soul was in sight.

I returned to the kitchen and headed toward a rear hallway. "Hello?" I tried again, my small voice sounding so timid to my ears. "Anybody here?"

Zip.

I passed a room filled with lockers and detected the faint sound of voices coming from farther up the hallway. My pink high-tops squeaking softly with each step, I crept toward a partially opened door just yards ahead. I could make out the noise of an argument between a man and woman, but caught only snatches of their low-pitched verbal battle.

". . . doesn't change anything. . . ."

". . . don't do this. . . ."

". . . the money. . . ."

". . . last night. . . ."

". . . not over yet. . . ."

I strained to listen, creeping closer and closer to the door, wishing they'd speak up, cocking my head toward their voices.

"The kitchen crew'll be in soon . . . you'd better scram."

That I heard, loud and clear.

The door flung wide open and, before I could get myself out of the way, Julie Costello barreled out and nearly knocked me down.

"Shit!" she cried out as I disentangled myself from her flailing limbs and stumbled backward onto my caboose, which, unfortunately, wasn't padded like my headlamps.

"Geez, sorry, I didn't see you," I apologized,

awkwardly picking myself off the floor, but she wasn't through yelling.

"Who the hell *are* you? And what're you doing here? You scared me outta my wits!"

From what I'd seen of her with Cinda Lou, that wouldn't be hard to do.

At least she didn't remember me hanging around the parking lot, watching Cinda do the interview. But the lights from the minicam had been in her eyes, and she'd paid no attention to anything but looking pathetic and skewering Molly.

"Who am I?" I stood and crossed my arms, buoying my inflated sports bra to utmost perkiness and giving her my most winning smile. The kind I used every time Cissy dragged me to one of her charity events.

Who *was* I? Did I use my real name? Something made-up?

"I'm pleased to meet you," I told her, avoiding the question entirely, and extended a hand, though she just stared at it blankly. "The back door was unlocked, so I let myself in."

"The restaurant doesn't open for another hour yet. Come back then," she said in clipped tones, but at least she wasn't shouting.

"I'm not a customer," I admitted.

Her heavily lined eyes looked me over from stem to stern. "Are you a reporter?"

She sounded hopeful, appearing visibly disappointed when I shook my head.

"I'm a waitress," I said. "I saw on the news

119

that a girl who used to work here got arrested, and I figured you'd need to replace her fast."

"You heard about the murder, huh? Did ya see me on TV by any chance?" She perked up, suddenly eager as a pup and nothing like Barbie's angry cousin Snippy, which she'd played to perfection when Cinda Lou had given her the mike. In fact, she seemed excited that I'd brought the subject up.

I fanned the flames, telling her, "Matter of fact, I *did* catch you on Channel 11 with Cinda Lou Mitchell."

"Really?" She flashed a perfect set of pearly whites and flipped a stray blond curl off her forehead. "What'd you think? How'd I look?"

She wanted a rating of her performance? Her hair and makeup? Can you say "self-absorbed"?

"Oh, gosh, I felt really bad for you. You seemed so sad." I remembered the single tear that had rolled down her cheek. Meryl Streep couldn't have played it better. "So you knew the guy who died?"

"Knew him?" She let out a deep sigh. "Bud Hartman was my boyfriend."

"Oh, wow, I'm so sorry," I said, praying that I sounded convincing. "That's gotta be hard, losing him like that."

"Harder than you can imagine." She bit her bottom lip, leaving a smear of color on her front teeth. "I can tell you're a sensitive person, er, what did you say your name was again?"

I hadn't.

"Andrea," I said, making a snap decision. If I used something fake, I might not come when I was called.

"Yeah, Annie, Bud's murder was a shocker." A pink-tipped finger twisted a lock of hair. "It's a nightmare really. Things were going good for us. The restaurant was doing great, and he promised to use me in the next ad campaign. He was getting me some purple pompoms so I could do a cheer, ya know, like J-U-G-S" — she whipped her arms in the air — "what does that spell?"

She suddenly hesitated. I wondered if the spelling part had stumped her. Should I give her a hint?

But she arched an artfully penciled-in brow in my direction and said, "I used to be a Cowboys cheerleader, as if you didn't know."

Oh, man, I wished I didn't have to do this. But I told myself it was for Molly and David. So I went for broke.

"Golly, yes!" I blubbered, drawing my hands to my mouth, fawning like an eleven-year-old gone gaga over the latest teen idol. "You were my absolute *favorite*. The games weren't the same without your high kicks."

"Damn right." Her eyes lit up, and she nudged me with an elbow. "Remember this?" She did a little pose with her elbows bent behind her head and lips puckered. "I was Miss August on last year's calendar."

"Amazing." I acted appropriately awed, which

121

wasn't hard to do. It floored me, how quickly she'd turned from being outraged at my presence to grieving over her lost beau to preening like a beauty queen. "So, what happened? Did you quit?"

She made a face. "Nope, got cut for being too friendly. Just because I hit it off with some of the guys."

Hit it off?

Interesting euphemism.

"Well, that sucks." I mimicked her pout.

Julie put her hands on hips encased in a shiny pink miniskirt, and she checked me over, up and down. "So you're a waitress, Amanda?"

"Andrea," I corrected. "And I'm the best waitress you'll ever hire," I lied, willing to do just about anything to get on the inside. If she didn't go for it, how else would I be able to help get Molly out of Lew Sterrett? "I . . . I can't imagine anything more fulfilling than working for a celebrity like you, Ms. Costello."

Her blue-lidded eyes watched me closely, and I wondered if I'd laid on the bullshit a little too thick. "Celebrity?"

"You're a . . . an example for women everywhere." I scrambled for the right words, a way to push her buttons to get what I needed. "You've shown that we don't have to sacrifice our femininity for strength."

Did I really say that?

Stewardess, a barf bag!

But Julie didn't seem as nauseated by my spiel

as I was making myself. She tossed her Heather Locklear hair and smiled beatifically. "You're a smart one, aren't you, uh . . . ?"

"Andrea . . . Andrea Blevins."

My pulse was beating faster than it ever did on the Stairmaster. Speaking of pulses, I knew Mother would have heart failure if she ever learned I'd used her maiden name as an alias to apply for the wait staff at Jugs. But I was under-cover after all. That was part of my disguise. Like a trench coat or Groucho Marx glasses.

"All right, Andrea Blevins," Julie drawled. "Leave me a number, and I'll think about it."

Think about it?

That's not what she was supposed to say.

In fact, it was the *opposite*.

"Can you show yourself out?" she asked and started to turn away dismissively. "I'm kinda busy."

No, no, no.

My brain swirled, searching for a way to turn this around and fast.

I had only a split second to react.

So I burst into tears.

Big, noisy theatrical tears that would've made Mrs. Coogan, the Hockaday drama coach, giddy with pleasure.

Through my suddenly gooey mascara, I saw Julie stop and swivel around.

"Please," I sobbed, "you *have* to give me this job. I . . . I have no one else to go to, and I'm in trouble. Deep trouble." The fear of being tossed out on my rear made me appear truly frantic, and the words came out in breathless gasps. *"Please."*

"Huh?" She stood stock-still, looking more stunned than angry as she had when she'd first discovered me lurking behind the office door. She blinked, probably wondering if I was crazy and if she should call 911 rather than hearing me out. "What the blazes are y'all talking about?"

I blurted out the first thing that came into my head. *"I'm pregnant."*

I'd dazed her. "You're . . . ?"

"Pregnant," I repeated, hating myself for fibbing so outrageously and proud at the cleverness of my lie at the same time. "You know" — I placed my palm over my button-down fly and made as pathetic a face as I could muster — "I'm with child, got a bun in the oven, knocked up, baby on board."

"Oh, sugar," she sighed. "You weren't taking antibiotics with your pills, were ya? That's what happened to Liz Hurley."

"Yes, yes, that's probably what it was. And now I'm all alone and unemployed," I rushed on, barely able to see with the clots of black sticking my lashes together. Damn that old mascara in my shoebox! It obviously wasn't waterproof. I took some deep breaths and made sad little gulps. "My, uh, boyfriend left me for another woman, and he wants nothing to do with the child. He won't give a dime for support, the lease is almost up, and I have nowhere to go, no money in the bank. Nothing." My chin was actually quivering, my heart banging hard against my ribs.

Would she bite?

Or had I gone too far?

Would she kick me out, call the police?

If she did, what would I tell Molly?

That I'd failed miserably? That I was a sorry excuse for a friend?

Now I really wished I'd called Reverend Jim Bob's prayer line.

I needed big-time help.

"I don't know what else to do," I sobbed, trying to blink hard and pry my congealed eyelashes apart as I waited for her to say something. Anything except "Buzz off."

Finally, I heard a rush of air escape her lips.

"Oh, Andrea," she cried and grabbed me in a bear hug that crushed the breath from my lungs. "You poor, poor thing. Of course, I'll help you out. What an awful, awful boyfriend to put you out on the street when you're in this condition."

I could barely see, but I didn't think anything was wrong with my hearing.

"You'll hire me?" I squeaked, sucking in my breath, as she finally pulled away and stared at me from arm's length.

She glanced down at my belly, which wasn't near as flat as hers to begin with, the slight curve only helping my cause. I just prayed she wouldn't pat it. Then she looked up at me, suddenly all business.

"How 'bout this, sugar? You can work part-time for now, which means no medical insurance or 401k, just minimum wage and tips. No maternity leave or anything like that, so you'd just better save up for Junior. And when you *really* start showing, I'll have to move you to the kitchen. Which, in your case, might be sooner rather than later."

My God, that sounded awful! Minimum wage? No insurance or 401k?

I nodded eagerly. "That seems fair."

"Can you start today?"

"Today?"

"You said you'd waited tables before, so you won't need training, right?"

"Uh-huh, that's right." I wondered if my nose was growing. "I'm great at waiting." Hey, that wasn't really a blooper. I was as patient as the next girl. I had never been especially skilled at skirting the truth. The flush in my cheeks and a slight stammer usually gave me away. Though Julie apparently mistook my ineptitude for anxiety.

"Well, at Jugs, it's not really the best servers who get the biggest tips, if you know what I mean." Her gaze touched on my chest, and I got the point fairly quickly. "I'm sure you'll do just fine," she said, and I realized my skills weren't nearly as big an issue as my cup size.

"I won't let you down . . . or Junior either," I

promised, and I settled both hands on my abdomen, because it added a nice touch.

Julie smiled benevolently.

"Let me give you the nickel tour before the crew starts to arrive."

"Sure."

"Just follow me. I'll take you to the lockers first so you can change and wash your face. You can fill out your paperwork later."

"Great."

I planned to delay filling out any forms as long as I could.

She trotted up the hallway, babbling over her shoulder about what my schedule would be for the rest of the week, but I hardly paid attention. I glanced back at the office through sticky lashes — like gazing through spider's legs — suddenly recalling the voice of the man she'd been arguing with. I wondered who it was. Someone involved in the business? Was it Bud's silent partner, perhaps?

If I could just take another look at the white Lincoln and jot down the license plate, maybe Malone could have the DMV run it and solve the mystery.

"Hey, c'mon, little mama, you're dragging your feet," Julie called out to me loudly enough to break my train of thought.

Little mama?

Lord, if my own mother ever knew what I'd just done, she'd have my hide.

"Sorry," I murmured and chewed my lip,

tasting Paradise Plum, a flavor more akin to crayon than tropical fruit.

"This way." She drew me into the room I'd passed earlier. She pointed at the row of yellow lockers and instructed, "Take any empty one you want. Go ahead and put away your purse and use the sink. I'll get you a uniform."

The infamous hot pants and cut-off shirt.

I could hardly wait.

Chapter 12

 Mirror, mirror, on the wall, who's the scariest chick of all?

It looked like the Maybelline factory had exploded on my face.

About half the liquid soap in the dispenser by the sink disappeared before I resembled a woman and not a raccoon. I didn't do quite as good a job replacing what I'd washed off with the meager supplies in my purse, but I didn't care.

I was *in*.

I never imagined I'd feel so giddy at the thought of waiting tables.

Once my makeup was under control, I dressed in about five minutes flat. Heck, there wasn't much to it. I felt naked in the skimpy outfit and grimaced as I caught my reflection in the full-length mirror behind the door. The purple hot pants barely covered my fanny, and the cropped T-shirt reached just below the line of my sports bra. Julie had advised going without underwear altogether, but I nixed the idea right off the bat. Frankly, I was more opposed to being panty-less than having panty lines.

Tugging the lavender spandex down as far as

it would go, I wondered how the waitresses could feel like anything but ponies led around the ring for show.

Well, this pony had a strong urge to race back to the stables.

The only thing that kept me from running was thinking of Molly and David. Otherwise, I'd be out the door faster than Seattle Slew.

If Mother had the faintest inkling of what I was up to, she'd probably lock me up in my old room — after dressing me in flannel and scrubbing my face — and summon the pastor from Highland Park Presby to exorcise the demons from my misguided soul.

The air conditioning blew cold against my skin, and I shivered, rubbing my arms to warm up.

I pictured a tearful David in my mind's eye and reminded myself he'd be without his mommy if I didn't do my part in getting to the truth of who killed Bud Hartman.

Somehow, the thought made wearing purple short-shorts bearable.

Julie had vanished while I'd changed, and she hadn't yet returned, so I took the time to poke around.

A few of the lockers had combination locks to protect them. The rest were unlocked and easy to inspect. But if I'd hoped to find a blood-stained sock or a confession written in lipstick, I was sorely disappointed. Instead, all my nosing around uncovered were assorted photos — including groups of Jugs's waitresses who all looked better in their tiny outfits than I ever would — boxes of tampons, sticks of deodorant, and bottles of perfume out the wazoo. Unfortunately, Bud had not been fatally doused with Calvin Klein's Obsession.

"You ready?"

I jumped at the sound of Julie's voice and slammed shut the door of the locker I'd been poking inside.

"Don't worry about anyone taking anything," she said, thankfully oblivious to the fact that the locker I'd been rummaging through a minute before wasn't mine. "Bud had a strict policy against stealing. He had ways of knowing right off the bat if anyone pinched something that wasn't hers. And he'd send 'em packing, too, just like that." She snapped her fingers and flipped her blond head.

"Bud must've been a tough boss," I said and casually squatted to tie my sneaker.

"Nobody messed with him, that's for sure. He used to play tackle for Texas Tech." Her eyes got dreamy all of a sudden. "Had the body of a Greek god."

"So you must've had some competition."

"What d'ya mean?" She frowned at me.

I shrugged. "Jugs has a reputation for its hot waitresses. How did you keep your leash on the guy?"

Her tiny nose tipped higher. "It's not Bud I had to worry about. The trouble was them goin' after him. Like Molly O'Brien."

"She was after Bud?" I stifled the urge to shudder.

"Like a cat in heat," Julie hissed, acting rather feline herself. "I know they had a fling, and I can't blame him for it, not the way she was always flaunting her goods in front of him. But then it was over as fast as it started, and Bud told me that he'd had to warn her to back off more than a few times." Her mouth puckered. "My guess is he brushed her off again, and she went psycho."

I nearly choked on my disbelief. The idea of Molly putting the moves on Bud was ludicrous. Either Julie wore blinders or Bud had been telling her some tales tall even for a Texan.

"Bud had a real power over women, you see," Julie explained, and a glassy look filled her eyes. "The guy had animal magnetism. He knew what he wanted in life, and he grabbed it. That power is mighty attractive. It's what made me fall for him." She rubbed her hands together, a little girl flush with delight. "It also made him rich and that didn't hurt, either."

I didn't want to hear any more about Bud's animal magnetism.

From what I'd learned from Molly, only the "animal" part applied.

"So business is good?" I asked her, changing the subject to something I understood all too well.

Money.

Something in her face closed off, as if she realized she'd said something she shouldn't. She remarked simply, "Business is great."

"And the murder won't hurt?"

"Where've you been, Andrea?" She actually got my name right, though she stared at me as if I came from outer space. "You can't pay for the kind of publicity we've been getting in the last twenty-four hours. It's free advertising, even if it is because Bud died."

She hesitated and squinted at the ceiling. For a moment, I thought she was dwelling on his untimely demise, pondering if he were in heaven.

I wanted to tell her she was gazing in the wrong direction.

Then she said, "Hmm, I might even have to add an extra waitress to each shift, maybe an extra bartender, too. I wonder if we should extend our hours? I should probably call our vendors and order more supplies. Definitely more booze. . . ."

"Julie?"

Yeesh, did she have ADD?

"Hey." I waved a hand in front of her to remind her I was there.

"The nickel tour?"

"Oh, yeah." She grabbed hold of my arm. "Lemme show you the kitchen first. That's where it happened, you know."

I let her draw me along and marveled at how she'd bounced back so quickly from the death of her lover.

And Bud not even as cold as the beer on tap.

133

The deserted kitchen of a half hour ago now percolated with people and noises. A crew of men and women in aprons and hairnets buzzed about, their animated voices rising above the hiss of steaming pots and the clang of pans on the grills. It didn't take a lip reader to realize what they were talking about.

They quieted instantly as Julie and I entered, their smiles replaced by taut mouths and serious expressions. A dark-skinned woman stepped away from the others and haltingly approached.

"We're all very sorry about Mr. Hartman," she said, though I didn't see a damp eye in the house. "We're a little surprised you wanted to reopen so soon." She paused, her brown features bemused. "Anyway, if there's anything we can do?"

"Thanks, Tasha, but I'm okay," Julie replied, a vague tremor in her voice. "Bud would've wanted us to go on without him. Business as usual, that's what he'd say."

Well, Julie was doing a fine job of that, I mused. I'd already gotten the picture she was one cool customer, though I wondered just how cool. Did she have enough ice in her veins to stab her boyfriend and then go on as if nothing had happened? And what would she have gotten out of it beyond the satisfaction of offing an unfaithful lover? Was there money involved? A piece of the restaurant?

I'd have to keep tabs on her, that's for sure. I'd

already gotten the impression that there was more to Julie Costello than frosted blue eye shadow and Heather Locklear's hairdo. She played the "dumb blonde" to perfection, but how much of it was an act to get what she wanted? Because I'll wager she didn't have much of a problem in that department.

"Everyone, this is Andrea," she announced. "Our new waitress."

My cheeks warmed as all eyes fell upon me, and I wished I'd had a towel to wrap around my half-naked self.

I did a soggy Princess Di wave.

But everyone was already turning away.

"Nice to meet you, too," I muttered to their backs.

"See the window there? That's where you'll pick up your orders." Julie tapped my arm and next pointed out the refrigerator that held extra tea if they ran out at the wait station, more jugs for beer, and the storeroom with ample supplies of napkins, condiments, and more.

I tried to focus on what she was saying but was distracted by the sight of a man busily chopping stalks of celery with a chef's knife grasped in a plastic-gloved hand. The sound of the blade's steady whack sent a shiver up my spine.

"You got any questions?" Julie asked, and I managed a shake of my head. "All right, then I'll take you to the wait station and the bar."

Before she dragged me out of the kitchen, I

caught a glimpse through the rear door as someone took a trash bag outside.

The white Lincoln was gone.

I cursed myself for not having paid it more attention. I couldn't remember a single letter or number from the license plate.

Some spy I was.

I also noted a panel of buttons blinking by the door. The alarm system. Something I'd have to figure a way around if I were going to do any after-hours snooping.

The sudden reality of what I was doing hit me like a speeding Humvee.

My heart fluttered, knowing I couldn't afford to slip up, not when Molly's hearing was a week away.

Julie pulled me with her into the dining room of the restaurant. "Over here is your station," she told me, indicating a patch of tables near the bar. "And in case you forget, there's a map at the hostess podium. Got it?"

I assured her I did.

As she nattered on about putting orders into the computer, I absorbed the room around me: the hillbilly décor complete with faux squirrel skins (at least I hoped they were faux), racks of shotguns, patchwork quilts and even an autographed photo of the guy who'd played Jethro on *The Beverly Hillbillies*. Rows of earthenware jugs lined the bar.

I wondered if Bud had thought himself clever when he'd named the joint. I imagined him howling with amusement as he'd come up with a list of euphemisms for "breasts" — knockers, headlights, melons — and then had crossed them off one by one until he'd found the right gimmick to hide behind. I mean, he obviously couldn't have called the place "Tits" and pretended it was a family restaurant.

Nope, Jugs had fit the bill. A straight-faced father could explain to his young son that a jug was used for drinking while elbowing his buddy in the ribs. If Bud had kept the secret to himself instead of putting up a billboard resembling a perfectly round pair of bosoms or dressed his waitresses more like Miss Ellie than Ellie Mae, then the Mothers Against Pornography would have stayed home.

Still, I'll wager Bud had seen the protestors as a perk, a way to draw extra attention to his business. The same way it pleased Julie to have more publicity even if the reason was homicide.

". . . push the bartender's specials, okay? Drinks add up, ya see? So do the jugs of beer at fifteen dollars a pop."

I blinked away my mental meanderings and focused on the tap Julie used to fill a jug with beer and neatly top it off.

"You've gotta be careful to avoid too much head," she warned, and I bit the inside of my cheek to keep from snorting. "Or the foam makes a really big mess."

"Got it."

"Usually the bartender will do this for you, but, if he's busy, you've gotta know the ropes."

I assured her I could manage.

She patted my arm and said, "Good girl." Which was better than "little mama" in a pinch.

By the time Julie had wrapped up my orientation and given me a laundry list of responsibilities, I'd picked out plenty of places where Bud's killer could have remained hidden until Molly had run out and Bud was left alone in the kitchen.

The only trouble was my suppositions were just suppositions. As Malone had so carefully pointed out, my imagination was not admissible in court. If I couldn't come up with anything more solid than "what if," how would I ever convince the Dallas P.D. that Bud's assailant was someone other than Molly?

I headed back to the locker room to realign the padding in my bra and to reapply my Paradise Plum lipstick. What I walked into was a scene straight out of Hugh Hefner's daydreams.

Three women disrobed in a flash of toned limbs, breasts, and rear ends. Memories of adolescent girls changing after gym class flickered through my mind, and I felt my cheeks warm. Modest as I was, I nearly raised my hand to my face to cover my eyes with my fingers until the coast was clear.

"Hey, you must be new." The tall brunette spotted me as she wiggled into her skimpy shorts. "Guess you'll be filling in for Molly, right? No offense, honey, but I do hope it's only temporary."

I suppressed the urge to grin. It was good to know that Molly at least had someone on her side.

"I'm Andrea," I said.

"Christie," she replied then gestured to the tiny redhead on her left. "This here's Ginger and this is Rhonda" — she hooked a thumb in the other direction, toward a dark-skinned woman with cropped black hair. All three had the rock-hard bodies of aerobics instructors.

Instinctively, I sucked in my belly. "Nice to meet you," I replied, quickly adding, "though I'm sorry about the circumstances. What a terrible thing, your boss getting killed." I wondered if that was the reason for their somber expressions. "It must be hard on everyone to deal with."

Tall Christie glanced sideways at flame-haired Ginger, who in turn looked at Rhonda.

"Yeah, we're sorry, too," Rhonda spoke up in a raspy voice. "Sorry that Molly's the one who got arrested. She's a cool girl. A real hard worker."

"I can't believe she stabbed Bud," Ginger said as she fashioned her locks into braids that looked not unlike Pippi Longstocking. "He must've really put the heat on her. The guy could come on real strong sometimes, and maybe Molly couldn't find a graceful way out."

"They'll get her off on self-defense, don't ya

think?" Christie asked her comrades, and their heads bobbed agreeably. "Bud could be so aggressive. Especially if he'd been drinking."

"Tell me about it," Ginger remarked and rolled her eyes. "Molly used to call him the octopus."

"He was trouble," Rhonda added.

Had they all endured Bud Hartman's come-ons? Because that's the picture I was getting. If so, it's likely that Molly wasn't the only waitress he'd tried to force himself on. What if someone else hadn't been able to get away? What if she'd come back and sought revenge after Molly had escaped?

I couldn't count out that scenario.

Crossing my arms, I leaned against a row of lockers and asked them, "If Bud was as bad as all that, why didn't anyone press charges?"

I'd posed the same questions to Molly and, though I understood her answer, it didn't make sense to me that seemingly intelligent women would routinely have subjected themselves to Bud Hartman's unwanted advances without doing anything about it.

"There are laws against sexual harassment," I said, and they all stared.

Rhonda jerked her chin, her expression strained so that pale creases stood out against her dark skin. "You got kids?" she asked.

"Not yet," I admitted, reminded of the fib I'd told Julie. Suddenly uncomfortable, I shifted on my sneakers, sensing where this was going.

"You got a man to take care of?"

"No." My mouth felt dry as Lubbock.

"You caught up on your rent? Is your car paid off? How about your credit cards? Got a zero balance there, too?"

I didn't answer. I couldn't find my voice with the three of them watching me so microscopically.

Rhonda pressed on, "Betcha have a mommy and daddy who'll slip you a few bucks when things get tight, huh?"

What was the deal? Did I have a neon sign on my face that said, ASK ME ABOUT MY TRUST FUND?

"You're wrong," was all I could squeak out, finding it harder to lie to these three women than to Julie Costello. "I've got no one to help me, and I've got a ba . . . a barrel of trouble in my life at the moment."

"Give the girl a break." Christie nudged her friend, and my shoulders sagged with relief that she'd come to my rescue. "Andrea wouldn't be here either, Ronnie, if she didn't have bills to pay."

Rhonda studied me, her features suddenly less fierce. "You're right. Hey, forgive me, Andrea. Sometimes I'm a pain in the ass. I'm just jittery is all. Like we didn't have enough to deal with before Bud got himself iced. Those Mothers Against Porn had already stepped on my last nerve. Get this. One of them tried to do another intervention with me last night in the parking lot." She rolled her eyes. "Since when is waiting tables a crime? There's plenty of filth on the Internet to keep 'em busy. All we do is serve burgers and beer."

Ginger finished applying crimson gloss on her lips and chimed in, "Guys bring their kids in, for shit's sake. It's all in fun, ya know? They just want to get an eyeful. Maybe the wife's not in such good shape. Maybe she's got stretch marks. So he wants to fantasize a little. It's not like we're doing lap dances."

But wasn't dressing up like this degrading?

And how about putting up with a boss who was constantly trying to cop a feel? Or worse?

Didn't that make their working environment less than ideal?

"There are always a few girls who can't hack it," Rhonda said as she ran a wide comb through her short dark curls. "Take that girl, Sarah whatever-her-name-was. She was all gung-ho for a week or two. Then she stayed to help Bud close one night and never came back."

"Really?" The hair stood up on my nape. "No one saw her again? What happened? Was it something Bud did?"

Christie sat down on the bench and laced up her Reeboks. "All I remember is Sarah seemed to have a crush on Bud, believe it or not." She made a face. "She followed him around like a love-struck groupie, batting her big eyes at him, which didn't sit well with Julie. Sarah was a cute kid, too. No more than eighteen, nineteen tops."

She paused, her expression shifting, as if she was trying to fit the pieces together. "She was only around for a couple of weeks before she split, so I figured Julie had Bud fire her. But no one ever had the chance to find out. She was gone when we showed up the next day for our shift."

"Didn't she come back to clean out her locker?" I asked.

The women looked at one another and shook their heads.

"Far as I know, she never set foot in Jugs again. She didn't even pick up her last pay-check," Ginger remarked. "If she left anything behind, I'd bet Julie threw it away."

"And no one knows where she went?" I asked, wondering what had made her vanish so abruptly.

Christie shrugged. "Probably ran home to mama. The girl still had a lot of growing up to do. She seemed really needy. Kind of lonely and pathetic."

"Prime Bud bait," Rhonda interjected.

"Yikes," Christie said and checked her watch. "Let's shake a leg, girls. Unless we want the cheerleader from hell chewing us out."

The trio headed toward the door, but I didn't move.

"You coming, Andrea?" Ginger asked, flipping red braids over her shoulders.

"In a minute," I told them. "Gotta use the john. Y'all go ahead."

Alone at last, I went into my locker and dug in my purse, retrieving my lipstick. Then I smeared some more Paradise Plum on my mouth and evened out my falsies with help from the mirror.

I looked at my reflection and sighed.

I hated pretending, hated lying to seemingly nice women I barely knew.

This was going to be harder than I thought.

But I had no choice.

When I stepped into the hallway, I glanced longingly toward the door to Bud's office. No doubt I'd find some answers there, if he had a computer. Which he must. No business these days did without one. If I could just get in and pull up his personnel files, I could track down the mysterious Sarah who'd quit so suddenly.

I wondered if the police had even attempted to interview any of the former or current waitresses at Jugs, though I doubted it strongly. Why use manpower chasing leads that could go nowhere when you had a bloody knife with fingerprints?

No, I'd have to dig up equally damning proof, evidence that pointed away from Molly and toward someone else.

I checked the hallway toward the kitchen and listened for the sound of approaching voices or footsteps. Hearing none, I crept over to the office door and put my ear against it.

Nothing.

Heart racing, I gave the knob a twist and

pushed, quickly poking my head into what had once been Bud Hartman's domain.

I spied the computer instantly, perched on an oak veneer desk scattered with papers. Nearby sat a console holding a TV, a VCR, and assorted electronics equipment that looked expensive and complicated. So many buttons, knobs, and switches made my head spin. Thank goodness his computer was a new-model Dell, one I knew had an internal zip drive. Nothing complicated there.

My fingers itched to get into his system, to see his programs and files, to poke through his books. Something told me a guy like Bud would probably have two sets of numbers.

It took real restraint to close the door and walk away.

I didn't have time to snoop now. I'd have to figure out a way to slip into Bud's office when Jugs had emptied out.

"Well, there you are. Did you get lost?"

Julie Costello marched toward me. Her round eyes lit up brighter than a bonfire.

"Uh, I had to use the restroom," I stammered out an explanation.

"Oh, sugar, I understand, you being in that condition," she said with a wink and a glance at my now mostly bared belly. "Hey, a big ol' crowd's already forming outside the doors," she said, sounding breathless. "The Moms Against Porn are in full force and a few reporters are still hangin' around, so I'll bet we double our receipts today. Come and see for yourself." She took my arm and propelled me forward into the dining room.

She hadn't exaggerated about the crowd.

Beyond the locked glass doors, a gridlock of people jammed together. I could hear shouts and spotted an occasional sign that popped up above the line of mostly male heads waiting to get in.

"Can you believe it?" Julie whispered. "If Bud could see this, he'd be grinnin' like a bull on a dairy farm."

A cry went up, and I watched as a sturdy gray-haired woman surged to the head of the pack and planted herself flush against the glass doors.

"Oh, God," Julie murmured. "It's the Wicked Witch."

"Who?"

"The mother of Mothers."

The woman in the pink scrubs looked familiar. Wasn't she one of the protestors I'd seen on last evening's news?

With a fist, she pounded on the glass, her voice too garbled by the glass for me to hear, and then strong hands drew her back and away.

"Thank God," Julie said when the woman was no longer visible. "I'd hate to have to call the police to haul her off. It might scare the customers."

And then she brushed past me toward the doors, keys jangling in her hand, preparing to let the lions into the Coliseum.

My chest clenched, and I tried to breathe,

praying I'd make it through my serving debut without spilling beer or splitting my hot pants at the seams.

Chapter 13

At the end of my shift, I nearly collapsed on the locker room floor.

I smelled like beer and French fries, and my feet — and the rest of me — ached for a soak in the tub. I'd had enough men call me "sweetheart," "babe," and "honey" to last me a lifetime. Two of my customers had suggested I meet them later for drinks (I'd politely declined). Still, it hadn't been as bad as I'd imagined, just so busy that I barely had time to breathe. I only mixed up one order and dropped an iced tea on the floor, barely a blip on the disaster meter.

My tips amounted to a hardly stellar hundred and twenty bucks, which I planned to put aside for Molly. I thought it might come in handy after she was released from jail and looking for work. Because I knew she wouldn't come back to Jugs. And I couldn't say that I blamed her.

I gratefully turned over my station to a woman on the dinner shift who introduced herself as Tiffany. With even less regret, I changed out of the tiny shorts and into my blue jeans. Tight as they were, at least they covered my skin.

Julie caught me on my way out the door.

"Bud's memorial service is tomorrow morning at ten," she said and grasped my arm so that I could go nowhere until she'd finished. "It's at the Church of Perpetual Hope in Plano. It'd mean a lot to me if you could come."

"Julie, I. . . ."

I hardly know you and mercifully never knew Bud, I wanted to say, but she wasn't about to take "no" for an answer.

"I felt this instant connection with you, Andrea," she insisted, though I was skeptical about that since it took her a while to get my name straight.

"Uh, I'm not sure I can. . . ."

"Great!" she cut off my stammering too fast for me to finish. "So I'll see you at ten sharp? And you, too, Junior," she added, leaning over to address my belly button.

Ugh.

"See you in the morning." She smiled and gave me an offhanded wave as she headed toward the dining room.

I stood and watched her as she sashayed toward a group of men in soccer shirts obviously high on hops.

Why me?

The last place I wanted to be the next morning was at a memorial service for Bud

Hartman at the Church of Perpetual Hope, which didn't sound like any church I'd ever heard of before anyway.

Wait a minute.

I did know of the place.

Well, I'd seen the name, along with the number for the prayer hotline. On the local religious channel with Reverend Jim Bob and Violet Hair, the pair that begged me to send money to save my soul (which might not have been a bad idea). I always wondered if those who did cut a check were sent bumper stickers that declared, WHO SAYS YOU CAN'T BUY YOUR WAY INTO HEAVEN?

It made me glad to be Presbyterian.

I headed out of Jugs and into twilight. A host of macho cars, mostly SUVs and pickup trucks, filled the parking slots around the restaurant. Across the shopping center, the Zuma Beach Club had switched on its bright pink and blue neon sign. A dozen cars lined up out front, though the place wouldn't be swinging for another couple of hours.

My Jeep sat around the corner, and I sighed happily when I reached it.

As I unlocked the door and yanked it wide, a hand clamped down on my shoulder from behind.

I spun around, my heart thumping.

It was the woman in pink from Mothers Against Pornography. The one Julie had called the Wicked Witch.

"Geez, Louise!" I exhaled sharply. "You shouldn't sneak up on people like that."

"I'm sorry," she apologized, "but if I don't catch you girls with a surprise attack, you'll break out into a run."

"I see what you mean."

Even with the falling light, there was sadness in her face that the dusk couldn't hide. With her close-cut gray hair and deeply shadowed eyes, she looked to be in her fifties. Though she may have been younger, and a hard life had left its mark on her features like water carving stone.

"Can I help you with something?" I asked. Nothing about her threatened me in the least, and I wondered why Julie seemed fearful of her.

"I was hoping I could help you," she said and touched my arm gently. "There are other places to work, you know. Places that don't exploit women and treat them as objects. I could steer you in another direction."

Steer me in another direction?

Oh, dear. Part of me wanted to laugh, wanted to tell her that she'd cornered the wrong person. I wondered what she might say if she heard the truth, that I was merely a mild-mannered web designer playing a role in order to bail out a friend.

"Honestly, I don't think. . . ."

"You seem like a bright girl," she cut me off and leaned nearer. "I could get you a job in an office where you didn't have to wear a skimpy outfit or get pawed by the wolves. It might not pay as much, but it would be honest work."

"Thanks for the offer, but I don't have much choice at the moment," I told her, feeling too pooped to hang around in the parking lot being lectured by a stranger, no matter how well intentioned. Inching my way into the driver's seat, I told her, "Don't worry about me, this is only temporary."

"That's what you say now." Her voice softened in the fading light. "But even one night of degradation is too much. I'm sure your own mother would agree with me, wouldn't she? Does she even know where you are?"

Perish the thought.

"I'm sorry." I was too tired for this. It was like an argument with Cissy that I was never going to win. "Excuse me, please, but I have to go."

I tried to close the car door, but she had her hand on it, holding it open.

She stuck her hand into a pocket of her smock. "Please consider what I've said."

"I will."

But before I could shut myself in, she reached inside and pushed a bit of paper at me. Then she hurried away, across the parking lot.

I locked the door and flipped on the overhead light to find a business card in my lap. THE WOMEN'S WELLNESS CLINIC, it read in discreet black script, listing an address and phone number. At the bottom, there was the name, PEGGY MARTIN, R.N.

The ringleader of the Mothers Against Pornography was a nurse at a clinic?

For an instant I panicked, thinking Julie had let it slip that I'd said I was pregnant, and somehow this Peggy Martin had gotten wind of it. Was that why she'd singled me out tonight? To rescue me and my make-believe baby? Or was it just that I was fresh meat?

I glanced out the window, but she was gone already.

Fresh meat, I decided.

I took a deep breath and settled down, stabbing the key into the ignition.

As Malone said, I had a vivid imagination.

I started the car, shifted into reverse, and maneuvered out of the increasingly crowded parking lot. I aimed the Jeep toward home, determined to wash up and change before I headed down to Mother's to see David.

The light on my Caller ID blinked incessantly as I walked through the door. I dialed my voice mail and listened as the messages played, wedging the handset against my collarbone as I loosened the laces on my high-tops and struggled out of my jeans.

Brian Malone rattled on about the final autopsy report being filed and Bud's body being released for cremation.

"Old news," I said aloud and smirked at the telephone, feeling smug that I knew where and when Bud's memorial service would be held, wondering what Malone would think if he learned I'd actually been invited to attend by the deceased's girlfriend.

". . . I don't trust you, Andy. You're up to something, though I'm not sure what," he said before he ran over the limit and cut himself off.

I pulled off my T-shirt and plucked the shoulder pads from my running bra, a little disappointed to see the cotton cups deflate so quickly.

A couple messages from clients followed Brian's. After that, two hang ups and then a strained voice with a crisp accent.

Hurriedly tucking a clean shirt into a pair of striped sweatpants, I held the receiver nearer to hear whatever sounded so urgent.

". . . it's Maria Rameriz calling for Andrea . . . a social worker was at the apartment today asking about *el niño.* . . ."

My limbs went numb.

". . . I told her I didn't know anything about where the boy was taken and that probably someone from Molly's *familia* had picked him up. . . ."

Dear God.

". . . maybe that will be that."

I dropped into the nearest chair, weak at the knees.

If I had left David with Maria, would he have been taken away to a foster home? Would Molly's worst fears have come true? What would I have told her then? She would have come apart at the seams.

I exhaled slowly, silently thanking my lucky stars that David was safely at Mother's. If, by chance, that social worker tracked down the boy's whereabouts, I knew Cissy would wave her magic wand and take care of things as she always did.

Though, as it stood, I already owed her.

Big.

I headed to the bathroom to wash off the mask of makeup from my skin, turning my white washcloth muddy in the process. After I'd scrunched my hair into a ponytail, I studied my face in the mirror and smiled as I recognized the girl who stared back. I felt like Dorothy returning to Kansas.

It took nearly twenty minutes to reach Mother's house on Beverly Drive. By then, the sky had lost all traces of pink and had settled into a deep navy sprinkled liberally with stars.

The lights glowed cheerfully in the windows as I pulled into the curving drive and parked in front of the door with its guardian lions.

When I entered the house, I pricked my ears at a noise I hadn't heard within these walls in quite a while. Not since Daddy died.

Laughter.

A boy's high-pitched squeal and a woman's throaty chuckle.

Dropping my purse on the bench by the stairwell, I gravitated toward the pleasant sounds and ended up in the kitchen.

I hesitated in the doorway for a moment,

simply watching as Sandy and David played cards on the glass-topped table. A bucket of the Colonel's finest had been pushed to one side as had plates heaped with chicken bones and half-eaten mounds of mashed potatoes. Various red-and-white-striped containers and plastic lids were scattered about the green marble counter-top. A sight I likely wouldn't see again in my lifetime.

So I soaked it in.

Leaning my shoulder against the jamb, I observed their goings-on with such delight that a shiver rippled through me. Memories rose to the surface, of long ago nights when Mother and Daddy had gone out, leaving me with Sandy to play game after game of Go Fish until well past my bedtime. I had loved every minute.

"Well, look who's here."

Sandy pushed away from the table and came toward me, arms extended.

"Hon, you're worn out," she said and pulled me into a rose-scented hug.

"I am that." My reply was muffled by her shoulder. "It's been a long day," I told her as she drew away, though I left out the details. I don't think she'd have been any less displeased than Mother to hear what I'd been doing.

"We've had a rather busy day ourselves," she remarked, her gaze shifting to David, who was gathering up their cards into a neat pile. "Cissy arranged for us to go to the zoo this afternoon."

"You're kidding." I nearly choked on the

words. It was pretty hard to image my mother at the zoo in her expensive pumps and Chanel suit. "*Arranged* being the key word, I presume? She didn't actually feed the elephants?"

"Oh, heavens, can you imagine that?" Sandy grinned. "No, it was just me and the kiddo." She glanced over my shoulder at David, now shuffling the cards at the table. "Cissy set up a private tour of the nursery, actually. David gave a baby chimp its bottle. It was truly amazing."

"Amazing," I repeated and felt my posture change as I said it. "Mother does have a knack for that, doesn't she?"

"Cissy is a wonder."

Mother did know how to make things happen, as Sandy had pointed out, though she didn't often do them quietly. She rather enjoyed being appreciated for her generous acts. I think a part of my mother was a frustrated actress who craved the spotlight and applause.

Only Joan Crawford had done Mother even better than Mother could. Though I'd never been yelled at for using wire hangers. Actually, I don't think I'd ever seen a wire hanger in the house.

I went to the table and sat down across from David. "What's your game, bud? Gin? Five-card stud? Twenty-one?" I asked, and he gave me a curious look.

He paused thoughtfully, then said, "Go Fish."

"Well, deal the cards, kid. But I have to warn

you, you're facing the unofficial Go Fish champion of Beverly Drive."

Sandy laughed. "Unofficial is right."

"Are we on?" I slapped my palms on the table.

David blinked his wide eyes and nodded. He chewed on his lip as he concentrated on dealing out the cards.

"Careful, David," Sandy said as she began clearing their plates. "She's a real shark."

"I was taught by the best." I looked up at her and winked. Sandy's face wrinkled with pleasure.

"Can I get you something to eat, Andy? We've got a few pieces of chicken left and some corn and mashed potatoes. I can heat them up in the microwave."

"No, thanks. I'm fine." I didn't tell her I'd eaten at Jugs on a ten-minute break. A greasy burger and fries that sat heavily in my stomach.

"Your turn," David prodded, and I fixed my attention on the cards in my hand, seeing his small face light up as we played. Seeing Molly in his smile.

An hour later, I called it quits. I could only lose to a six-year-old so many times before my ego suffered.

"I surrender!" I announced and threw down my cards. "Guess I'll have to turn over my title as champion to you now."

"I'm the champion?" David's cheeks warmed to pink.

"You bet."

"I think it's time for the newly crowned champ to hit the sack," Sandy said, looking tired herself.

I told David "goodnight" and Sandy followed him upstairs to make sure he brushed his teeth. Afterward, she'd tuck him in bed and tell him a story. She had an endless cache of them, each of which I'd probably heard a dozen times.

I wondered if David would cry himself to sleep, but hoped he wouldn't. He seemed to have settled in remarkably well. Sandy had obviously taken him under her wing. And Mother wasn't doing so bad with him, either.

He'll be fine, I told myself. And it was just temporary, right? Until Molly could get out of jail and go home.

Quiet filled the kitchen without Sandy's voice and David's giggles. I pushed away from the table and headed for the downstairs den. With a grateful sigh, I sank into the rose-patterned chintz cushions on the overstuffed sofa and propped my feet atop the coffee table, something I couldn't do if Mother was around.

I flipped on the TV perched in the cherry armoire and caught the nine o'clock news starting on Channel 11. They led off with a piece about fighting in the Middle East, then segued to a press conference with the mayor. Just when my eyes began to glaze over, they switched to a shot of a reporter standing in front of Jugs. She proceeded to give an update on the murder of Bud Hartman.

I sat up straighter and leaned my elbows on my knees as a familiar face appeared on the screen.

Peggy Martin. The mother of Mothers Against Pornography. The not-so-wicked witch who'd approached me in the parking lot as I was leaving.

Turning up the sound, I listened as she remarked with dismay about restaurants like Jugs infiltrating the suburbs, reinforcing the stereotype of women as sexual objects, and bringing crime along with it.

"Look what happened to Mr. Hartman," she said, and the camera zoomed in to catch the despair drawn on her wrinkled face. "He treated women like toys and paid the ultimate price for his bad behavior."

The reporter tied things up with a pithy remark about that being a sad epitaph on Hartman's tombstone.

Only, he wouldn't have a tombstone, I mused. He was being cremated.

I pushed the buttons on the changer and moved through the stations to find Channel 3 on Mother's cable.

Ah-ha.

A handsome man in crewneck sweater and tan slacks sat on a gilt-framed sofa beside a Technicolor woman with bright makeup and a lavender wig built like a beehive. Stained glass windows lit up the background and blood-red carpeting smothered the floor underfoot.

"We do so much to help the poor in Third World countries," the man said, and the woman nodded her head and replied, "Amen, Reverend Jim Bob. Amen."

"Those kids in Guatemala that we took the toys to last Christmas . . . Lord, I've never seen such gratitude in anyone's eyes. It was as if they were touching heaven, and it was just a box of GI Joes."

"Praise God," his purple-wigged cohort cried again and raised her hands. "Hallelujah and Amen."

A phone number and message ran continually across the bottom of the screen. Reminding me of a tornado warning, it begged me to PLEASE GIVE TO THOSE LESS FORTUNATE . . . THE CHURCH OF PERPETUAL HOPE BLESSES YOU . . . COME PRAY WITH US AT THE CORNER OF PRESTON AND PARKER ROADS IN PLANO.

So that was where Bud Hartman's memorial service would be held. At least now I had the address.

I found it hard to believe Bud had been a churchgoing man, and I wondered what his connection was to Perpetual Hope. Or had the choice of location been Julie Costello's and had nothing to do with Bud's religious preference? I had no problem imagining her falling under Reverend Jim Bob's spell. He was a good-looking fellow with rugged features and thick salt-and-pepper hair.

Reverend Jim Bob and Beehive continued to

babble about all the missions they'd undertaken to touch the lives of toyless children, and I yawned loudly, feeling fatigue run through my blood like Novocain.

I shut off the tube and dragged myself from the overstuffed couch. Weariness slowed my movements, and I shuffled through the house, my flip-flops slapping on the tiles.

The towering grandfather clock in the foyer chimed half past nine as I took the stairs up to the second floor and padded down the hallway toward my old room.

I opened the door and switched on the ceiling light, illuminating the tableau of my youth, a reflection of my own tastes superimposed on my mother's. The frilly canopy bed dripped with scarves in wild prints. The white French-style desk and ornate chest of drawers had flowering vines crawling up the sides, and the entire wall behind them had been painted to mimic Monet's garden in Giverny, down to the water lilies. Mother had shown great restraint in letting me augment the perfect girlie room her interior designer had supplied. It had not been done without a great deal of sighing on her part — with reassurance from my father that walls could always be repainted and furniture replaced — and had taken me an entire summer to finish.

As I stood there, looking in, the sight tweaked a happy chord inside me, knowing that Cissy hadn't hired someone to obliterate my creations with a bucket of Benjamin Moore.

Above the escritoire on which my old computer sat, the shelves overflowed with books, including a perfectly preserved set of Nancy Drews with yellow spines. Mother hadn't touched those either.

It was déjà vu all over again.

Nothing had changed since I'd headed to college.

As if I could come back anytime and pick up where I'd left off.

I went over to the bureau, catching my reflection in the mirror, half-expecting to see a skinny kid with braces and pigtails.

My fingertips drifted across the sterling set of combs and brushes with my monogram etched into the polished backs. A collection of perfume bottles with glass stoppers crowded atop an art nouveau tray. Mother had encouraged me to collect them. But she'd been the only one of us who'd taken an interest in that.

Daddy had done better with his idea of the perfect collection, giving me leatherbound copies of classics, like *Black Beauty*, *Heidi*, *Rebecca*, *Jane Eyre*, *Pride and Prejudice*, and *Wuthering Heights*, which I'd read at night before falling asleep, sometimes beneath the covers with a flashlight for fear Cissy would notice a glow slipping out from under my bedroom door past ten.

It pleased me immeasurably that Mother had never given away any of my books to charity or the church rummage sale. I still had hopes that someday I'd have a daughter of my own to pass them on to. Although, with my luck, she'd get Cissy's designer genes and be more interested in perusing the latest issues of *Vogue* or *Town & Country*.

The cadre of Madame Alexander dolls I'd received for Christmases and birthdays in my girlhood still occupied the shelves of the large armoire, though their original clothing was packed in a drawer. Instead, each of them, from Heidi and Red Riding Hood to the Little Women, wore creations whipped up by Molly O'Brien. Little miniskirts and halter tops cut from Cissy's outrageous pink and green Lilly Pulitzer castoffs made them resemble a line of spaced-out go-go dancers with their round blue eyes and mouths in a perpetual moue.

My own castoffs filled the walk-in closets. There were enough shoes alone to make Imelda Marcos pea green with envy. There were little- or never-worn taffeta party dresses for dances at the country club or one of Mother's benefit galas, and there was, of course, the specially made white Vera Wang gown I was supposed to have worn for my debut.

I wondered if Mother kept it on hand as a reminder of the disappointment I'd caused her. Though I'd told myself many times since that, where I was concerned, she should have been used to not always getting her way well before then.

Seeing the gown caused a little lump of regret

in my throat, but only because it made me think about what life would have been like if Daddy were still around.

If wishes were horses.

It did no good at all to dwell on "what ifs."

I crossed the room and sat down on the bed, picking up the nearest silver-framed photograph from the nightstand.

My father and me. His near-bald head pressed to mine. His eyes mere slits, his smile so wide. My mouth was open in a fit of giggles.

My throat tightened, and I set the photograph aside.

There was another of me with Cissy, both of us wearing pained expressions, as if our shoes pinched our feet.

It was taken during my thirteenth-birthday luncheon at the Junior League. She'd made me wear a hat. I looked like a Jackie Kennedy wannabe. Mother had drawn up the invitation list and had conveniently left off Molly's name, though I'd told my friend to come just the same. She had, which was probably the reason Mother's otherwise perfect face showed strain. The frown on my lips had more to do with the location. I wanted to have my party at the skating rink, but that hadn't been an option.

I shook my head and set down the picture, then fingered one of Molly and me. I couldn't even remember when it had been taken. We must have been about fourteen with long straight hair and chubby cheeks.

We'd taken it ourselves, holding the camera an arm's length away. We looked clownish, our faces tinted too brightly with pink blush and pearl-blue shadow swiped from Mother's vanity. We were pretending to be society ladies, though it impressed me now that we looked more like call girls in training.

Who would have ever thought back then that one of us would end up in a cell at Lew Sterrett, accused of murder?

I toed off my flip-flops and sagged into thick layers of lacy pillows. Shutting my eyes, I tried hard to make sense of what had happened and how to fix it. The hazy pieces of the puzzle didn't fit together yet, but they would soon, I was sure.

I recalled how easy it had been to slip through the unlocked rear door of Jugs that morning and how I'd wandered through the restaurant undetected until Julie Costello had bumped into me.

Wouldn't it have been as simple for Bud's murderer to linger behind in the restaurant after the late shift when the alarm was still shut off? As I'd seen for myself, there were numerous places to hide. It would have been a piece of cake for the killer to stay out of sight and wait until Bud was alone. Then he could've picked up the knife from the floor where Molly had dropped it and finished Bud off with a stab in the back.

The knife.

I'd told Malone the killer could have worn

gloves, which would explain why Molly's prints were the only ones found on the handle. When I'd been in the kitchen at Jugs, I'd noticed the food handlers had worn plastic gloves from boxes kept by the gross in the storeroom.

How hard would it have been for someone to yank out a pair and pull them on before picking up the knife?

Anyone could have done it. Any one of the waitresses whom Bud had manhandled, any one of their angry boyfriends or husbands.

Or Julie Costello.

Or Bud's mysterious partner whose name Molly didn't know.

If the strip mall security guard, Fred Hicks, had been occupied with a couple of drunken college boys at the Zuma Beach Club — as he'd professed in his statement to the police — he could have missed the real killer's exit entirely.

And there was still the matter of the disappearing bank bag. Who had taken it? Couldn't the cops track down that sort of thing by getting warrants to check bank records?

That alone could lead them to the killer.

My mind raced.

There were so many "maybes" to follow up. Too many to make me feel anything but unsettled.

If only Brian Malone would help me out.

I frowned.

Malone thought I was little more than a

screwball artist vainly trying to save an old friend who looked guilty as sin.

I rolled onto my side and curled into a fetal position, wishing I had something more than theories and gut feelings.

The whir of the air conditioner kicked on, and the noise of it lulled me, until my brain felt too groggy to think.

In my dreams, I saw children holding hands in a circle, playing "Ring Around the Rosie." Then they turned into shouting women bearing protest signs who flew away on broomsticks.

At one point in the night, I awakened to feel a soft touch on my forehead, and I peered into the dark to smell my mother's perfume.

"Go back to sleep, baby," she whispered, and I closed my eyes and drifted off again.

Chapter 14

Sunlight streamed through the windows, spilling onto the silk rug that covered the floor, nearly touching the ruffle of the bed skirt.

I blinked against the brightness, disoriented, trying to remember where I was and how I'd gotten there. Slowly, it came back to me. Dropping in to see David at Mother's house, reminiscing in my old room, and curling up on the bed to rest. The scent of Cissy's perfume tickling my nose as I'd slept.

My contacts stuck to my corneas, and I squished my eyes open and shut until I felt them loosen up. Then I glanced at the clock.

Nine-fifteen.

Oh, crap.

I threw aside the blanket that Mother must have draped over me during the night when she'd come in to check on me, and I hopped off the bed, my pulse jumping, wondering how I was going to get dressed for Bud's memorial service and make it out to the Church of Perpetual Hope in only forty-five minutes.

Shedding my rumpled clothes into a pile on the bathroom floor, I turned the shower on as hot as I could stand it and scrubbed the smell of Jugs from my hair and skin with a scented bar of Crabtree & Evelyn soap.

Ever the perfect hostess, Mother always kept fresh towels on the racks, and I rubbed myself dry, then wrapped the soft Egyptian cotton around my damp head as I rummaged through the depleted medicine cabinet to scrounge up a spare toothbrush and tightly rolled tube of Crest. I located a sample-sized mascara with a crust of black around its rim and dabbed at my lashes, pinching away any clumps. A dried-up stick of deodorant nearly crumbled to pieces in my armpits.

An ancient 1,200-watt dryer I'd left behind still worked, though so slowly I thought I'd turn gray before my hair felt less than damp.

My old dresser drawers yielded faded pairs of floral panties and bras with tiny bows between the cups. My slept-in clothes held little appeal, and I decided clean and out-of-date was better than day-old, no contest.

The simple Liz Claiborne black dress that I'd worn to my father's funeral still hung in the back of the closet where I'd stuffed it years before, hoping never to see it again. Definitely hoping never to wear it. Now I held it in my hands with the clock ticking, debating whether to slip it on or go to Bud's service in the cranberry moiré number I'd once worn to the

Dallas Symphony Association's fundraising ball.

"Sorry, Daddy," I whispered and dropped the black dress onto the bed.

I went through several balled-up pairs of pantyhose before I found one without runs. Then I zipped myself into my funeral dress and slid my feet into the only pair of black shoes I could track down. Pappagallo pumps with Minnie Mouse bows that were so old they were probably back in style.

Gathering up yesterday's clothes and sneakers into a ball, I raced downstairs and snatched up my purse from the bench in the front hall where I'd left it the night before.

I heard voices in the kitchen, but I didn't have time for morning chitchat.

My watch showed twenty to ten, and I'd need every one of those minutes to reach the Church of Perpetual Hope before the memorial service started. Even though I didn't want to go, I had a thing about being late.

I had the front door open and one foot outside when Mother's voice stopped me cold.

"Just where do you think you're skipping off to without so much as a 'good morning'?"

I cringed at her tone and slowly turned around. "Good morning."

Her eyes raked over me, and her perfectly made-up face frowned. "Why are you wearing black? Isn't that the dress you wore to Daddy's . . . ?"

"Yes, yes, it is," I cut her off and self-consciously held my purse and bundled clothes against my belly.

She crossed her arms, willing to wait me out. "You look like you're on your way to a funeral."

"You're right. I am."

"Anyone I know?"

"I don't think so."

"Andrea?"

I mumbled the name.

She wrinkled her nose. "What was that?"

I sighed. She wasn't going to let me off that easy. "All right, already. I'm going to Bud Hartman's memorial service in Plano," I told her, enunciating crisply so she wouldn't miss a word.

"The man the police think Molly O'Brien murdered?"

"The very same."

Her mouth fell open. It was one of those rare — and I do mean rare — moments when Cissy was speechless.

Of course, I took full advantage of it.

"I've got to go."

My watch showed a quarter till ten. At this rate, I would be late even if I drove like Jeff Gordon.

"I'll phone you later," I called over my shoulder and leapt down the front steps to my car.

The worst of the morning traffic had already passed, and I made good time north into Plano, an area best known for its ever-expanding neighborhoods and new shopping malls that seemed to proliferate like oversexed rabbits.

Unlike Highland Park or University Park, which housed the campus of Southern Methodist University, the residential areas up north were newer, the houses all very similar in architecture, and the yards sorely lacking in things green and leafy. From what I knew of Dallas real estate, fully mature shade trees on the property could boost prices higher than in-ground pools. Heck, pools were a dime a dozen. But honest-to-God thirty-foot maples or oaks, now those were as rare as an honest politician.

I could only imagine how the market values in Plano would shoot up when the omnipresent saplings had a chance to mature in another decade or two.

Speaking of time, it was five past ten when I approached the intersection at Parker and Preston. I squinted past the glare of sun on my windshield, looking for the Church of Perpetual Hope amidst the grocery stores, retail outlets, and restaurants that crowded side by side in every direction.

As the light shifted from red to green, I finally spotted a billboard beyond the bull's-eye of Target. The towering sign depicted soaring doves and clouds with silver linings. COME SAVE YOURSELF, COME PRAY WITH US, the words beckoned, and a lightning bolt pointed down to a spot just beyond the Black-Eyed Pea restaurant, where I assumed the church was located.

Yep, there it was. A golden dome came into view as I rounded the corner and drove about another half a block.

"Oh, my," I breathed as I pulled into a parking lot as big as the one outside Texas Stadium.

Come to think of it, the church itself gave the Cowboys' home a run for its money.

It was hardly an ordinary white clapboard structure with a bell tower in its steeple.

All chrome and glass that glinted fiercely beneath the sun, it appeared to be the same size as the Wal-Mart SuperCenter in Mesquite. The place must've covered five acres. And that was a conservative guess.

A small herd of cars occupied the spaces in the first few rows nearest the entrance. I wondered if they belonged to church staffers or if they were mourners come to pay their last respects.

Leaving the Jeep in the first open slot, I hurried toward the building, bypassing Julie's red Corvette in a square marked RESERVED well in front.

I slowed my steps as I spotted a second car that looked familiar.

In the adjacent reserved parking space sat a shiny white Lincoln Town Car with pockmarks on its otherwise pristine surface.

The same car I'd seen at Jugs yesterday.

A butterfly took flight inside my stomach.

He was here at the church.

The mystery man I'd heard arguing with Julie in Bud's office. The one I suspected might be a partner in the restaurant.

I reached inside my purse and pulled out the tiny notebook I kept for grocery lists and appointments. I removed the pen from its spine and jotted down the three letters and three digits that made up the Texas license plate number. This time, I'd be safe rather than sorry.

MCY 653.

Then I returned the notebook to my bag and entered through the glass doors.

A receptionist at a moon-shaped desk in the subdued blue lobby pointed me toward a carpeted hallway, which I followed like the Yellow Brick Road until I came to a pair of closed doors.

The air conditioning must've been set on "frigid," and I shivered as my body tried to adjust from the tepid morning to the chilly temperature.

I rubbed my arms and drew in a deep breath, then I pushed past another set of doors to find myself at the rear of an enormous room the shape of a baseball diamond. Polished beams rose heavenward toward a skylight through which hazy rays of sun descended. The entire wall behind the pulpit was stained glass. Images of Jesus, Mary, and Joseph, of various creatures and biblical scenes came alive as the sunlight breathed movement into the riot of color.

Cushioned pews that could have held hundreds remained mostly empty save for a smattering of people scattered in the foremost rows.

A table up front held a lidded brass pot surrounded by vases full of white lilies, and I figured the pot contained Bud's ashes.

It seemed impossible to believe that a man who'd caused so much trouble, whose death had put Molly behind bars, now was little more than dust.

". . . ashes to ashes, dust to dust . . . ," the preacher intoned as if reading my thoughts.

Red runners led up to the apse and carved pulpit. A tall man in robes helmed it like a ship's captain, his voice reverberating through the auditorium as he spoke of Bud Hartman "going home."

The carpet masked my footsteps as I tiptoed forward. I saw Julie's blond head bobbing as the eulogy went on, the booming bass of the minister's voice thumping inside my skull.

I glimpsed Rhonda, Christie, and Ginger clustered together in the row behind Julie. I recognized a few others from the restaurant. The rest were strangers to me.

Sliding into an empty pew several rows back, I set aside my purse and clasped my hands in my lap.

My gazed focused on the preacher's face, and

it dawned on me that I recognized him. It took but a second for it to register that he was the Reverend Jim Bob Barker in the flesh.

What had Bud Hartman done in his lifetime to rate Jim Bob's presence at his memorial service?

How could a man busy with raising funds to buy toys for children in undeveloped nations have time to eulogize a murdered restaurateur? Especially when that restaurant was Jugs, which I doubted was a place the Reverend Jim Bob would take Mrs. Jim Bob to dine unless he was looking to sleep on the couch.

It made no sense.

Other than the rise and fall of the preacher's voice, reverberating like a rumble of distant thunder inside the cavernous space, the only sounds I detected were sniffles from the front row.

Solitary sniffles.

Julie Costello seemed to be the only one grieving over Bud's passing, and, if what I'd seen yesterday was any indication, that barely registered a one on the Richter scale. By all accounts, theirs had been an open relationship, one where Bud had been able to have his cake and eat it, too.

So what if Julie had gotten tired of his tomcat ways? What if she'd wanted monogamy, maybe even marriage, and he'd refused to give it? She appeared to be a take-charge kind of woman — despite her ditzy facade. I couldn't imagine she'd be okay with a boyfriend who ran around with his hired help right under her nose.

Such behavior had to be a slap in the pom-poms for the former Cowboys cheerleader. Maybe she'd returned to the restaurant that fateful night, had found Bud all over Molly, and had decided to put an end to his extracurricular activities once and for all.

Could've happened.

Julie was hardly in the clear, as far as I was concerned. Especially after eavesdropping on her argument with the mystery man yesterday morning. Maybe there was more involved here than Bud's sex-capades. Maybe she was the one stabbing Bud in the back with someone else, for business or pleasure.

Which led me to the matter of Bud having a partner in the restaurant. If this was the case, as Molly had suggested, why wasn't anyone stepping forward? Who was he? And was he tied to a murder plot?

I'd have to ask Malone to check into the business, see if there was partnership insurance and whose name was on those papers. Perhaps Bud had been killed for the time-honored motive of money.

Last, but not least, there were the Jugs waitresses. I wasn't entirely convinced that someone hadn't paid Bud back for his harassment by sticking that chef's knife between his ribs after Molly had run off.

Christie, Rhonda, and Ginger had all complained about Bud's unwanted advances. Who's to say the killer wasn't one of them?

I counted suspects on my fingers until I ran out of digits.

Bud had more enemies than Osama bin Laden.

Unfortunately, the police didn't seem to care, not as long as they had Molly's fingerprints on the knife and Molly herself locked up snugly in Lew Sterrett.

". . . as Jesus gave his life on the cross, so shall we be saved . . ."

Reverend Jim Bob thundered on, and I stifled a yawn.

Ever since I was a child, church services had made me sleepy. I'm not sure what it was. The repetitive phrases I'd heard time and again. The hum of the air conditioning. The way I had to sit so still.

My eyelids began to droop, my chin sloping toward my chest only to snap up again as the preacher's voice rose emphatically.

Someone coughed — probably trying to stay awake as well — and I forced my eyes wide, making a concerted effort to concentrate as Reverend Barker wrapped up the eulogy with a few more flowery phrases about Bud's return to the arms of Our Loving Father, and then concluded with a persuasive, "Amen."

I glanced at my watch and noted it was ten-thirty, and I sighed with relief that the service had been mercifully short.

Reverend Jim Bob stepped down from the pulpit and strode toward Julie, his hands outstretched, his graceful robes swaying.

Glancing to my right, I watched Ginger, Christie, and Rhonda scoot out of their pew and make a beeline toward the aisle. All three were dry-eyed. They looked anxious to escape, and I realized they'd probably come for the same reason as I had: because Julie had left them little choice in the matter.

I recognized several faces from the kitchen staff and a few other servers. If not for Jugs employees, I wondered if anyone would have shown up at all.

Slipping my purse over my shoulder, I slowly rose and inched my way from the pew onto the line of red carpet. I followed it forward, passing others leaving, and approached Julie and Jim Bob Barker.

They leaned into one another, speaking in hushed voices. Julie dabbed at her eyes. His hand rested on her shoulder, gently kneading. The gesture appeared rather intimate, and I wondered if the preacher gave all his lambs such personal attention. Or maybe it had more to do with Julie's snug-fitting black lace dress that showed off her curves so unchastely. Her stockings had seams up the backs, and her stiletto heels made her legs seem endless, though perhaps the short length of her skirt aided in that illusion.

Like the well-mannered woman my mother

brought me up to be, I softly cleared my throat to announce my presence.

Jim Bob's head fast drew apart from Julie's, and he dropped his hand from her shoulder to clasp the other in the folds of his black robes. He smiled at me, and I was struck by what a truly good-looking man he was, even more so in person than on TV. His eyes were a clear and piercing blue and seemed to cut right through me. His gray-streaked hair was neatly combed away from his chiseled features.

I understood why he'd attracted such a following. Though he was surely old enough to be my father, I felt a tingle down yonder. The man was a hottie.

"Andrea," Julie greeted me, miraculously getting my name right. She sniffed and blinked teary eyes, though her mascara remained perfectly unsmudged. Must be industrial-strength waterproof. I wondered what brand it was. "You made it after all," she said. "I didn't see you before the service started."

"I was running late. I'm sorry."

"No, it's okay. I'm just glad you're here. Everyone else only came because they were afraid I'd dock their pay if they didn't. But I think you came for something else, didn't you?"

"Something else?" The hairs on my neck bristled like a prickly pear. Did this have to do with my undercover act as an unwed mother-to-be? Was she going to have Reverend Jim Bob do a laying-on of hands and banish Satan from my soul for all the lying I'd been doing?

"Don't look so worried." She reached out and squeezed my hand. "I know you came because you're a good person. You really care about people. I could tell that from the moment I met you."

I felt Reverend Jim Bob staring at me, and I prayed he couldn't read the guilt on my face. If I'd been wearing pants, we'd need an extinguisher to put the fire out.

"Who might this be, Julie?" he asked, and I was actually glad for the distraction.

She quickly made the introductions. "This is Andrea Blevins." She waved her hand at me as if I were a letter Vanna White had turned around. "She's a waitress at Jugs. Just hired her yesterday as a matter of fact. She appeared out of the blue when I needed her most." Her gaze drifted down to my belly. "And when she needed me."

"Ah, a gift from Heaven for you both," the preacher remarked with an ephemeral smile. Then he nodded at me. "Lovely to meet you, Andrea," he said in a smoky warm tone that made me quiver. "You can call me Jim Bob. Everyone does."

"The Reverend Barker is a big celebrity in these parts," Julie jumped in, using his formal title all of a sudden, I noticed. Trying to create a little distance for my benefit? "He's got his own TV show and a big billboard right on LBJ. He's a busy, busy man, always out doing the Lord's work," she finished, staring hard up at the pastor, though he kept his eyes on me.

He shifted his shoulders beneath the purple mantle that topped his robes, clutching his hands together. "It's good to have you in my church, young lady, despite the circumstances. Did you know Mr. Hartman?"

"No," I told him, glad I didn't have to lie this go-round. "I never had the pleasure." Okay, so that was a stretch. I waited for lightning to strike, but merely heard the air conditioning click on again.

"Reverend Barker was a friend of Bud's," Julie said, and the preacher's face tightened visibly. "They had a lot in common."

"Oh, now, Julie, I wouldn't say that," he murmured, and I detected a faint flush to his cheeks.

"Well, you were both successful businessmen with humble beginnings," she remarked, but I had a feeling that was not all she'd meant.

Which left me to wonder how Reverend Barker knew Bud.

Through the church?

Though Bud's being a dutiful member seemed highly unlikely. Although I reminded myself that greater sinners than he were members of congregations all over the place. Even Highland Park Presbyterian.

Maybe Bud had donated to one of Jim Bob's causes?

If only Julie had a string in her back like my old Chrissy doll, I'd give it a tug and make her explain her comment.

"Was Bud a member of Perpetual Hope?" I asked. Well, it couldn't hurt to try to figure it out on my own.

Julie laughed.

"Er, not exactly." The preacher tugged back his sleeve to check his watch, a gold and diamond Rolex Presidential that winked beneath the lights. "We were acquainted through my charitable activities. He often collected toys at his restaurant during the holidays for our annual drive." His reply was so smooth I almost bought it.

"There were lots of things about Bud people didn't know," Julie jumped in, and Jim Bob's expression went from benign to unreadable. I bet he beat the socks off his buddies playing poker.

"I don't doubt that," I said, finding it impossible to believe the Bud Hartman I'd learned so much about in the last two days had been generous without something in it for him.

I couldn't help but wonder what that might have been.

The preacher did another watch check. "Oh, my, I didn't realize it was so late. I've got an appearance to make at the Parents for Public Morality luncheon at the Adolphus, and then I have a board meeting with my wife's diabetes foundation." He touched his wedding band. "I'm sorry, ladies, but I must go."

He nodded at me, then grasped Julie's hands. "Be brave, my child," he told her. "This is not the end."

"You know it's not." She tipped her pretty face up toward his.

He let her go.

She frowned, her eyes following his imposing figure as he sauntered off, black robes snapping at his heels.

Her small hands clenched to fists at her sides, and I noticed the red imprints of his fingers on her white skin.

Ouch.

"Have you ever seen Mrs. Jim Bob?" Julie asked out of the blue, her gaze still fixed on the doors that the minister had disappeared through.

"No," I said, because I hadn't. Unless she was the woman with the purple beehive on his cable show.

"She looks like somebody blew her up with a tire pump," Julie said and sounded pleased as punch. "That's probably how she got diabetes, from eating too much sugar."

"I don't think. . . ."

She didn't let me finish. "Walk me out to my car?" she asked brightly.

"Sure."

She picked up the brass pot from the table amidst the lilies and nonchalantly tucked it under her arm.

"Let's hit the road."

I followed her outside while she babbled on about the pretty flowers, the lovely service, and how tickled Bud would have been to hear Reverend Jim Bob paint him in such a positive light.

"You'd have thought Bud was Mother Teresa," she said with a giggle. "He would've gotten a real kick out of that."

Once past the glass doors in the lobby, the humid air hit me hard, and I felt my breath catch in my throat. Within seconds my clothes stuck to my skin, and perspiration molded stockings to flesh. I could only imagine the temperature inside my Jeep.

Hot enough to roast a turkey.

"Where's your ride?" she asked.

I hooked my thumb across the lot toward the Wrangler, its black hard top baking beneath the sun.

"Four-wheel drive?"

"Yeah."

"Bud had a Cherokee," she said and sighed. "Now it's on probation."

On probation?

Did she mean in probate?

I cleared my throat, working hard to keep a straight face. Sometimes I couldn't tell when she was doing her dumb blonde routine and when she was serious.

Julie's red Corvette sat right out front, but the white Lincoln was gone from its reserved parking spot.

"Hey, I've got a favor to ask you," she said and paused beside the driver's side door. She dumped the brass pot none too gently on top of her sports car and left it there while she dug her keys from her purse.

"What kind of favor?" Hadn't I done enough do-gooding for one day?

"Tiffany called me this morning and told me she couldn't make her shift," she replied and scrunched up her face. "Says she's sick, but, knowing her, it's nothing contagious. Just PMS. Which is just as well, because she scares the customers when she's in hormone hell. Can you fill in?"

Another shift would give me more time to poke around. "Sure," I told her. "No problem."

"You're a doll," she squealed, and I wanted to laugh, that coming from a woman who looked like Barbie. "I'll see you later then. Oh, and Junior, too!"

"Right." Ha, ha. I was getting tired of her "Junior" routine already.

She hesitated for a minute and tipped her head, squinting at me over the roof of her car. "You look different today, Andrea. Though I can't put a finger on it. Thinner, maybe? Must be the black."

"Gee, thanks." I think.

With a shrug, she dove into the Corvette and slammed the door. The engine roared to life, and the car started to back up when I realized she'd forgotten something.

"Julie, stop!" I shrieked at the top of my lungs.

Luckily, she did.

I ran over to the Vette and removed the brass pot, which had skidded precariously close to the edge of the roof, the hot pavement below.

She lowered her window, and I shoved it through.

"Oh, hell," she said, then raised the window and drove off.

Shading my eyes with my hand, I watched the sleek red car skim across the parking lot and disappear into the street.

"You look different today," I mimicked and headed toward my Jeep. *"Must be the black. Right,"* I muttered and smoothed my fingers over the crepe fabric. The dress was a size six and still fit, so it must've been the too-tight Calvins yesterday that had her confused.

Or else . . . my heart stopped.

I glanced down.

And realized something was missing.

I could see all the way down to the Minnie Mouse bows on my shoes without obstruction.

Uh-oh.

Yesterday, I was Marilyn. Today, more like Twiggy. No wonder Julie had thought I'd lost weight. I was minus two full cup sizes, front and center.

"Good going, Kendricks," I said aloud and unlocked the Jeep.

I doubted if Mata Hari had ever had to worry about stuffing *her* bra, for Pete's sake.

Chapter 15

I headed back to my condo, mulling over my observations from the memorial service as I drove.

What kept running through my mind was the sight of Reverend Jim Bob's hand on Julie's shoulder after the eulogy was over and the way they'd been speaking to each other in such hushed tones, heads bent together so intimately my gut told me there was more to their relationship than shepherd and sheep.

Were Jim Bob and Julie having an affair?

Was that what she'd meant when she'd suggested the televangelist and Bud had had something in common?

Her, perhaps?

I remembered, too, the way the preacher had gripped Julie's hand so tightly before his departure.

What the heck was that about? Was he angry with her for some reason? Was it a warning to keep quiet?

Might it have anything to do with Bud's death?

189

I could be way off base, but I'll wager I wasn't far afield.

Julie and Jim Bob Barker? I mused and shook my head.

The more I dwelled on the idea, the less it seemed so far-fetched.

I mean, why not? The Rev was a great-looking guy, though twice her age. And he certainly had enough money and power to appeal to her baser needs. For heaven's sake, Bud had been two- or three-timing her, if what I'd heard from the other waitresses was correct. So what would have prevented her from taking another lover?

But what if Bud had found out? What if *he* wasn't big on sharing?

Or maybe he'd seen dollar signs. A business opportunity.

Maybe he'd tried to blackmail the preacher. He could've had Julie followed, come up with photos that would've tarnished the preacher's squeaky-clean image. Could Julie have even been in on it?

Well, it was possible, wasn't it?

And it was a damned good motive for murder.

The theory sent a charge through me, a sudden surge of hope tempered only by my worrying whether or not Malone would think it was worth looking into. Or, worse, would he tell me I was grasping at straws?

Once home, I changed out of my funeral attire and into a pair of jeans and a T-shirt from Operation Kindness, a local non-kill animal shelter I'd done some pro bono web design work for. Peeling off the sticky pantyhose had taken a bit of doing, but it was pure joy to throw the damp wad of nylon into the trashcan and wiggle my bare toes in the carpet.

Having skipped breakfast that morning for lack of time, I fixed myself a quick peanut butter and jelly sandwich and considered it brunch.

The phone rang just as I took a bite. I picked up the receiver and uttered a gluey "Hello?"

"Andy? Is that you? It's Malone."

Speak of the devil, I thought, as I forcibly swallowed down the lump of peanut butter and bread.

"Anything new?" I asked, hoping he'd found some glitch in the prosecutor's case, some way to get Molly out of jail so I could drop this Nancy Drew act and return to my slightly less theatrical existence.

I heard him shuffling papers in the background. "I've been doing some digging on my own," he said, "and I found out a few things about our friend Fred Hicks, the helpful security guard who so fortuitously spotted Molly running from Jugs just before one o'clock on the night of the murder." Sarcasm edged his usually even-keeled voice.

"And?" I twisted the cord around my finger, waiting for him to finish, knowing it had to be something good to have gotten a rise out of him.

"He's not as clean as the cops made him out to be," Malone remarked, sounding triumphant, and I realized he wasn't nearly as disinterested in this case as he'd appeared in the beginning. "Hicks has a record of two arrests for theft, though charges were dropped when he paid restitution."

"Theft of what?"

"Cold hard cash."

"So how could he keep working as a security guard?"

"He was an unarmed guard, Andy. Some companies still don't do background checks these days, which is how pedophiles end up working in day care."

Fred Hicks was a thief.

The tip of my finger went from blue to white, and I unwrapped the cord from around it as fast as I could. My heart was pounding hard inside my chest.

"Do you think he went over to Jugs, found the door unlocked, and tiptoed in to rob the place? Maybe Molly was still in the locker room" — she'd said Bud had been watching her from the shadows — "so maybe Hicks slipped in, found the bag with the day's deposits sitting there on Bud's desk and tried to run off with it, only to get sidetracked when Bud attacked Molly. He might've witnessed the struggle before she ran out." The more I talked, the less idiotic the scenario seemed. "So then Bud turns around and catches him with the loot in his sticky fingers."

Malone did one of those, "Whoa, Andys,"

that he was getting so good at. "I agree that the police need to look at Hicks more closely, but let's not jump to conclusions, okay? As much as I'd like to clear Molly, we have to approach this realistically. First off, how would Hicks have even known where Bud's office was, much less that the day's receipts would be sitting on his desk?"

"You said he'd been working at the Villa Mesa shopping center for almost a year." My brain clicked into overdrive. "The guy probably had the layout of every retail establishment down cold and everyone's habits memorized. I'm sure he knew Bud left the restaurant with a full bank bag at around midnight or shortly after. Maybe he was desperate or greedy. . . ."

"Andy," he tried to cut me off, but I didn't let him.

"And if he deposited all that cash in his bank account, we'd have him by the balls, wouldn't we? So check his balance, Brian, that's all I'm asking. You can do that, can't you?" I was not about to let him drag me down when he'd just ripped a seam in the D.A.'s case.

He sighed. "I'll see what I can do, but it's a long shot."

Geez, did the guy cry at parties? Did he talk about the divorce rate when he went to weddings?

"C'mon, Malone," I prodded, because even a long shot was worth aiming for. "If Hicks *had* tried to steal from Bud and he'd been caught red-handed, Hartman would have pressed charges. There's no way Bud would've let the guy off with restitution. And I'm sure Hicks would have done just about anything to prevent that, like picking up the knife Molly had dropped and using it to stop Bud permanently. He could've worn the gloves they keep in the kitchen."

"Gloves in the kitchen? How would you know about that?" His voice cracked like a kid in puberty.

"Oh, er, isn't that standard these days after all those hepatitis scares?" I rushed in to rescue myself, hoping to avoid a train wreck. "Really, Malone, it would explain why no one else's prints were on the murder weapon but Molly's, and if you'd just for one minute pause and consider. . . ."

"There's plenty I'm considering, but it's hard to get a word in edgewise," he grumbled. "If you'd quit talking long enough for me to tell you what I'm thinking, you might actually hear me say I agree with you."

"You do?"

Really, I was stunned. Not quite speechless, but stunned nonetheless.

"Yes, I do. About one thing, anyway. That Hicks may have been the one to take the bank bag, though I'm more inclined to believe he snatched it after the fact. When Bud was already dead and couldn't put up a fight."

"After Bud was dead?" I echoed and my heart

sank like a stone. Why did he have to be so damned logical? "Which hardly gets Molly off the hook."

"The cops think Molly took the money," he said, "which gives her a motive for murder, right? So if we can trace the stolen cash to someone else, that'll weaken the prosecutor's argument. See, Andy, you and I are on the same side of this thing. We just seem to take different paths to reach the same conclusion."

"That's one way of putting it," I remarked, buoyed a bit by the thought that, while we weren't always on the same page, at least we were reading the same book. At least he sounded positive, for once. "It is nice to know I'm not working alone."

Dead silence.

"Malone, are you there?"

"Wh-what exactly do you mean about working alone?" he blasted into the phone, a cannonball made of words shot directly at my eardrum. "Please, tell me you're not doing anything stupid." This time, he sounded more concerned than angry.

"Aw, so you do care." I grinned.

No doubt his cheeks were red as Mother's English roses. "Tell me what you're up to, Andy. If you're involved in anything that might jeopardize. . . ."

"Oh, for crying out loud," I stopped him midstream. "I'm not doing anything illegal and certainly nothing to hurt Molly. And, believe it or not, I've come up with a few things you might find interesting."

Talk about a pregnant pause. I pictured Malone removing his glasses and pinching the bridge of his nose to prevent a migraine from attacking.

Finally, he sighed. "Go on."

So I did breathlessly. "Bud's got a secret partner."

"Not so secret."

"You know who it is?"

"It's a corporation. ERA, Inc., to be precise."

So Malone hadn't been twiddling his thumbs while I hustled tips at Jugs and played the busybody. "Was there partner's insurance?"

"Yes, ma'am."

Why did he always make me drag it out of him? "Did the corporation hold the policy on Bud Hartman?"

"You bet."

"How much?"

"Ten million bucks."

"Ten million?" My pulse banged against my temples. "My God, that's like hitting the jackpot."

"A small jackpot these days."

But his remark did nothing to dampen my excitement at his news. "It's worth killing for, wouldn't you say?"

"Possibly."

Oh, fudge, but he was a killjoy. "So what's ERA?"

"I'm working on that, Andy. There's a lot of red tape involved. Somebody wanted to keep the information buried."

I rolled my eyes. "Well, dig fast, would you? We don't have much time."

"Any more instructions before I go?"

"Yeah, smart aleck," I said because there actually was something I needed him to do. "Hold on a sec." Wedging the receiver between my jaw and shoulder, I grabbed my purse and pulled out my notebook, flipping through the pages until I found what I was looking for. "Can you get someone to trace a license plate number?"

"A plate number? Hell, Andy, what exactly *are* you up to?"

"Do you really want to know?"

A pause, then a soft, "Probably better for my health if I don't."

"Ready?"

"All right." He caved. "Lay it on me."

I gave him the letters and digits I'd copied from the plate of the white Lincoln Town Car, repeating everything twice just to be sure. Then I asked him to call me ASAP when he had anything.

"That's it?" Why did he sound so anxious?

"For now," I assured him.

"You stay out of trouble, you hear me? Don't stick your nose where it doesn't belong. Molly's in deep enough already."

"I'll do what I have to."

"Whoa, whoa. . . ."

"Goodbye, Malone," I said and hung up.

I finished my peanut butter and jelly sandwich, washing everything down with a glass of cold milk. Then I checked my mail, paid a few bills, and got a handful of invoices ready to send.

Since I wasn't working at Jugs until the late shift, I decided to go downtown and visit Molly. I doubt she'd had anyone come by that day except perhaps Malone.

And I figured she could certainly use some encouragement after that.

Chapter 16

Molly looked worse than she had when I'd visited her two days before. But then being locked up at Lew Sterrett was hardly comparable to a pampering at the Greenhouse Spa.

The shadows beneath her eyes had darkened. Her skin seemed gray, the line of her mouth more grim, though the hopelessness in her eyes lifted briefly as she caught sight of me beyond the Plexiglas barricade.

"Don't give up," I said the instant she grabbed the black receiver and put it to her ear. "We haven't lost the battle yet."

"Then why am I still here?" she demanded. "Why haven't they caught the real killer so I can go home to my son? Or aren't they even looking for anyone else? Oh, God, they're not, are they, Andy?"

"*I'm* looking," I told her, but that didn't seem to give her much more confidence than it had Malone.

"I didn't do it, I swear." Her eyes glistened with unshed tears, and she bit at her lip to fight them back. "Bud was a creep, for sure, but I didn't murder him. He wasn't worth my losing everything. Hell, he wasn't worth the price of a burger."

"You don't have to convince me, Mol," I assured her, wishing I could leap past the clear partition and give her a hug. "I've believed from the beginning that you're innocent. So does Malone," I added, sensing after my last conversation with Brian that this wasn't stretching the truth anymore. "You have to trust us. We're doing all we can to fix this mess."

"I know you are, Andy," she said, but didn't appear any too encouraged. "And I can't thank you enough for that."

I leaned nearer the Plexiglas, as if I could whisper my next words to her instead of breathing them into the receiver. "I got the job at Jugs," I informed her, and her eyes widened. Though I left out the sob story about my pretending to be alone, penniless, and pregnant. She might think my artful lie was imitating her life a tad too closely. "I started yesterday, and I'm working the dinner shift today."

"Have you found out anything new?"

"A few possibilities."

She leaned forward, eagerly. "Spill."

I hardly needed prodding. "Well, for one, you're certainly not the only waitress who felt Bud was an octopus. I met Rhonda, Christie, and Ginger, and each of them had stories about Hartman coming onto them, despite his so-called relationship with Julie Costello."

"It's like I said, Andy." She frowned, tension pinching her features. "Bud was a big guy. He was physically powerful. If he wanted something, he just took it. What a waste of nice packaging. If only he hadn't been such an ass on the inside."

"Well, someone other than Julie must've ignored what was beneath his slick-boy exterior. I heard about a girl named Sarah who worked at Jugs for two weeks, then abruptly disappeared. The other waitresses said she had a thing for Bud."

Her brow wrinkled in concentration. "Yeah, I remember her. Cute girl. She was young, maybe eighteen."

"Bud bait," I repeated what I'd been told. "How well did you know her?"

Molly pursed her lips. "I didn't get a chance to talk to her too much. I mostly worked the late shift, which can be crazy. Lots of guys coming in after softball games or hanging out to watch sports. But, the few times I did speak to her, she seemed too anxious for me to like her. Like she was desperate for a friend."

"Did she really follow Bud around like a puppy?"

"Some girls have no taste." Molly smiled shakily. But it was short-lived. "Sarah was supposed to help Bud close the restaurant one Friday night a while back. I was actually scheduled to work with her the next day. But she never showed. All Bud would say was that she wasn't coming back, but I had a feeling something happened between them when they were alone."

"Do you recall her last name?"

"Oh, damn." She squished her eyes closed, and I crossed my fingers, hoping she could retrieve the information from wherever it was buried in her mind. Then she opened them and said, "Sarah Craven. Wait, no. That wasn't it. Carson? Something like that, anyway." She looked crestfallen. "I'm sorry, Andy. We're pretty much on a first-name-only basis at the restaurant."

"It's okay," I assured her. That shouldn't be too tricky to find out.

"I just wonder . . . ," she said, but the words trailed off.

"Tell me, please."

She whispered into the receiver, "I wonder if what happened to me, happened to Sarah. Only what if she didn't get away from him?"

I had been wondering the same thing. Yet, I figured that, if Bud had actually assaulted Sarah, she would have filed a police report. Which, I assumed, she hadn't. Otherwise, the cops would've taken Bud in, and, the way the grapevine moved at Jugs, everyone would've heard about it. There's no way Bud could've hushed that up.

Maybe there was nothing nefarious about Sarah's no-show at Jugs at all. What if she'd been convinced not to return by a sweet-faced woman in the parking lot?

"What do you know about the Mothers Against Pornography?" I suddenly asked her, thinking of Peggy Martin and her contingent of female crusaders. "Are they harmless? Have they ever kidnapped anyone? Like the people hired by parents to snatch brainwashed kids from cults?"

"Kidnapped?" The tension in Molly's face eased, and her mouth twitched, like she wanted to chuckle. "My God, Andy, I doubt they'd abduct a girl just to keep her from doing her shift in hot pants. I mean, the worst they ever did was corner me in the parking lot and try to convince me to quit degrading myself by serving beer 'half-naked,' as they put it." She smiled weakly. "One of them even offered me a job at a doctor's office, filing papers for seven-fifty an hour." She shrugged. "It was annoying sometimes, but I actually felt safer when they were there. I never had to worry about some creep lurking around my car."

Although a lurking Mother can be creepy enough, I thought.

"Did you know the shopping center security guard, Fred Hicks?"

She shrugged. "I saw him around sometimes. He'd tip his hat to me. Usually when I left, he was hanging out at the Zuma Beach Club. Sometimes he'd be talking with a few MAP members in front of Jugs."

Did Peggy Martin know Fred Hicks? I wondered.

Molly's eyes suddenly darkened, and her forehead puckered. "Oh, man."

"What?"

"I just realized something. If I'd gone home after my shift, the Mothers would have been around. But since I stayed to help Bud close, all the Moms Against Porn had packed up hours before. Too bad, huh? Because otherwise one of them might've seen something or someone. . . ."

"Or clobbered Bud with a protest sign," I remarked.

Molly brightened. "I could've sold tickets for that."

"Standing room only."

She nodded, her gaze drifting off for a moment, so I could tell her mind had shifted elsewhere. Not surprisingly, she asked, "How's my baby?"

Beyond the ache in her voice, it was plain in her face how much she missed him.

"He's doing great."

"Yeah?"

"He's the newly crowned Go Fish champion at Mother's house," I told her, causing a smile of pure delight.

"The kid's a con man."

"You're telling me."

She chuckled, eyes bright for a moment before the sadness crept back in. "He's the best thing that ever happened to me, Andy. He's the only thing I've done right. I can't let myself imagine not being able to hold him again. It's too awful to even consider."

Her eyes filled with tears, and I felt my throat constrict as I watched her brush them away with the back of her hand.

This wasn't right, I kept thinking. It wasn't right at all.

I changed the subject, as much for my sake as for hers. "You don't happen to have the password for Bud's computer, do you?"

Molly blinked. "You're planning to break into Bud's system? You've gotta be shitting me."

Why did she look so surprised? Computers were my forte, not serving beer in tight shorts to guys who thought every woman's name was "babe."

"Hey, I'm dying to check out the books, see if Bud was doing a little creative cooking. And I wouldn't mind peeking at his payroll records, which would give me our elusive Sarah's name and address. If I could find her, she might have something worth saying."

"Just when do you plan to do this?" she breathed into the receiver, sounding as nervous as I felt merely saying it out loud. "Because, I guarantee you, Julie will find out if you're up to no good. She's got eyes in the back of her head."

"She won't find out."

"No?"

Well, at least I hoped she wouldn't.

I swallowed, not letting her anxiety deter me.

It was the only way. "I'll wait until the restaurant's closed and everyone's gone. Julie won't even know."

She stared at me. "You're insane."

"But in a good way, right?" I grinned like it was no big deal, telling myself it was simply an adventure and probably less dangerous than Cissy's matchmaking.

Still, I'd never broken into anyplace before. And it wasn't something I wanted to do more than once. So I had to do it right the first time.

Which reminded me.

"Did the police confiscate your key to the restaurant?"

"They took my purse, and it was on a ring with everything else."

I chewed on the inside of my cheek.

Okay, no big deal. It just meant I couldn't deadbolt the door behind me. Maybe no one would notice if the self-locking mechanism at the handle was set. It was a chance I'd have to take.

I quickly moved on.

"If you closed up the restaurant, you must know the code to the alarm system," I said, remembering the blinking keypad by the back door. All I needed was to trip that up and have the cops catch me red-handed. Then the jig would be up for good, and I might be joining Molly behind the Plexiglas.

She gnawed on a nail as she spoke into the phone. "Yeah, I've got the code. It's 1-9-8-9.

206

The year Bud got kicked out of Texas Tech and ended his football career."

I dug out a pen from my purse and scribbled the number on the inside of my hand.

"Usually Bud would close up Jugs and turn on the system. On rare occasions, Julie did it, but otherwise it was usually me."

I smiled and flashed her my palm. "Now I know it like the back of my hand, or the front, anyway."

But she didn't smile back. Her face looked more pinched and worried than it had before, if that was possible.

"Is there a motion sensor?"

"No." She bit her bottom lip.

"Hey, relax. It'll be a piece of cake," I promised, wondering if that's what Bonnie had told Clyde before bullets rained down on them.

"Please be careful," Molly whispered. I could see how tightly she gripped the receiver. "If anything happened to you because of me, I'd never forgive myself."

"What could happen?" I ignored the knot in my belly and flashed what I hoped was a devil-may-care grin. "If worse comes to worst, I can always make up a story. Say I went back for my purse and got locked in. That I was sick and passed out in the bathroom. I've got a million of 'em."

Molly hardly looked reassured.

"Look, if they toss me in jail, I'll have Mother bail me out. Can you imagine that? I'd be the first deb dropout to make the Metro crime report *and* the society page with my mug shot."

Molly didn't laugh.

"It'll be okay," I told her. "Really."

The guard approached, and Molly glanced up at the uniformed woman and nodded before turning back to me and saying quickly into the receiver, "Oh, God, I almost forgot. It's pecker."

"What?"

"The computer password. Julie only told me because she'd dreamed it up and thought it was ironic."

The fact that Julie even knew what irony was seemed ironic to me.

"Pecker?" I repeated, still not sure I'd heard correctly.

"I gotta go, Andy."

She hung up, and I watched the guard lead her away. Slowly, I replaced the receiver, but I sat there for a moment, not moving.

Pecker.

The password was *pecker?*

Classy.

As I left the downtown jail and walked toward the lot where I'd stashed my Jeep, a thought flashed across my brain. Something Cissy had once told me.

We'd been watching *To Kill a Mockingbird* on video, because I'd read the book for school and wanted to see the story come to life. Halfway through, my mother had sighed in a very unmother-like fashion and had remarked on how attractive Gregory Peck was. Only she'd called him "Gregory Pecker." When I'd giggled, she'd realized what she'd said and had confessed that it's what she and her school chums had called the movie star way back when.

Even now, thinking of the oh-so-dignified Cissy Blevins Kendricks saying the word "pecker" made me grin.

Slang wasn't exactly my mother's style, especially when it referred to a man's private parts.

But what had amazed me even more was to imagine Cissy as a teenager, hanging out with her friends, going to the picture show, eating popcorn, and gushing over a movie star like Gregory Peck.

I'd always envisioned Mother emerging from a giant clamshell — like Venus — a full-grown society maven clad in a pink Chanel suit with matching bag and pumps.

Which was far easier to believe.

Chapter 17

Sweat dripped down my back as I slid into my Jeep and turned on the AC, which blasted warm air for what seemed the longest time before it finally cooled down. I maneuvered my way through the one-way streets downtown, bypassing the steel and glass tower that housed Malone's firm, finally getting onto the northbound tollway toward home.

The ever-brilliant sunlight glinted fiercely off the windshield, and I blindly rummaged through my purse on the passenger's seat, foraging for my shades. I was afraid to take my eyes from the road as a gray Cadillac ahead of me — its driver on his cell phone — wove unsteadily across the lanes and back again.

When I finally located my Ray-Bans, I grabbed the wheel with both hands, pressed my foot on the accelerator, and surged around him before he caused an accident that might involve yours truly.

Cadillacs, I smirked and shook my head once I was safely past, though I realized Daddy was surely driving one in heaven.

Acuras, Infinitis, and Beamers with vanity plates zipped by me as if I were moving at a snail's pace though my speedometer registered sixty-five. If I drove any faster, I couldn't concentrate. And there was much on my mind to think about.

I mulled over all I'd learned thus far about Bud Hartman's life and death, frustrated by the loose ends still dangling. There were too many unanswered questions, though I knew I was inching ever closer to finding the truth.

If I were lucky, Bud's computer would yield a few answers.

If I wasn't so lucky, I might be sharing a cellblock with Molly at Lew Sterrett by morning. And orange didn't exactly become me.

Exiting the tollway, I took 635 to the Preston Road exit, fighting a nervous stomach all the way to the condo.

There were no messages on my voice mail, not even a wrong number. So I grabbed an apple from the fridge, settled down in front of my Dell desktop, and started working on some ideas for the children's artwork web site. A local cancer society and the Children's Medical Center had hired me — okay, I'd basically volunteered — to put together some pages that featured drawings by kids with cancer. The artwork was featured on note cards and calendars that could be purchased online or in the hospital gift shop, and all profits would help fund research.

I spent a couple hours immersed in the pages, happily arranging the drawings into categories: flowers, pets, hearts, places, and people. I loved looking at the colorful ways the kids had expressed themselves, each one so joyful and vibrant: families holding hands, a cluster of smiling daisies, cats and dogs rubbing noses, a curious moon peering down at the Earth from space.

Mother didn't understand why I took jobs that paid pennies or, sometimes, nothing at all, especially when she had wealthy friends with prosperous businesses that could afford to shell out generous fees.

"This is why," I wanted to tell her, as I smiled at my monitor. Besides, taking a handout from Cissy — or one of her cronies — put me in her debt, and I could only afford to do that sparingly. I was surprised she didn't understand the choices I'd made, especially when she'd spent her whole life giving her time to worthy causes. Though I had a feeling she wouldn't have been so preoccupied with my balance sheet if I'd been married. As far as my mother was concerned, being somebody's wife solved just about every problem on the planet, including the greenhouse effect and nuclear proliferation.

My father had understood, even early on when I wasn't sure how I would use my passion for art in the real world.

Daddy had run a pharmaceutical company, one his grandfather had built from the ground up and his father had helmed before him. He'd been working on contracts, sitting at his desk in his study on Beverly Drive, the day he'd died, and I'm sure he'd wanted it that way. "You have to love what you do, baby girl, or it's not worth getting up everyday."

I do, Daddy, I wanted so badly to tell him, though I figured he knew.

The sun had shifted, weakening the light that filtered through the window blinds, as I signed off and shut down my computer.

I checked my watch, noting I had enough time to heat up a Stouffer's lasagna, eat, and change before I was due at Jugs for the six o'clock shift.

Between bites, I threaded a needle and secured the shoulder pads into the seamed cups of my running bra so they'd stay put. I didn't need any added distractions.

In another half-hour, I'd curled my hair and teased it to unnatural heights, applied enough Mary Kay cosmetics to hide every pore, and slipped several empty zip disks into my purse, just to be safe. I'd dressed in black jeans and Tee, my favorite uniform, and a color scheme that seemed to be the primo choice for burglars. I definitely didn't want to make a fashion faux pas while breaking and entering.

When I pulled into the parking lot at Jugs, the sun had set, and the neon sign at the Zuma Beach Club flashed hot pink.

I settled the Jeep into a spot near Zuma, figuring that if I planned to be at Jugs after closing, I didn't want my car in an obvious place.

The Mothers Against Pornography were on the march again, about a half-dozen of them anyway, and I ducked around parked cars to avoid the sign-wielding contingent as I made my way to the restaurant's rear entrance and slipped inside.

The kitchen hummed with activity. Steam rose from grills, and the smell of spices and frying burgers filled the air. I hurried up the hallway toward the lockers.

A few of the servers from the early shift dressed in their street clothes while the rest of us changed into our skimpy outfits.

Several women I recognized from Bud's memorial service nodded at me, introducing themselves over naked shoulders as they pulled on cropped T-shirts and hot pants.

I gathered up my order pad and pen, shutting the door to my locker and heading into the dining area, which seemed even more crowded than the day before. I spotted a few women and children among those seated at my station but, like yesterday, most of the customers were men.

Halfway through the evening, Julie Costello tapped my arm as I stood at the bar waiting for two jugs of beer to be filled.

"There's a guy came to see you, Andrea," she said into my ear, her voice raised to be heard above the noisy crowd and the Mavericks basketball game playing on the television. "He's preppy, but cute. Asked specifically for one of your tables, though he called you Andy Kendricks. I thought your name was Blevins?"

"It is. Uh, I'm divorced," I told her, the first thing that came to mind.

She nodded sympathetically. "Gotcha. Anyway, I went ahead and seated him myself. In your section."

"Where?"

"Right over there." She pointed her finger across the room, and I followed it with my eyes.

Oh, hell.

It was Malone.

"Everything okay?"

"Yeah, fine," I murmured, though my pulse kicked into overdrive. What in God's name was Malone doing here? How had he known where I was?

"You don't look so good all of a sudden." Her heavily made-up eyes dropped to my belly. "Can you get morning sickness in the after-noon?"

I stared at her, speechless, and shook my head. *Please, please,* don't let her have mentioned my "condition" to Brian.

"I'm fine."

"You sure?"

"Oh, I get it." She nudged me with an elbow. "He's the one who dumped you?"

"No. I mean, yes. Er, no!" Even I was con-fusing myself. "It's kinda complicated," I explained, my lies becoming more convoluted than a soap opera plot.

"Is he Junior's father?"

"Oh, geez, Julie, of course, he's. . . ." — *not,* I was going to say, but clamped my mouth shut and debated this one for a moment. Interesting suggestion. Still, it didn't seem right to make Brian out to be the heel who'd left me high and dry, not even if it was all pretend.

"He's what?" She poked me again.

This was one lie I didn't want to tell, so I did the next best thing. I exited, stage left.

"Excuse me, would you? I've got customers waiting." I picked up the two jugs and delivered them to a table of unruly guys who were yelling at the Mavs game and consuming copious amounts of buffalo wings and chips.

One of them patted my butt as I turned to leave. Oh, boy, was I *so* not in the mood for that. I spun around with a frozen smile and leaned into his face. "Do that again, buster, and the next jug of beer's on your head. You got that?"

He uttered a word that rhymed with "itch."

I guess I could forget about a tip.

I wove through the tables, approaching the one where Brian Malone sat. He was studying a menu, head tipped down, brown curls falling onto his brow and glasses slipping halfway down his slim nose.

"What the hell are you doing here?" I hissed at him in lieu of the usual "Yee haw, y'all, and welcome to Jugs" shtick.

He glanced up calmly and pressed a finger to the bridge of his tortoiseshell frames, pushing them higher. *The better to see you, my dear.* "I should ask you the same thing. Does your mother know you're working in this place?" he asked point-blank.

He sounded like the woman from Mothers Against Porn, which only made me all the more ticked-off at him.

I put my palms on the table and glared at him. "Of course she doesn't!" I hissed through clenched teeth, "Not unless somebody told her."

He wriggled a finger beneath his collar, like he needed more air. "Do I look like I have a death wish?"

I squinted at him, thinking that, if he wasn't telling the truth, that death wish might come true.

"How'd you find out, by the way, because I don't recall mentioning it?" I was nearly nose to nose with him now.

He shrugged and fiddled with the gingham-checked napkin. "Maybe I figured it out on my own, did you ever consider that? I could've asked myself, 'What's the craziest, stupidest thing Andy could do to rescue her friend?' And I came up with this."

"If that were true, then you win what's behind door number two." But I didn't believe it for a minute. He was a far worse liar than I was.

"Hell, it doesn't matter how I found out." He didn't appear amused. "How *could* you?" he said under his breath. "This is insane."

"It's part of the plan, Malone, which you're going to send up in flames if you hang around here, spilling the beans about me to Julie Costello."

"I can't believe you're doing this, Andy."

"How else am I supposed to help Molly?" I asked him, feeling steamed. "It was the only way to get inside and find out the truth about Hartman and who wanted him dead." I looked past Malone's shoulder and saw Julie near the bar, watching us with unbridled curiosity. "I just hope you haven't blown my cover."

His bespectacled eyes flickered over me in a less than lawyerly manner. "I'd say you're hardly covered at all."

"Stop it," I warned and felt heat rise in my cheeks.

His gaze froze on my breasts. "My, how you've grown."

I straightened up and crossed my arms over my chest. "Give it a rest, four eyes."

He grinned. "I think I like this side of you, Kendricks. Tiny shorts, big hair and even bigger. . . ."

"Finish that thought," I cut him off, "and I'll have Mother spread the word at the firm that you're a cross-dresser."

He looked tempted, but he closed his mouth like a good boy.

Julie still hovered at the bar, making no attempt to hide the fact that she was keeping tabs on Malone and me. I quickly pulled my pad and pen from the band of my hot pants and held them poised in front of me.

"So, seriously, how'd you know where I was?" I asked, pretending to scribble an order as we spoke.

"Molly phoned me from jail."

What?

I nearly dropped my pen. *That* wasn't what I'd wanted to hear. "How much did she tell you?"

He wiggled a finger at me and I bent nearer. "Oh, maybe just that you plan to do a little breaking and entering tonight."

Gulp.

Shit, meet fan.

Now I was going to have to come clean.

"I've got no choice, Malone," I pled in a whisper and stared at him, daring him to try to convince me otherwise. "So don't try to talk me out of it. It won't work. I've made up my mind."

He lifted his hands in mock surrender. "I swear, Officer, I didn't know a thing about theft of computer records. In fact, I don't even recognize this woman."

He laughed.

I didn't.

Instead I stared at him, daring him to stop me. "I'm not changing my mind, okay? So if you're through pestering me, you're free to leave."

"Andy. . . ."

"I mean it."

He nodded, and I started to go.

But he reached out and caught my hand, holding on tightly for a moment before releasing me. "Can you sit down for a minute? I've got something for you. It's about the license plate you asked me to run a check on."

"Now?"

"Pretty please?"

I eyed the bar from where Julie had been keeping vigil, but she was absorbed in conversation with a bulked-up guy in snug jeans and a Tommy Hilfiger shirt.

So I reluctantly took the seat catty-corner from him and waited.

Malone removed a folded paper from the breast pocket of his white button-down. He spread it smooth on the table in front of me. "The tag number was issued to ERA, Incorporated."

My mouth hung open for a moment before I had the presence to close it. "That's the company that holds partner's insurance on Bud Hartman."

"One and the same."

Curiouser and curiouser.

"It gets better," Malone assured me, excitement coloring his face. "I tracked down the only name I could find listed on the corporation papers. This guy was pegged as the CEO, president and chairman of the board."

"Hartman?" I guessed.

But Malone shook his head. "Larry Jones."

"Who?"

The name meant zilch.

"He lives in Pine Bluff, Arkansas," he continued. "Just a good ol' boy from the sound of it when I called him and mentioned I was an attorney from Big D. He must've thought 'lawsuit,' because he made no bones about telling me he wasn't anything more than the company figurehead. Said it was done to keep the privacy of the real partners, one of whom happens to be his brother-in-law, who resides in Plano, Texas. A certain James Robert Barker. Ever heard of him?"

James Robert Barker.

It took a few seconds for the proverbial light bulb to flick on.

Oh, Lord.

"The Reverend Jim Bob," I said in a breathless rush. "The pastor of the Church of Perpetual Hope, where Bud's memorial service was held this morning."

"You went to Hartman's service?" Malone squinted at me. "Hell, Andy, what else haven't you told me?"

That Malone was miffed made no difference, not when I was too pumped up to think of anything except the fact that my hunch had paid off.

221

So there was a real tie between Bud Hartman and the Reverend Jim Bob. A legal and financial bond. Only it didn't make much sense.

"Why would a prominent church leader who runs a big television ministry and preaches about morals and family values involve himself with a guy like Hartman?"

"You've got me," Malone agreed, apparently through giving me a hard time. At least for the moment. "The plot thickens all the time. I only wish I could flip straight to the last chapter and find out how it ends."

I echoed his sentiments, but my voice was drowned out by a loud call of, "Hey, babe! We need more beer!"

"Babe?" Malone repeated, his mouth lurching into a smirk.

"Shut up." I sat and rose from the chair with a push, scrambling to keep from losing my pen and order pad. "I'll bring your order when it's ready."

"My order?" he yelped. "What order, Andy?"

I gave him a wave over my shoulder and headed off.

Fifteen minutes later, I unloaded a basket of wings, a jug of beer, and a Jethro burger with "the works" in front of him.

He looked stunned. "You expect me to consume all this?"

"You're a full-grown man." I patted his back. "You can handle it. Just don't forget to leave a big tip."

"Oh, I've got a tip for you all right." He stared up his thin nose at me. "If you knew what was good for you, you'd drop this charade and go back to your web designs."

"That kind of tip you can keep to yourself," I shushed him and skirted the table, vanishing to the kitchen to pick up my next order, telling myself to forget about Brian Malone and the ketchup stain on his silk tie.

I wasn't gone more than a couple of minutes; but when I returned with a loaded tray balanced carefully at my shoulder, I nearly dropped everything and fled.

I blinked twice to make sure the blur of blue was no mirage.

But the specter I saw didn't go away.

Cissy stood at the hostess podium, wearing pearls and a robin's-egg blue Escada silk suit, her blond hair, as always, perfect. She looked as out of place at Jugs as George Hamilton at an albino convention. I could smell her Joy perfume through the stench of hamburgers and fries, and my stomach turned.

She must've just walked in, because it didn't look as if she'd spotted me yet — or Brian, for that matter — so I still had a chance to run. Then her head tilted toward Danielle, the buxom brunette playing hostess. Danny nodded, glanced around, and raised her arm to point me out.

Dear God.

I pirouetted in my sneakers like a prima ballerina, and I hurriedly set the tray down on the nearest table before I lost my grip.

I gulped in air and slowed my racing heart enough to avoid passing out, though fainting wouldn't have been such a bad idea if so much spilled beer hadn't made the linoleum stickier than flypaper.

"Andrea!"

My ears rang with the sound of my mother's voice as I forced myself to turn around.

"What in God's name are you doing?" Cissy's tone rose well above its typically well-bred decibels and pierced the noisy buzz of conversation, the clink of dinnerware, and the Maverick's ball game with the power of a bullhorn. I felt the place go silent around me. Or maybe it was my imagination. It was as if she wanted everyone to hear her.

I stood and stared, my sneakers glued to the floor, my feet unwilling to move, despite my brain telling me to run, to throw a block on Cissy and rush her out the door.

"Poor misguided child, this is no place for you!" she trilled.

I stayed motionless, my mouth open but producing no sounds, as my mother came toward me, stopping only long enough to yank a checkered cloth from an unoccupied table, sending the condiments and jug of wildflowers crashing to the ground.

Julie Costello shrieked at the bartender.

Malone leapt to his feet.

But not fast enough. Not before Mother approached and threw the tablecloth around me, her powdered face wearing a horrified expression that made Munch's *The Scream* look like a yawn.

"Have you no pride?" she cried out, holding the ends of the checkered fabric closed around me and pulling me forward at the same time. "Whatever possessed you to work here? I wouldn't believe it if I hadn't seen you with my own eyes."

I couldn't even respond.

Malone scrambled to intercept Mother on the front end, and I glimpsed the bartender — a beefy weightlifter named "Bulldog" — coming at her from behind. I had a mental flash, of Bulldog tossing her across his shoulder like a sack of designer flour and hauling her outside. As appealing as that might have seemed for a very split second, I didn't want my mother humiliated. She was worried about me, and I couldn't blame her.

"Get her out," I snapped at Brian, sure that he was the reason Cissy had shown up. How else could she have known? I felt pretty confident that Molly hadn't called *her* up from Lew Sterrett.

"Mrs. Kendricks, please, come with me," Malone cajoled and pried her hands from the cloth. "You'll spoil everything," he beseeched, repeating my earlier warning.

Cissy stopped resisting him and looked right

at me. "Leave with me, Andrea," she instructed in that overloud voice, and I detected a flicker of something in her eyes. Something a little off.

"Mother, please," I whispered. "I have to do this."

"So do I." This time, she lowered her tone for my ears alone, and damned if she didn't wink at me. It was so subtle, I thought I'd imagined it.

She backed away with a frown, her features settling into the composed countenance I was used to, and she turned to Brian. "No need to trouble yourself, sir. I can find my way out."

She tugged on her jacket, lifted her chin, and strode through the glass doors.

Conversations resumed, utensils clanked, and someone notched the sound higher on the Mavericks' game.

My knees nearly buckled.

"It's not what you think," Brian said softly. "I didn't have anything to do with this, though I might've mentioned to J.D. that I was coming by to see you, but he wouldn't have told your mother about it, would he?"

"Save it." I wadded the tablecloth and pushed it at him.

I cleared my tray, my hands shaking as I distributed burgers and fries to a quartet of college boys who merely gawked at me. When I'd finished, I headed back to the restroom.

I was holding onto the sink and staring at myself in the mirror, utterly confused about what had just gone on, and hoping everything wasn't ruined, when Julie trotted in after me, wearing a full-blown pout.

"Oh, girlfriend, are you all right? That Mother was pretty riled up about you being here. Do you know her?"

"What?" I met her eyes, reflected in the silver glass.

"That woman who came after you. She's one of those Mothers Against Porn, isn't she?"

I couldn't believe this. It was like being handed a hall pass when I'd been caught smoking in the bathroom after the bell rang. My cover wasn't blown at all. In fact, Cissy may have actually done me a favor.

"Oh, yeah," I agreed. "She's a mother, all right."

"The best-dressed one I've seen, for sure."

"That was a nice suit." I had no earthly idea where this was going, so I fudged my way along.

"Looks like she's on your case, big-time."

Only all my life.

"You're just the second waitress they've ever come inside to grab like that."

This had happened before? "Who was the first?"

"That nitwit Sarah who drooled all over Bud." She patted my arm, her Barbie doll features pinched. "Just watch your butt, okay?"

Not bad advice. Mother had always said I'd never be too old to spank.

"Thanks, I will."

I splashed some water on my face and patted my cheeks dry with a paper towel.

Still, I felt as if I'd stepped into an episode of *The Twilight Zone*, and I didn't know how to get out.

By the time the restaurant closed at midnight and Julie had locked the front doors, my mother and Malone were long gone.

Brian left me a ten dollar tip, the bill folded over a piece of scratch paper on which he'd scribbled two words, "Be careful."

And I knew he didn't mean safe sex.

While the busboys cleaned up tables and mopped floors, Julie cleared out the register and disappeared into the back office, closing the door.

I peeled off the shorts and too-small top and redressed in black jeans and shirt, taking a bit longer than usual. As the other waitresses left for the evening, one by one, I hung around the locker room as long as I could. I brushed my hair a hundred strokes and reapplied my lipstick almost as often until I was sure no one had forgotten anything they'd need to come back for.

I used the time to pull myself together. I had to be sharp, in control. I couldn't dwell on the surreal episode with my mother. One thought of David and Molly and what might happen to them if I didn't do this right, and I felt more focused than jittery.

I stepped into the hallway and stopped to

listen, but heard no footsteps on the tiles but my own.

I walked toward the office and knocked on the door, pushing it wide to find Julie at Bud's desk, counting cash and credit card receipts.

She glanced up as I entered.

"Just wanted to say goodnight," I told her. "Guess I'll see you tomorrow on my regular shift." As if I had a regular shift.

Her smile was weary. "Yeah, see you tomorrow, sugar. It's been a long day for us both, huh?"

"Too long." And it wasn't over yet.

"I can't believe that Mother barged into the restaurant tonight, on top of your old boyfriend dropping by," she said just as I was heading for the door. "If it helps at all, the guy looks like he still has the hots for you. So maybe he'll take you back before the baby's born. Hey, you never know, right?"

Malone looked like he had the hots for me?

Something tickled in my chest, and I bit back a smile.

"We'll see," I told her.

Julie wiggled her fingers, a sure sign she wanted me to scram. "Make sure the back door locks behind you, sugar."

"I will." Not.

I ducked out and hummed loudly as I headed toward the kitchen and rear exit.

The place was deserted. The dining room was dark, and the kitchen only dimly illuminated. The whir of the dishwashers filled my ears with white noise, but it didn't completely block out the anxious thump of my heart. My mouth felt dry and no amount of swallowing could moisten it.

I pulled open the heavy back door and let it drop closed with a clang, then I tiptoed to the supply closet and slipped inside, drawing shut the door so that only a sliver remained open. Enough for me to see out so I'd know for sure when Julie left the premises.

Which, I hoped, would be soon.

I pressed the knob on my watch that made the face glow an eerie blue.

Twelve thirty-five.

I settled atop a plastic crate and waited, one eye on the crack in the door.

Twenty minutes later, my chin propped on my knuckles, I heard footsteps and sat up straight. A few ticks after, I caught a flash of pale arm through the shadows as Julie walked past the supply closet and through the kitchen.

I detected the beep-beep of the alarm as she punched the keys to turn the system on.

Then the back door thunked as it shut.

I didn't dare move, my pulse pounding, afraid she'd come back and catch me with my fingers on Bud's keyboard.

The dishwasher had stopped nearly ten minutes before, so I could clearly hear the noise of a car engine revving up. The squeal of tires ensued, and I finally let out a held breath.

I sighed and rose from the crate, stretching my arms and legs, working out a crick in my neck.

Then I slipped my purse strap over my shoulder and escaped from my hiding place, scurrying up the hallway to Bud's office.

Chapter 18

There were no windows to the outside, so I risked turning on the ceiling light.

"Okay, here we go," I whispered as I took a seat behind the desk. I removed the empty disks from my purse and set them down on the blotter before I reached across to turn on the tower and monitor. The familiar Windows logo appeared and asked for my password. My fingers quivered as I typed in the word "pecker" and prayed that no one had changed it since Julie had mentioned it to Molly.

When the sound of thunder rumbled from the speakers and a disembodied voice said, "Welcome," I smiled, rubbing my hands together with relief as the Quicken icon lined up with the rest.

So far so good.

I clicked on the icon and got into Bud's payroll files first, running down the list of names that appeared on the spreadsheet. I scrolled past Julie, Rhonda, Christie, Ginger, Tiffany, Molly, and at least a dozen others before I found what I was looking for.

A paycheck from the month before that had never been cashed.

There was a notation, stating that the employee had not returned to the restaurant to pick up the money. It was signed BH.

I wondered why Bud had never tried to mail it.

The payee was Sarah Carter, the only Sarah I could find on the list of Jugs's employees, past or present.

One mystery solved anyway.

I jotted down the name, address, and phone number, hoping they weren't out of date. I prayed Sarah hadn't truly vanished into thin air and could perhaps tell me something about Bud that would shed some light on what had happened to him.

Then I opened up Bud's files of invoices, noting the regular payments to vendors, to the utilities companies, to TCI Cablevision, and to specialty grocers. All involved memorized transactions that appeared at monthly intervals.

Except for one.

An invoice paid two months earlier to Hi-Tech totaling $15,000. I did a search but found no other checks written to that company.

What was Hi-Tech? I wondered. If I had to guess, I'd say they had something to do with electronics. No matter; it should be easy enough to find out.

So I copied down the check number, date, and name.

The phone rang.

The shrill noise sent me half out of the chair.

A red light blinked, and I stared at it hypnotically, counting each subsequent ring until a loud beep sounded, followed by the click of a machine turning on.

"You've reached Jugs, the best down-home restaurant in town. We're closed for business right now, but we'll open again tomorrow from eleven 'til midnight. Mosey on by and check out our hot vittles not to mention our hot waitresses. If you've been here before, y'all come back, ya hear?"

The machine shut off, and I heard the brief sound of a dial tone before that, too, was gone.

I sat as still as a rock.

Barely breathing.

The voice on the message was Bud's.

It had to be.

Gooseflesh danced across my skin.

"I think I've had enough," I said aloud and quickly shoved a zip disk into the drive to back up the files on the Quicken program. I didn't even need the second disk I'd brought along. My pulse pounded faster as each second passed, which only further assured me that I wasn't cut out for the criminal life.

The message on the machine lingered in my head as I shut the computer down and turned off the monitor.

Skittishly, I stuffed the disks into my purse and hurried from the room, hitting off the lights as I went. Stumbling through the darkened hallway I fairly cried with relief when I reached the back door.

And then I came to a dead stop.

The alarm light glared at me through the darkness.

I was so jittery, my brain wasn't thinking straight.

What was the damned code? The year Bud got booted from Tech?

I checked out the palm of my hand, but the numbers I'd written there had smeared, probably from all the sloppy jugs of beer I'd handled during my shift.

C'mon, Andy.

It was there, in the back of my mind.

Squinting at the keypad, I punched in 1-9-8-9.

I nearly screamed with relief when the red light turned to green. I scrambled to unlock the deadbolt and grabbed the door handle. Then I reset the alarm and slipped out the door, not daring to exhale until I heard the self-locking mechanism safely click closed behind me.

Standing on the back stoop, I peered into the darkness to see only the garbage Dumpster hulking like a dinosaur beneath the faded glow of a streetlamp.

Otherwise, the coast was clear.

Though the strong thump of a bass beat from music at the Zuma Beach Club pulsed through the night air, I saw no one and quickly slithered out the door, rounding the corner of the restaurant, making a dash toward the club where my Jeep was parked.

I cut behind a line of cars, scurrying over to my car, when a hand grabbed hold of me and jerked me around, pushing my back flat against the Wrangler's side.

I gasped for air and tried to scream, but a palm clamped over my mouth.

"Andy, it's me."

My heart, which had almost leapt out of my chest, stuttered to a near stop.

Malone's shadowed face came into focus, stooping down so we were brow to brow.

Slowly, he peeled his fingers from my mouth as if still afraid I might scream even though I'd clearly seen him.

"Don't look so pissed. I've been waiting here for hours," he explained. "I wanted to make sure you were all right. I promised Cissy."

He what?

I balled my hand to a fist and threw it into his stomach with as much force as I could muster.

"Ugh." He grabbed his belly and reeled back a full step until the side of a Ford Focus stopped him from staggering farther. "W-why'd you do that?"

"Are you an idiot?" I cried.

"Hey, keep it down, all right?"

But I was too mad at him to care that I had raised my voice. Besides, I didn't see anyone else near enough to eavesdrop. Not even the helpful Fred Hicks, who seemed to have gone conveniently missing since the murder. "I can't believe you! First, you have the nerve to turn up unannounced at Jugs and then you drag my mother into it besides."

"D-drag her?" he stuttered. "Whatever Cissy did was *her* idea!"

So that explained the wink.

Did Mother assume she was now my sidekick?

Dr. Watson in pearls and Escada?

Dear God.

"What have you done?" I moaned, talking to myself, but Malone obviously thought the words were meant for him.

"I'm only trying to protect you, Andy."

"You're lucky I wasn't armed."

"You own a gun?" He looked mortified.

"No, but I've got pepper spray," I told him and dug the can from my purse to prove it. "And I'm not afraid to use it. So piss me off again, and you'll get it right in the eyes. Blind you for hours."

He carefully peeled his hands away from his stomach and lifted them meekly. "Okay, okay, you've made your point."

"I can take care of myself, for Pete's sake. I don't need you hovering about and waiting for me to send up a distress signal. And I certainly don't need my mother sticking her neck in." I returned the pepper spray to my bag and squared my shoulders. "I'm fully capable of handling things on my own. You should know that by now."

"Let's just say I'm learning more about you everyday."

That hardly sounded like a compliment, but I let it pass.

I reached back into my purse to withdraw the loaded zip disk and held it up to Malone, who plucked it from my grasp. "Find out what Hi-Tech is and why Bud Hartman shelled out fifteen thousand dollars to them eight weeks ago."

"Yes, ma'am."

"You might also want to get a copy of Bud's bank records and see if the deposits match the information on Quicken."

"Anything else?"

I thought of the white Lincoln I'd seen parked alongside Julie's red Corvette at Jugs the morning after Bud's murder, and I knew without a doubt the car belonged to Reverend Jim Bob. Which meant he'd been the man I'd heard arguing with Julie, something to do with nothing changing just because Bud was dead.

"I wouldn't be surprised to learn that Hartman was blackmailing the Reverend Jim Bob," I remarked aloud.

"You think Bud was blackmailing his own partner?" Malone leaned nearer.

His breath brushed my cheek. "Yes," I whispered. "I do."

The doors to the Zuma Beach Club burst open and a couple staggered out, a blast of ear-splitting rock music emerging with them.

Malone pulled away, and I turned to open the door to the Jeep. Before I got in, I looked back at him and said, "Call me when you know something more."

He pocketed the disk. "I'll get on it first thing in the morning."

"It is morning."

"Are you always right?"

"Like Avis, I try harder."

He shook his head. "Man, you are something." He smiled at me in a way that made my mouth dry all of a sudden. Then he turned and sauntered off.

Well, okay.

I climbed up behind the wheel of my Wrangler and started the engine. As I pulled out of the Villa Mesa parking lot onto Belt Line, my heart still pounded. Whether from my escapade or the strange way Malone had stared at me, I wasn't sure.

It was nearly three A.M. when I got home, but I was too wound up to go to bed.

There was a message from Cissy on my voice mail that casually asked, "Did I pass my screen test, darling?" Which only confirmed what Malone had suggested, that she'd learned what I was up to (probably from J.D.) and, for some insane reason, had decided to play along.

It could've been worse, I told myself.

She could've thought I'd lost my mind completely and had me kidnapped by the folks who stole brainwashed kids back from cults.

"I have to do this."

"So do I."

How could she not have warned me?

I should know to never underestimate my mother.

Cissy had skills that I could never learn, like how to make a seating chart for six hundred that kept apart ex-wives and ex-husbands, Democrats and Republicans, vegetarians and cattle ranchers. She could juggle schedules, florists, caterers, distillers, and decorators without dropping a single ball or putting anyone's nose out of joint.

"Someday, baby girl," Daddy had once said, "you'll look in your mama's eyes, and you'll see part of yourself staring back."

Maybe that's what Mother's wink was about.

It was a nice idea anyway, whether or not it was true.

I donned a cotton nightshirt and poured myself a glass of milk before I settled onto the sofa to sort out a few things rattling through my brain.

Bud and Jim Bob.

Jim Bob and Julie.

Bud and Sarah.

My mind stuck on the latter pairing, and I wondered who this young woman was, what Bud might have done to her to make her take off so abruptly. She hadn't given notice. She hadn't cashed her last paycheck.

Something was very wrong with that picture.

I drained the milk from the glass and curled up on the couch, closing my eyes.

The next morning — actually this morning — while Malone tracked down Hi-Tech, I'd drive over to the Addison address for Sarah Carter listed in Bud's computer files.

I had questions for her. Tough questions.

With that settled, I forced myself to get up, switching off the living room lights as I headed off to bed.

Chapter 19

 The phone rang, and I cracked open my eyes, grabbing clumsily at the receiver on my bedside table.

"Yeah?" I croaked.

"Andy, it's me."

"Malone?" I dragged myself into an upright position and glanced at my clock. It was already eight, so I could hardly bawl him out for waking me at an unseemly hour.

Dang.

"You still there?" He sounded even more anxious than usual.

I yawned and did a little scratching. "Barely."

"Turn your television on and flip to Channel 11 *now!*"

Whatever had gotten his knickers in a twist must've been good, so I snagged the remote from my nightstand, pushed the power button, and pressed in the number eleven.

I winced, unprepared for a close-up of Cinda Lou Mitchell first thing in the morning. And she was wearing her "I'm-a-serious-reporter" face, too. So it had to be bad news.

"What's up?" I started to ask Malone, but he quickly shushed me.

So I turned the sound up.

". . . the body of Frederick Hicks, a guard employed by Lone Star Security, was found slumped over the wheel of his car behind a boarded-up building that once housed the Nude 'n Naughty gentleman's club. Reportedly, Hicks had a suitcase in the trunk and was on his way to Love Field, though no one's sure why he took this deadly detour."

There was a noisy rumble, and the camera panned away from Cinda to showcase a blue-bellied Southwest Airlines jet streaking across the sky.

"Hicks was rushed to Parkland Hospital in a coma, and we're told he's in critical condition. Authorities can't tell us any more than that at this juncture. Hicks recently helped police track down the alleged killer of restaurant owner Bud Hartman. We'll let you know of further developments. Back to you at the news desk, Vivian."

Shutting off the TV set, I sank back into my pillows, suddenly lightheaded.

"What the hell is going on?" I murmured into the telephone receiver. "How can this be happening?"

"Looks like Hicks was on his way out of town," Brian said, as if that part needed explaining. "He had a suitcase in his trunk, and he was headed toward the airport. Maybe he pulled over to take a leak and had a heart attack or something."

"Why would Hicks be skipping town?" I asked, because it didn't make sense. He'd been conspicuously absent from his guard duties since the night Bud was killed. I figured it was because he needed a few days off after the trauma of finding Bud's body, but maybe there was another reason. What if he *had* taken the cash from the bank bag, and he worried that the cops would find out? Could be he figured it was time to take a little vacation.

Nope, something just wasn't kosher about him.

"I'll see what I can find out from the D.A.'s office, Andy, and from the hospital. When I know something more, I'll tell you. So far, all I've been able to learn is what you saw on the news. The man's in a coma, and my sources tell me it's probably irreversible."

I popped upright, wide-awake suddenly as I wondered what this could mean for Molly. "If Hicks can't testify. . . ."

"There's still his sworn statement, Andy. She's in as much trouble as before, more if we can't tie the missing money to Hicks."

"Spoilsport."

"Well, here's some news guaranteed to improve your mood," Malone piped up. "I'm heading over to Hi-Tech in an hour. They're a specialized electronics company. They deal in customized nanny cams and top-of-the-line digital surveillance equipment."

Customized surveillance equipment.

Who was Bud spying on?

"They weren't very forthcoming over the phone, so I figure if I show up in person and threaten them with a subpoena, I'll get the answers I'm looking for." He sounded as excited as a kid on Christmas morning.

He was right. My mood did improve.

"Good thinking," I told him.

"Uh, I wondered if you'd like to meet me for lunch," he suggested. "Say, noon at the Mansion? Then I could fill you in on whatever I turn up."

Had Malone just asked me out?

I could swear he'd said he wanted to do lunch at the Mansion on Turtle Creek, a spot that had long been one of Cissy's favorites for Sunday brunch. Even I had to admit that the place had real class. Men were required to wear coats and ties to get service, not just shirts and shoes.

"Andy?"

"Did you say noon?" I repeated, wanting to be sure I hadn't misinterpreted him in my sleepy state.

"I did."

I almost said "yes," until I remembered I was supposed to take the early shift that day at Jugs. I had to be there a half hour before it opened at eleven.

"I can't, Malone," I told him, hearing his silence on the other end and wondering if he was as disappointed as I was. "I'm on duty."

"At the restaurant?"

"Uh-huh."

Silence.

"How about a rain check?" I quickly filled in the void before he had a chance to launch into another lecture. "Maybe a late dinner after work?"

"I'll clear my calendar."

That sounded like a "yes."

I pushed tangled hair from my eyes and caught my blurry image in the bureau mirror across the room. Sometimes it paid not to have 20/20 vision. "We'll talk later, okay?"

"I'll touch base with you after I pay a visit to Hi-Tech."

"Great."

"Oh, and Andy." He paused before turning serious and telling me, "Don't do anything stupid."

The line clicked as he hung up.

More slowly, I replaced the receiver, ignoring his parting words and dwelling instead on his invitation.

A date with Malone.

I pushed the covers away and swung my feet over the side of the bed, planting them firmly on the floor.

Maybe things were looking up already, I thought, as I shuffled into the bathroom for a leisurely shower.

The address for the apartment complex where Sarah Carter had lived was just off Belt

Line, several miles west of the Villa Mesa Shopping Center, behind one of the hundred or so restaurants that lined the busy street.

I parked in front of Building B. Apartment 252 was up a narrow metal staircase that vibrated with each step.

When I got there, I knocked soundly on the door.

No one answered.

"Sarah?" I called, pressing my face near the weather-beaten wood. I pounded that much harder. "Sarah, are you there?"

"She's gone."

I turned to find a slender black woman standing outside the apartment two doors down.

"You're looking for Sarah Carter, right?"

I nodded. "I need to find her." Almost without thinking, I added, "It's her paycheck. She never picked it up from the restaurant." I patted the purse hanging over my shoulder. "It's her money, after all."

The woman crossed her arms and leaned against the doorjamb. "Well, you won't find her at this address. She moved out, I guess a couple weeks ago."

My heart did a back slide into my stomach. "Do you happen to know where she went?"

She shook her head. "The girl didn't talk much except to say 'hi' now and then. She kept to herself mostly. Didn't hardly ever see anyone come visit her, although I caught a man leaving her place early one morning when I went out for a paper." She lifted a hand about six inches above her crown. "Big guy. All muscles and hair gel. He looked like a player, you know, 'cuz he was even checking me out."

Sounded like Bud Hartman.

"You said she left?"

"A truck came by and loaded up her stuff, though Sarah wasn't around when they did it. Just some older woman I figured was her mama."

Damn.

"Sorry you missed her."

"Me, too," I said and started down the steps, feeling more dejected with each one I descended.

"Hey!"

I paused halfway down and looked up to see the woman bent over the railing, waving at me.

"Check with the manager in the office. It's Building A. There's a sign so you can't miss it. Maybe he'll know where Sarah's gone to."

"Thanks, I will."

I got into the Jeep and drove over to Building A, braking in front of a sign marked BLUEBONNET VILLAS — OFFICE.

An overweight male wearing a UT-DALLAS T-shirt rose from behind an oak-veneered desk as I entered.

He smiled eagerly, the same way the saleswomen at Saks did when they saw Mother coming.

"Hi, there. Can I help you? Are you interested

in leasing a place here at beautiful Bluebonnet Villas?"

I hated to disappoint him, and I knew I would. So I got right to the point. "Actually, I'm trying to locate a change of address for a former tenant of yours named Sarah Carter. I know she lived here until a couple weeks ago, and I've got her paycheck from work. She never came back to pick it up, and no one knows where to send it." The fib had seemed to work with Sarah's neighbor so I spun it again. "Could you tell me if she left a forwarding address with you?"

The smile disappeared completely. The young man's cherubic face looked suddenly suspicious. "Are you a relative?"

"Well, no. . . ."

"Then I'm not allowed to give out that information. Sorry." He rounded the desk and plunked his oversized body into a less-than-comfortable-appearing secretary's chair.

If there's one thing I'd learned from my mother over the years, it was never to take "no" for an answer. Though, come to think of it, I don't recall ever hearing anyone refuse Cissy anything to begin with.

How about Julie Costello? She always seemed to get what she wanted with just a sway of her hips. Couldn't hurt for me to try to use my feminine wiles.

With a sigh and bat of eyes, I approached and leaned on the desk, twirling a stray hair around my finger and going for an expression that was both cute and needy. "C'mon, um" — I desperately sought a name plate on the desk only to come up empty — "uh, sweetie pie." I tried to mimic Julie's drawl, as my years in Chicago had practically erased mine. "It's not like I'm asking for her Social Security number or the PIN for her ATM card. I just need an address so I can hand over her money."

Maybe it was the term of endearment that did the trick. He blushed and squinted up at me like he was almost ready to give in. "I dunno. My boss would have my job if I gave out personal information. Though for what he pays me. . . ."

He let the sentence trail off, and I wondered if something other than my molasses-sweet voice was drawing this fly in.

Dropping the hair I'd been twirling, I hastily reached into my purse and removed my wallet. Thankfully, I had a twenty-dollar bill, which I slipped out and placed in front of him. It always worked in the movies.

"Just write down the address, would ya, sugar?" I tried again, noting that his eyes were glued to the cash. Definitely a good sign, right? "I'm sure Sarah would be very grateful."

He hesitated, but only for a second. Then he palmed the bill and stuck it into his shirt pocket. "Let me find her file," he said and began to rummage through the desk, finally emerging with a slim manila folder that he placed in his lap and opened wide.

"Hmmm." He ran a finger down a page until

he stopped midpoint, obviously finding what he was looking for. He grabbed a Post-it from a pad and scribbled something on it before handing it over.

"This is all I've got. It's not an official change of address or anything, like at the post office. It was for in case she left anything. Which she didn't."

"I understand." Hey, something was better than nothing, which is what I'd had when I'd walked in.

"Hey." He half-rose from the chair, the faux leather making noises like breaking wind — at least I hoped it was the faux leather — and he leaned across the desk, eyeballing me in the same way my second cousin Henry had when we were eight and he'd tried to coax me into the coat closet with bribes of watermelon Jolly Ranchers. "You want to, maybe, hang out with me later? I get off at six. There's a *Star Trek* marathon on the SciFi channel, and my folks have a big screen"

Was he kidding?

I was at least ten years his senior, and, God help me, but he looked like the Kewpie doll I'd seen appraised on *Antiques Roadshow*. All he was missing were the red-and-white-striped pajamas.

Still, it was flattering, in a rather weird way.

"Oh, geez, love that Captain Kirk, but I'm busy tonight," I said and backed away from the desk. "Live long and prosper!" I wiggled the slip of paper at him before I high-tailed it out of there.

Well, I *was* busy that night.

I might even have a real date if I didn't blow it.

I was so relieved to escape the office that I didn't look at the note until I was settled in the Jeep and had the air conditioner running. Then I flattened it out on my thigh.

His handwriting was miserable to read, but I looked it over several times and finally figured it out.

Sarah Carter
7000 Walnut Hill
Dallas, Texas

Why did that address seem so familiar?

I chewed on it until something clicked.

Wait a doggoned minute.

I dug inside my bag and found the business card that the ringleader of Mothers Against Pornography had pushed at me the other night.

THE WOMEN'S WELLNESS CLINIC
7000 WALNUT HILL LANE
PEGGY MARTIN, R.N.

Well, look at that.

Did Sarah work at the Wellness Clinic? Had Peggy Martin's crusade convinced the former Jugs waitress to leave behind the lavender short-

shorts and panting men for a gig in the medical field, filing for seven-fifty an hour as Molly had mentioned?

Or was she a patient?

Had Bud's "attentions" somehow required her to seek a doctor's care?

Though it seemed strange for her to leave a medical office as a forwarding address for her apartment manager.

I mean, I adored my gynecologist, but I don't imagine she'd appreciate my using her place of business as a return address.

Whatever the answer, I didn't want to wait any longer than necessary to find out. I put the Jeep in gear and headed off for the Women's Wellness Clinic, determined to find Sarah.

Chapter 20

I took Central Expressway, driving south to Walnut Hill.

The clinic was situated just off the exit ramp, and I made a fast right into its small parking lot after leaving the highway. The building was a squat red-brick number with stickered windows and signs stuck in the dirt warning of monitoring by Smith Alarms. There were bars over the windows, something that was becoming more common in the neighborhood, despite its close proximity to Presbyterian Hospital and the seemingly omnipresent traffic.

When I entered the front door, a security guard in blue uniform gave me the once-over, then nodded as I passed. I thought of Peggy Martin protesting outside Jugs and wondered if the Women's Wellness Clinic hadn't experienced some protests of its own.

The receptionist glanced up from behind a Formica countertop as I emerged into a utilitarian-looking waiting area. Atop her cropped brown hair sat the band of a telephone headset, the gear reminding me of the clunky retainers kids used to wear.

She smiled nervously as I approached. "Can I help you, ma'am? Do you have an appointment with the doctor?"

Despite her calling me "ma'am," I smiled back and said, "I'd like to speak with Sarah Carter, if I could."

The curve of her lips disappeared. Her nervousness didn't. "Sarah Carter?" she repeated.

Maybe the earphones made it hard for her to hear.

"Yes, Sarah Carter. Does she work here? Or maybe she's a patient? Either way, I need to find her, and I was given this place as her forwarding address. I hoped she might be around."

"You were given our address . . . for Sarah?" She looked at me oddly, and I started to feel self-conscious. Maybe I should've talked to Malone before driving down. If Sarah were a patient, they were hardly obligated to reveal that information.

"Please, it's a matter of life or death." As soon as it was out of my mouth, I could hardly believe I'd uttered the cliché. It sounded so dramatic, though I reminded myself it was true.

"Maybe you should talk to Ms. Martin." The guarded expression softened the slightest bit, and I saw her fingers punching buttons on the telephone, even as she suggested it.

"Peggy Martin? She's the nurse who runs Mothers Against Pornography, right?"

"Yes."

So Peggy knew Sarah? Had she stopped her in the parking lot after her shift at Jugs one evening, just as she'd done with me? Had she convinced her not to return? Maybe that was the reason behind Sarah's disappearance. Bud could have abused her one time too many, until she'd had it, paving the way for Nurse Peggy to ride in to the rescue.

"Your name, please?"

"Andy Kendricks," I told her, even spelling it. "I met Ms. Martin the other night at Jugs. She might remember me. Tell her I was the girl in the Jeep."

The receptionist blinked, light dawning in her eyes, and I could practically see her brain shifting gears. "Oh, you work at Jugs. I see," she murmured and watched me closely as she fiddled with her headset, probably listening to the telephone ring in another part of the building. "She's not answering her extension, so she must be with a patient. I'll try buzzing that exam room."

I tapped my fingers on the counter and waited.

After a few seconds, she nodded and said, "Will do," into her headset. Then she looked up at me. "If you'll have a seat, Peggy will be out in a few minutes."

"Thanks."

There were only a few other women in the waiting room: a very pregnant one who seemed about my age and another who appeared far too young to have even driven to the clinic on her own.

I sat down in the nearest blue vinyl seat and picked through a ragged pile of magazines on the adjacent table. *Parenting Today, Good Housekeeping, Highlights for Children*. Not exactly my cup of tea.

Selecting the topmost issue of *Good Housekeeping*, I thumbed through it to find page after page torn in halves or fourths or missing altogether where someone had apparently lifted the recipes.

"Miss Kendricks?"

Setting aside the mutilated magazine, I rose to my feet and smoothed the wrinkles from my khakis. Peggy Martin's familiar round face with the worried eyes stared at me from the doorway. She had on pink scrubs and Reeboks with reflector strips on the sides that made her look as if she were about to go for a run.

"You wanted to see me?"

"Could we talk privately?" I asked, not wanting any stray ears to hear the questions I needed to ask her.

"Of course." Her brows arched, betraying her curiosity. "Follow me."

She led me up a narrow hall past those metal scales that always added five pounds to your weight, between walls plastered with posters depicting the dangers of STDs and diagrams graphically depicting a woman's body in the various stages of pregnancy.

I actually felt relieved that I was sleeping alone by the time I'd walked that gauntlet.

She entered the first opened door on the left, and I followed her inside to find an exam room with a stool, a single chair, and a paper-covered table with metal stirrups that made me want to cross my legs.

Peggy shut the door behind us, but remained standing. I sat on the stool and surveyed the blue countertop behind the examining table. There were glass containers with tongue depressors, gauze, and huge Q-tips as well as labeled boxes full of disposable thermometer tips, syringes, gloves, and other sterile items.

Cabinets above the shelf and drawers below likely hid even more interesting medical paraphernalia. Things that poked and prodded and generally made me want to stay out of doctors' offices as much as possible.

I swallowed hard and turned away.

Peggy was watching.

"Uh," I started, ever eloquent, "I don't know if you remember me, but we met the other night in the parking lot of Jugs."

"Oh, I remember you, dear." She smiled, and her Moon Pie face crinkled. "I'm so glad you're here. It gives me great comfort to know that I've reached just one of you. That it's not too late."

I shifted on the stool. "Actually, I haven't come to talk about myself. I'm hoping you can help me find a missing person."

"A missing person? I don't understand." Peggy did a quick look-see at the door, as if to make certain she'd closed it. Then she took a step forward, her hands clasped. "Who are you trying to find?"

Obviously, her receptionist hadn't mentioned to her that I'd asked about Sarah. Or maybe she had and Peggy was purposefully avoiding the subject.

Suddenly uncomfortable, I shifted on the stool, unsure of how to do this. Lying to Peggy Martin didn't feel right. So I said without further preamble, "I need to find a woman named Sarah Carter who used to waitress at Jugs until a couple weeks ago."

"Why would you assume I'd know anything about this missing waitress?" Peggy's expression remained benign, so I couldn't read anything into it.

"I dropped by her apartment this morning, but she'd moved. The only address the manager had was this one . . . for the clinic, so I figured she was an employee or possibly a patient," I plunged ahead, finding myself more discomfited with each word and not entirely sure why. But I didn't back down. There was too much at stake. "So is she here?"

Peggy tapped a finger to her lips. Then she dropped the hand to her side and shook her head. "I can't discuss personnel information with you or confidential patient records for that matter," she said firmly, so I figured she'd take a lot more convincing. "What do you want from her, anyway?"

"I'd like to ask her some questions."

"About what?"

Man, she wasn't giving an inch.

I held my purse tight against my belly, needing something to clutch. "About Bud Hartman," I said. "About why Sarah left Jugs so abruptly and never returned, not even to pick up her paycheck."

Peggy crossed her arms over her chest and said nice as you please, "I'm sorry, but there's nothing I can tell you."

So why didn't I buy it?

It had partly to do with my gut, and even more to do with a remark Julie Costello had made earlier.

"You're only the second waitress I've ever seen them come inside to grab like that."

"Who was the first?"

"That nitwit Sarah who drooled all over Bud."

Mothers Against Porn had been awfully intent on removing Sarah from the restaurant, even against her will from the sounds of it.

So I couldn't help wondering why Nurse Peggy was giving me the brushoff, when there was obviously so much more to this.

I hesitated, wetting my lips, trying to formulate what to say next to make her understand, because I knew she wasn't getting the full picture.

"Please, Ms. Martin, if you know where Sarah

260

disappeared to, tell me now. I don't want to get her in any trouble, but I have to find her. I think she might know something that may help clear an innocent woman. My friend's future is at stake because of Bud Hartman . . . because she was arrested for killing him . . . but she didn't do it. Someone else did."

She stood still, not interrupting, which I took as a good sign. At least she appeared to be listening.

So I went on. "The waitress who was arrested is Molly O'Brien. She's my friend and the mother of a six-year-old boy." I thought of David and my voice softened. "He's the light of her life, and she misses him terribly. As we speak, she's sitting behind bars at Lew Sterrett, and she wants nothing more than to go home."

"I still don't see what Sarah has to do with any of this," Peggy muttered, but so half-heartedly that I figured she wanted to hear the rest.

"The reason I've been working at Jugs," I confessed, "is to search for the truth behind the murder. Someone has to, because the police have stopped looking. They think Molly's the killer, but I know she couldn't have done it. If only because she loves her son too much to let him grow up without her. Surely you can understand."

"You've been undercover? Are you a cop?" She seemed confused.

"No," I admitted. "I'm an artist."

"You're a what?" She cocked her head, studying me, probably thinking "con artist" from the skeptical look on her face.

"A web designer, actually. I'll admit, what I'm doing is unorthodox, but I didn't feel like I had a choice in the matter."

"You're working at Jugs to clear your friend?"

"Yes."

I sat quietly, waiting, hoping Peggy Martin would fess up to whatever she was keeping secret. And it had something to do with Sarah Carter. I was certain of it.

With a weighty sigh, she leaned her back against the door and closed her eyes. "I'm sorry," she whispered. "I'm truly sorry for this girl, Molly O'Brien. It isn't right that she's in jail for stabbing Bud Hartman to death. He was a terrible man, a dreadful excuse for a human being. The police should be giving her a medal for fighting back. Someone should have done it a long time ago."

I'd heard her belittle Bud's character on the evening news, but there was something in her tone now that I hadn't caught before.

There was more to Peggy Martin's dislike for Hartman than the fact that he'd opened a restaurant where the servers wore hot pants.

It sounded personal.

"Did Bud ever hurt you, Ms. Martin?" I asked cautiously.

Maybe Hartman's bad behavior wasn't limited to the women who worked within the restaurant walls. Men who forced themselves on others often didn't care much about who their victims were, so long as they had the right equipment.

"Please, talk to me," I urged her.

"I can't." She wouldn't even look at me. She stared at the opposite wall, though there was nothing more interesting pinned up than a diagram of the digestive tract.

It was apparent she was struggling with the decision of whether or not helping Molly was worth spilling her guts.

"Did he harass you, too?" I pressed, not willing to let this drop. "Or is it someone else? Have you treated women who've been his victims? Some of the waitresses, perhaps?"

Her eyes brimmed, her anguish painfully apparent. Whatever she knew — whatever had happened — had her pretty torn-up. "There are always going to be people in the world who prey upon the weak, upon those who don't know any better. Bud Hartman was one of them. What else do I need to say?"

"She seemed sad. So anxious for me to like her."

I recalled Molly's comments and ventured to ask, "Weak people, like Sarah?"

For a second, I thought I'd gotten her. That she was about to confess whatever it was she was holding back.

She took a step away from the door, brushing her hands on the front of her scrubs, clearly agitated. "Do you want me to tell you that I've seen more than my share of women who've been taken advantage of and made to feel that they're less than human because of men who get their ideas about relationships from dirty magazines, from strip joints, and places like Jugs, where females are dehumanized? Well, I have. Is that what you came for?"

Not exactly, but at least she was talking.

"You think Jugs is as bad as all that?" I asked, recalling I'd felt the same thing once, before I'd become acquainted with the women who worked there. Most of them seemed strong and fully capable of managing their own lives, ignoring what was ugly and focusing on what was important.

"Jugs is worse than that, and I'll tell you why." Smudges of red stained her cheeks. "The place masquerades as a family outfit, which makes it all the more offensive, don't you see? It's merely another haven for males who see women as objects. Are there any men on the wait staff? Not a one. They wouldn't suffer the indignity of wearing such skimpy outfits."

I couldn't disagree with her there.

"Bud Hartman set the tone for that place," Ms. Martin went on. "He had no respect for us, and his customers could sense it."

No respect for *us?*

"I went there several times to eat, to give the place a chance to prove me wrong, but my visits only confirmed everything I'd heard about it and seen on TV. It was degrading, even as a customer." She clicked tongue against teeth. "To witness those poor half-naked women have to endure the leers and the suggestive comments." Her nostrils flared. "It's hard to believe such dens of iniquity exist in the twenty-first century."

Considering that I was one of those "poor half-naked women," at least for the time being, I couldn't argue with her about the leers. Still, she was avoiding my question about Sarah Carter by filling my head with her Mothers Against Porn rhetoric. Maybe I even agreed with her, but that's not why I was here.

"Do you know if Bud sexually assaulted any of the waitresses?" I went straight for the jugular, fairly sure at this point that's why Peggy despised him. "If that's the case, maybe one of them had wanted him dead . . . and went through with it. Maybe someone like Sarah."

Her face shut off.

Like a bank safe locking. I swear I heard the click.

Her eyes cooled, her expression strangely stoic as she told me, "If you're trying to pin the blame on Sarah for Bud's death, you're barking up the wrong tree. She wasn't even in Dallas when it happened. She was long gone by then."

So she did know something.

Far more than she'd told me.

Maybe Sarah had sought refuge at the clinic after suffering at Bud's hands. Had Peggy Martin and her staff sheltered her? Helped her move?

So where was she now?

And why was Peggy Martin protecting her so fiercely?

"Please, tell me where Sarah is, and I'll ask her myself." I sounded desperate, but I didn't care. Molly was counting on me, and all I kept turning up were more and more people who seemed pleased as punch that Bud was mincemeat. I could do eeny-meeny-miney-mo and land on someone who had the motive and means to have stabbed him. "Maybe Sarah could give me some answers that would lead me to the real killer."

Peggy shook her head. "I can't do that."

"Why?"

"She's been taken advantage of enough already." She sliced a hand across the air and stated emphatically, *"No more."* With that, she turned away and shuffled toward the door. She grabbed the handle and jerked it open. When she looked back at me, all the fight had gone out of her face. "I think you'd better go."

The last thing I wanted to do was to give up and leave. I'd had every intention of leaving the Wellness Clinic with Sarah Carter's new address, but instead I was being kicked out before Nurse Peggy had spilled the beans.

I'd seriously flunked the Jessica Fletcher test. My questions hadn't elicited any gut-spilling confession. Why wasn't real life ever like television?

Peggy Martin cleared her throat and tapped the watch at her wrist. "I have patients to see,

Ms. Kendricks. I'm asking you to leave so I can do my job."

"Only if you'll think about what I've said."

She sighed. "If it will make you go away."

Well, that was good enough for me.

I got up from the stool, hiked my purse over my shoulder, and aimed for the door.

Our eyes met as I passed her on my way out, and I realized I'd gotten from her all I was going to get, at least for now.

Still, I wasn't backing down.

I couldn't.

As I crawled into my steamy Jeep, I told myself to think like a detective.

What would Nancy do? I asked, not for the first time. If Bess and Ned were busy, no doubt she'd talk to her dad.

But since my father wasn't around, that left only one option.

Cissy.

An involuntary groan escaped my lips.

What could I possibly say to my mother after the show she'd put on last night? I had half a mind to critique her performance, and the rest of me figured I owed her an apology for embarrassing the Blevins and Kendricks alike by wearing lavender hot pants.

I cringed as I imagined the story she'd tell her socialite chums at her next bridge game at the Junior League. . . .

Hold on a dad-gummed minute.

Cissy's chums.

Mother and her cronies helped to organize charity events to raise money for women's health issues ranging from breast cancer to varicose veins, dealing with muckety-mucks at hospitals and clinics across the metroplex.

If anyone could dig up the dirt on Peggy Martin, R.N., and the Wellness Clinic, she could. It could be her encore performance. Lady Snoop's Grand Finale.

I checked my watch and realized I had more than an hour before I had to show up at Jugs for my shift, so I put the Jeep into drive, cranked up the AC and cruised toward Buckingham Palace.

Chapter 21

 After a slight change in plans, I ended up in Highland Park Village, near the intersection of Mockingbird and Douglas.

I'd called Mother's on my cell to warn Sandy I was on my way, only to be told that Cissy had buckled David into the leather passenger seat of her Lexus and had taken him to Paciugo Gelato for ice cream.

Stop the presses!

Can you blame me for dropping the phone in sheer astonishment and nearly running a stop sign while reaching down for it between my feet?

Cissy Blevins Kendricks buying David a gelato?

The woman didn't know a Popsicle from a drumstick.

Andy, Andy, Andy.

Okay, I was a wee bit jealous, I'll admit. When I was a girl, I would've killed to have Cissy whisk me off for an ice cream. But she'd always been too busy with her garden clubs, church meetings, and charity events. If it hadn't been for Sandy, I never would've seen the inside of a Baskin-Robbins.

Still, it didn't take long for the envy to ebb and for real pleasure to set in. The more I thought about what my mother had done, the wider I grinned.

Maybe Cissy was truly getting into the swing of things, even feeling charitable toward Molly. Despite all the fuss she'd put up in the beginning.

I parked in the shadows of the Regent Highland Park Theater, perspiration dampening my skin despite the short walk into the air-conditioned building. Paciugo Gelato was in the downstairs foyer of the theater, and, judging by the number of people milling about, fiercely studying the selection of thirty-two rotating flavors, it was probably the most popular place in town on this hot, humid day.

I spotted Mother and David easily enough.

As odd a couple as Felix and Oscar.

Cissy had on bright yellow, one of her new Ralph Lauren ensembles, her pale hair perfectly brushed off her face and enormous pearl clips at her ears. Her young male companion wore a Harley-Davidson T-shirt, one of the spares Maria had stuffed into his knapsack. It's a wonder Mother had let him out of the house in it.

I found an empty chair and dragged it over.

Cissy glanced up, plucked brows arching deliberately as she remarked, "Well, look who's here. And she's got all her clothes on."

I gave her the evil eye and turned to David. "Whatcha eating, buddy?"

David poked his plastic spoon into his cup and brought up a dripping mess for me to see. "It's Cookies 'n Milk. That's the kind of ice cream."

"No, honey, it's gelato," Cissy corrected, brushing his bangs from his forehead and ignoring my surprised look. "That's Italian for 'better than ice cream.' "

"Yeah, better," he echoed and stuck the loaded spoon in his mouth.

"You doing okay?" I asked him, and his head bobbed up and down. I glanced at my mother, who nodded as well.

"David's been a very brave boy," she said. "Haven't you, sweetie?"

He beamed at her, then turned his head to say excitedly, "Cissy's takin' me to a movie."

I set my purse in my lap and propped my chin up with a fist. Otherwise, my jaw would've dropped to the ground "You're kidding. Which one?"

"Something about a yo-yo and LifeSavers," Mother drawled.

Which set David to giggling. "Yoda, not yo-yo!"

"And I think you mean light sabers," I teased her.

"Of course." A smile twitched on her perfectly painted lips.

"You're seeing the latest *Star Wars*?" I could

271

hardly believe it myself. "I practically have to call a tow to drag you with me to the Magnolia for an art film."

"The child wanted to go, and Sandy had some work to do for me." She shrugged casually, toying with the remains of her lemon gelato that, not surprisingly, matched her suit.

I squinted my eyes and peered at her closely. "So who are you and what've you done with my mother?"

"Don't be silly."

"Are you channeling Mary Poppins?"

"Hush, Andrea, you're setting a bad example for the boy." Mother stole a glance at David, who alternated between slurping down gelato and coloring on a tablet with a set of brand-new crayons. "After the show, I thought I'd take him to Harold's to get a few things."

"How about Baby Gap," I suggested. Did Harold's even have stuff for kids? Mother was a tad out of her element where children's clothing was concerned. When I was little, I'd been dressed strictly in Florence Eiseman from Marshall Field's.

"Baby Gap? They don't have Harley shirts, do they?"

"Not that I'm aware of."

"Good." She put a little spit on a napkin and worked some gelato off David's chin.

I watched, amazed.

If I hadn't seen it with my own eyes, I wouldn't have believed it.

The six-year-old son of "that scholarship girl" had wrapped Cissy Blevins Kendricks, queen of Dallas Society, snugly around his little finger.

I was tempted to phone "Ripley's."

I couldn't wait to tell Molly.

"Why don't you join us for the picture show, Andrea?"

David looked up at me eagerly.

"I wish I could, but I've got an early shift. . . ." — oh, hell. I cut myself off cold.

"An early shift?" Cissy stared. I could see what was coming, but I just couldn't stop it. "At Jugs?"

I placed a hand over hers, checking to make sure David had gone back to his drawing. I lowered my voice. "I'm begging you. Stay out of this."

With her free hand, she patted mine, and it scared me, the way she smiled. "Why should you have all the fun, darling? You're not the only Kendricks who can be rebellious now and then."

"Mother," I groaned. Rebellious to Cissy meant carrying a handbag from last season.

"I'm concerned about you, Andrea, that's all." She let go of my hand. "Mr. Malone understands that, the nice man. Which reminds me, I hear you're going to dinner with him tonight, yes?"

"As a matter of fact, I am" — How did she know? I hadn't let it slip, not even to Sandy — "but that has nothing to do with the case."

"Doesn't it?" She touched a pearl earring, a smug little gesture that told me plenty.

My spine went rigid. "Mother, you didn't."

"Didn't what, sweetie?"

"You *did*," I hissed under my breath, glancing over to make sure David had lost interest. His crayons were in motion, thank goodness.

"You called Brian."

"He's with the firm, darling. I often have occasion to discuss legal matters with my attorneys."

"With Malone?"

"Settle down, for heaven's sake. Don't make a fuss. Yes, I've spoken with Mr. Malone now and then. He has a fine legal mind," she drawled. "J.D. has great faith in him, and he's often remarked about his potential in criminal defense."

My throat closed up. I nearly had to shield my eyes from this epiphany. It blinded me more than those halogen headlamps.

No, don't even think of it, Andy.

Even Mother wouldn't go that far.

Would she?

"Please, please, don't tell me this was a setup from the start," I croaked, the words struggling to come out because I didn't want them to be true. "Tell me you didn't have J.D. send Malone to the North Dallas substation to take Molly's case because you wanted me to meet him."

Her hands primly went to her lap. "I merely inquired if he was available."

I groaned, dropping my head in my hands.

"Oh, God, I can't believe this! You used a homicide as an excuse for a blind date!"

"Well, he's taking you out tonight, sweetie, so it must've worked."

I peeled my fingers from my face, feeling the heat of my skin, trying to take a deep breath and keep any words I'd regret from spilling from my lips.

Cissy daintily spooned gelato into her mouth, then leaned over to whisper something to David.

He giggled and glanced at me before turning back to his artwork.

I tried not to glare at them both.

"I can't believe it," I muttered and started to get up, ready to stomp off, thinking I'd call Brian on my cell and cancel our date this evening, tell him to forget about Molly and find someone else to represent her, until it struck me that he was as much a pawn as I.

I'll wager he didn't have a clue about Cissy's plot to throw us together.

We'd both been duped.

Poor bastard.

He couldn't understand what he was up against.

Sighing, I settled back into the chair. I couldn't walk out on my mother, not yet. "In between trying to run the world — or, at least, my life — could you do something for me?"

"Besides babysitting?" she said innocently.

"Yes, besides that." I tried not to be testy.

Begging for favors from Cissy was an art, and tone of voice was an important part of that. Ever so sweetly, I asked, "Could you check into the Women's Wellness Clinic on Walnut Hill Lane?"

"Are you sick?" Her brow crinkled.

"No, I'm not sick." I brushed her hand away from my forehead. "See if the name Sarah Carter comes up. Also, pretty please, could you find out about a nurse named Peggy Martin? She apparently runs the clinic and she's also the leader of the Mothers Against Pornography. They've been protesting outside Jugs recently."

"Ah, yes, MAP," she remarked.

"Do you know much about them" — I paused, feeling my eyelid start to twitch — "besides pretending to be a card-carrying member last night? Because I'd like to learn more about what they've done in the past."

"For your information, Buffy Winspear asked me to chair a musical fundraiser with her called *Rap for MAP*, about a year ago or so," Mother drawled, always one step ahead. "She was negotiating with a fellow named Puffy to appear, but I was doing a gala for GLAD at the time. . . ."

"The gay and lesbian group?"

"No, honey." She let loose a throaty chuckle. "The Golden Ladies Alliance of Dallas. They're an organization of women over sixty who knit caps for the homeless."

"Ah."

How did I ever spring from this woman's womb?

It was one of those questions that would forever remain a mystery.

Like cats without hair.

Or crop circles.

There was a message from Malone on my voice mail when I got home. He sounded jazzed and asked me to return his call just as soon as I could. Whatever he'd gotten from Hi-Tech must've been good, I mused as I dialed the number for Abramawitz, Reynolds, Goldberg, and Hunt, then asked for his extension.

"Malone," he said in a brisk lawyerly tone.

"It's Andy."

"Oh, man, wait'll you hear what I've found out. You'll never believe what Hartman was into," he said in a verbal wind sprint that nearly left him out of breath.

"First, listen to this," I said, derailing his excitement for long enough to tell him about my visit to the Women's Wellness Clinic down on Walnut Hill and what Peggy Martin had said — or rather, what she hadn't said — about Sarah Carter. I didn't leave out my suspicions that Bud had scared Sarah into hiding and that, perhaps, she'd dropped by the restaurant the other evening to settle the score with him. Maybe it was a simple act of revenge.

Malone made appropriate "uh-huh's" and

"maybe so's," but I could sense he was itching to give me his news.

"Now what did you want to tell me about Hartman?" I asked, figuring that there was nothing about Bud that would surprise me.

"The subpoena threat did the trick. I got the Hi-Tech guy who sold Hartman the equipment to open up like Old Faithful. And when he finally started talking, he wouldn't stop. I think he wondered himself what Hartman had up his sleeve."

"C'mon, Malone, spill," I prodded, tired of listening to him yap without saying much of anything.

"I'm getting to it, Andy."

"Well, do it faster."

"Okay, okay." He paused for effect, I was sure, because I wanted to scream. "Hartman hired Hi-Tech to install digital surveillance equipment in the locker room at Jugs and in the bedroom of his condo."

Cameras in the bedroom hardly seemed shocking, what with Bud being such a creep. But the locker room?

I wondered if Julie knew about this.

"Why?" I squeaked.

"Because he, uh, wanted to tape himself having sex with different women," Malone offered rather timidly.

"You think?" That part I didn't need pointed out to me. "No, I mean, why the locker room at Jugs?"

278

"Uh, to see women undressing?"

I sighed noisily. What had I expected? Malone was a man. He just saw the obvious. "There has to be more to it than that. Hartman was sleazy, but he was also slick."

"All I know is he made the guy show up at four o'clock in the morning so he could rig up the equipment without anyone knowing it was there." Papers rustled, then Malone surged ahead. "There's a light-sensitive infrared camera up in the ceiling fixture of the changing room. It has a wide-angle lens so it picks up everyone and everything inside those four walls. He had a wireless transmitter sending signals to a recording device, basically a VCR hidden in a locker, so he got every moment on tape. All Hartman had to do was pop in fresh tapes every few days. Then he could play them at his leisure."

"Or someone else could," I said, thinking of all the stories I'd heard about landlords putting hidden cameras in their tenants' bathrooms to catch them naked and then doing a little "pay per view" on the uncensored Internet.

Was Hartman selling his homemade movies or even the live feed to voyeurs online?

Had anyone else known about it, if he were?

His partner, Jim Bob, for instance?

Could the Reverend Barker have wanted out of his business ventures with Bud, only to find himself trapped? Wasn't that enough motive for murder?

"The technician said he set up pretty much the same equipment in Hartman's bedroom," Malone kept talking, and I felt sick to my stomach. "Probably cut down on his visits to the back room at the video store."

Brian was kidding, I knew, but the joke wasn't funny. Not to me.

Was I on the tape in the locker room, in and out of my clothes?

My mouth went dry at the thought.

"Andy, are you okay? You went quiet all of a sudden."

"Bud Hartman really was an animal," I said, a bad taste in my mouth. "Maybe he did get what he deserved." I echoed what I'd been hearing over and over the past few days. I gripped the telephone receiver tightly, hearing the anger in my voice, feeling it in my body. "It wasn't enough just to harass his hired help, he had to play Peeping Tom, too. And who knows what he did with the tapes."

"He told the guy from Hi-Tech that the setup was for security reasons, to make sure no one stole from the lockers."

"Right," I barked, clearly as skeptical as Malone. "And he had his bedroom done to make sure no one plumped his pillows when he wasn't looking?"

Malone chortled. "The Hi-Tech guy figured he walked on the kinky side, but he said it wasn't his job to ask questions of his customers. He mentioned that Bud seemed like someone destined for trouble, so he wasn't too shocked when he saw on the news that he'd been murdered."

"So why didn't this geek go to the police when he learned about Bud's death?" I demanded, because it was logical. Because the cops would've known about Bud's surveillance equipment by now, which might've led them on the path to a suspect other than Molly.

"I asked him the same thing, Andy," Malone assured me. "His answer was that it wouldn't have made any difference at that point, especially since the cops seemed to have caught their killer."

But it would make a difference now. I was sure of it.

"So what do we do with this information, Malone? Because we're sure as hell not keeping quiet about it."

"Whoa, Andy. I'm ahead of you there. I've already talked to the D.A.'s office and told them everything, including the fact that the videos Bud made might provide new evidence in the case. They're getting their paperwork done now to go after the equipment at Jugs and in Hartman's bedroom. There might be something on the locker room tape from the night of the murder that'll give us a clue to what really happened."

Renewed hope danced in my chest.

"You think Bud might have caught his killer on tape?" I suggested, sure that was exactly what he was thinking.

"I do believe we're finally on the same page."

"Did the D.A. tell you when they'd be at Jugs?" Because I wanted to be there, too, watching their every move, making sure they didn't miss a thing.

"They're looking to search his condo tonight. They'll probably have the warrant for the restaurant by tomorrow morning."

That was music to my ears. "We still on for a late dinner?"

"Definitely."

I brightened up measurably.

"You want to go to the Mansion?" he asked.

Oh, Cissy would love that, wouldn't she? She'd probably even put a bug in his ear about it. So it was up to me to toss in a little wrench.

"How about something less fancy?"

"Truluck's on Belt Line?" he suggested.

I was already drooling, thinking of the fat piece of carrot cake with gobs of cream cheese icing I'd have for dessert, the restaurant's specialty. "You read my mind."

I knew there was something I liked about the guy.

"I'll pick you up at Jugs after your shift."

"How about I meet you there? I wouldn't want Julie to see us together again. I think she already smells something fishy."

"Seven o'clock?"

"Perfect."

I hung up and grabbed a quick bagel with cream cheese to quiet my stomach's grumbling.

I had only fifteen minutes to curl my hair, apply the Miss America mask of makeup, and don my padded sports bra before I was off to Jugs to "suffer the indignity of wearing such skimpy outfits," as Peggy Martin had so eloquently put it.

Hey, a spy's gotta do what a spy's gotta do.

At least that's what I told myself as I shoehorned my butt into the purple spandex hot pants one more time, praying I'd never see another pair once this jig was up.

Chapter 22

My mind definitely wasn't on serving beer and buffalo wings.

All afternoon, I kept thinking of the things that weren't adding up.

Bud and Jim Bob Barker's partnership in Jugs and the ten-million-dollar insurance policy. The preacher's oddly cozy relationship with Julie Costello. The disappearing waitress, Sarah Carter, and her connection to the Mothers Against Porn. Bud's cameras in his boudoir and in the locker room (prompting me to dress in a bathroom stall) and exactly what he may have been up to with those tapes. And, last but not least, the security guard, Fred Hicks, who'd turned up comatose in his car near Love Field with a suitcase in his trunk.

It was enough to make my head spin, which might be why I had more than a few orders mixed up.

I found Julie's eyes on me whenever I turned around, a funny look on her face, probably thinking she should've scheduled Tiffany for the afternoon shift, despite her dreaded PMS.

Each time I blundered, she was at my side, asking how I felt, if I needed to sit down.

"I'm fine," I kept telling her. "I'm not an invalid."

"Well, sugar, you're serving like one."

Ouch.

At around five o'clock, she insisted I get something to eat and relax for fifteen minutes. I passed on the food, since I was meeting Malone in a couple hours for dinner at Truluck's. But I did take her up on the break, heading back to the empty locker room to sit and think. This detective work was harder than I'd imagined. It wasn't anything like the reruns of *Murder, She Wrote*, where suspects constantly blurted out confessions to Angela Lansbury at the end of an hour.

I sighed, feeling depressed, and my eyes drifted to the ceiling, to the light fixture where the Hi-Tech nerd had told Malone he'd wired a camera.

Even when I squinted hard, I still couldn't find it.

I glanced around me at all the yellow doors, wishing I could pinpoint which locker held the rest of the equipment.

Half of them had combination locks, but I wouldn't know which belonged to Jugs's waitresses and which Bud might've used. There were so many. I couldn't locate any wires protruding from anywhere, even when I got up and poked around. Probably remote controlled with antennae and radio waves or something equally sci-fi.

Ah, well, the police would show up the next morning — if Malone had his facts straight — and, if we got lucky, Bud might have actually caught his killer on tape. Then everything else would be a moot point.

I realized the Dallas P.D. could well be at Bud's townhouse at that very moment, going through those videotapes and uncovering more of the randy restaurateur's dirty little secrets. Then it shouldn't be hard to persuade them that there were plenty of motives to go around.

Revenge.

Blackmail.

Jealousy.

Insurance money.

Missing cash.

Just to name a handful.

When the cops heard what else Malone and I knew, they would *have* to start looking harder at other suspects. They'd *have* to let Molly go while they investigated further.

Wouldn't they?

"Hey, are you okay?"

It was Julie.

I hadn't heard her come in. She stood beside the bench where I sat with my head in my hands.

"You need some water, sugar?"

I peeled my fingers from my face and wet my lips, thankful only that she didn't know what I'd been thinking in the moments before. "I'm fine, really."

She didn't look as if she bought it. She crossed her tanned arms beneath the large breasts barely concealed by the cut-off shirt. "You know, Andrea, there's something not right about you."

Uh-oh.

"What's not right?" Had one of my falsies come unfastened, giving me unbalanced boobs? *Please, let it be that simple.*

"You're not on your game today." She patted my shoulder. "It's probably hormones, what with your condition. So why don't you duck out early tonight and take tomorrow off? We'll talk after that, see how you're feelin'."

"No." I tugged my too-short shorts down from where they'd crept and stood facing her, nose to nose-job. "I don't need any time off. Honest." Oh, God, I couldn't screw this up, not just when I was getting so damned close to finding out who'd really killed Bud. "I've had a lot on my mind lately, but I'll try harder, I promise."

"Maybe Junior needs his mommy to stay off her feet. . . ."

"My feet are fine!" And besides, I wanted to blurt out, there *was* no Junior! "Look, Julie, it's just that. . . ."

I was tempted to tell her why I was pretending to be someone I wasn't. To explain to her about Molly's and my friendship, about David missing his mommy. Who knows? She might even want to help me out, to fill in some of the blanks that no one else could.

Unless she'd murdered Hartman.

Maybe she and Jim Bob had both wanted Bud dead. It didn't seem at all illogical, the more I thought about it, recalling what I'd overhead between them when I'd barged into Jugs the morning after the murder. They'd mentioned "the money" and "last night" and something that was "not over yet."

I couldn't trust her.

For all I knew, I was standing a foot away from a killer.

I found myself studying the pretty painted face and trying to figure out if Julie had it in her to commit such a violent act. She'd been nothing but kind to me, though I'd heard that Jeffrey Dahmer's neighbors had said the same thing about him.

"It's just what?" she prodded.

"Never mind." Now was not a good time to play confessional. There was still too much to be sorted out, and, if Julie really had killed Bud and I tipped her off, Molly might not be the only one whose life was at stake. "Unless you're firing me, I'm heading back out there to finish my shift, and I'll be here again in the morning."

She shrugged. "Hey, sugar. I'm only lookin' out for your own good." She shook a pink-nailed finger at me. "You're lucky I'm in charge now. Bud wouldn't have been so sympathetic about your situation. He never would've hired you. The baby thing."

"He didn't like children?"

"No, silly." She slapped my arm lightly. "Pregnant waitresses."

"Ah."

"You take it easy, little mama, and get back to your tables." Julie moved down the rows of lockers and popped one open. "I've got to change and head out into that godawful heat."

"Hot date?"

"A prayer meeting," she replied with a straight face.

A prayer meeting?

You've gotta be kidding.

"It's how I've been getting over Bud being gone," she said as she wiggled her top off and pulled on a lacy black bra before I could avert my eyes. "Sometimes it helps to talk about your troubles, you know? Give them up to a higher power."

I had to bite my tongue to keep from asking if that "higher power" was named Jim Bob Barker.

She shimmied into a purple spandex dress that didn't look like proper attire for any Bible study I'd ever been to at Highland Park Presbyterian. In fact, it seemed to be made of the same material as the short-shorts I was wearing. Could be Bud had gotten a cut-rate on the clingy fabric, had used at least a yard on fifteen pair of hot pants, and had enough left over to make Julie an outfit akin to colored Saran Wrap.

"Yoo hoo, Andrea?" Julie wiggled her fingers in front of my eyes until I blinked. "You sure you're all right?" she asked again.

"Peachy."

"Well, then *hasta la vista, mamacita*," she said and slammed her locker door shut. She waved at me over her shoulder as she sashayed from the room in a pair of high heels that would've toppled a lesser mortal.

I lifted my head to the light fixture, wondering if a tape was running. On the off chance that it was, I stuck out my tongue for good measure before I left the room.

The sun was setting as I drove up Belt Line toward Truluck's Steak and Stone Crab, which wasn't more than a mile or so west of the Preston intersection.

The restaurant was casual upscale with dark wood, large booths, and a 1940s décor that, coupled with the dim lighting, felt more than a little romantic.

Malone was already there when I arrived, and I was quickly led to his table.

"Hey, Andy."

He half rose as I scooted into the booth on the opposite side, and I noticed he'd already ordered a beer for himself and an iced tea for me. I took a long sip before I even said "hello." Then I cupped my hands around the cool glass and met his eyes.

"So tell me about the search of Bud's place." I

kept my voice low, and he leaned toward me. "Did the police find all his smutty tapes?"

"He had shelves full of them behind the clothes in his closet. Hundreds, at least. It was unbelievable." Malone looked flushed. Could've been from the heat. "There were dozens marked 'Jugs' that were dated, but nothing more recent than last week. Got a glimpse of one of 'em that Jed Lindstrom — he's the assistant D.A. — played on Hartman's VCR, and it wasn't anything you'd show your mother."

"Never underestimate my mother," I said to him, though I was thinking about the snowball's chance in hell that Cissy Blevins Kendricks had ever seen a kinky movie (and, if she had, I surely didn't want to know). Instead, I considered what I'd learned at Paciugo Gelato earlier that day. And I wasn't about to tell him that my mother had asked J. D. Abramawitz to put him on Molly's case because Cissy was playing matchmaker and that his skills as a litigator had *nada* to do with it.

I didn't want to hurt his feelings.

He continued in a low voice, "They found some files on Bud's computer and corresponding financial records that pretty clearly suggest he was marketing his homemade porn to subscribers on a web site he'd set up called HotLove.com. He kept a pretty detailed list of the ladies who are, um, shown in compromising positions with him."

"What a creep." I felt my stomach lurch.

"Lindstrom said they'd try to match up the women's names to waitresses at Jugs, past and present."

"Molly's name wasn't there, was it?"

Malone's mouth pressed into a tight line.

"It was?" My heart sank.

"I'm sorry, Andy."

Molly said she'd slept with Bud once, had made a mistake, and realized it soon after. But even if she'd found out about Hartman peddling the sex tapes on the web — and surely she would've at least mentioned it if she had — it still didn't mean she'd stabbed him to death.

But maybe someone else had.

"What about Sarah Carter?" I ventured to ask. "Was she on the list?"

He took a sip of his beer, then ran the back of his hand lightly across his mouth. "Yeah, she was. Julie Costello, too."

I had figured as much. That Sarah had gotten herself in deep with Bud, maybe deeper than she'd intended to.

"She's been taken advantage of enough."

I remembered what Peggy Martin had said and wondered if she'd meant the videotapes. If Sarah had found out that Bud had recorded their most intimate moments together and was offering them to a paying public on the Internet, would she have freaked out? Lost her mind for even the moment it took to pick a knife from the ground and lash out? Then what if she'd run to the Wellness Clinic for help, and Peggy had gotten her the hell out of Dodge?

It wasn't entirely inconceivable, was it?

But the tapes also gave Molly motive. At least, the police would see it that way, I'm sure.

Aw, cripes. The last thing I wanted to do was help the Dallas P.D. find more nails for Molly's coffin.

I didn't want to think about it. Didn't even want to talk about it any further.

"You all right, Andy?"

"Yeah." Just depressed that nothing seemed to be going Molly's way.

"I've got more news about Fred Hicks, if you want to hear it."

I perked up. "Fire away."

"One of the paramedics drew blood for testing while he did the IV start in the ambulance, and one of the results came back abnormal."

"Did they find alcohol or drugs?" That's the first thing that came to mind.

"Nope." Malone got a funny look in his eyes. "Acute hypoglycemia."

"Low blood sugar?" I shrugged. "Maybe he was diabetic."

"They searched his suitcase and his car, Andy. There were no prescriptions found in his belongings besides some arthritis medication." He scooted forward, so his elbows crossed the center of the table. "They also ran something called an insulin C-peptide level, which showed

293

the combination of very low blood sugar and a normal C-peptide."

"Which means, in plain English?"

He gushed, "That someone likely administered insulin from an outside source, an IV or possibly a syringe. The police are investigating it as a suspicious death."

"So Hicks didn't have a heart attack?"

"No."

I shivered, knowing what that meant. And, just in case I couldn't put two and two together, Malone said it outright: "Someone tried to kill him."

"Tried?" I sniffed. "He's in an irreversible coma, for God's sake. I'd say they did a bang-up job."

"But, Andy, you're not seeing the bright spot in all this. Whoever murdered Bud Hartman likely went after Fred Hicks. It can't be a coincidence."

"If that's true" — I looked him straight in the eye — "does it mean the police will let Molly go home?"

He leaned away from me, settling back against the booth. "Not exactly."

"Then how does this help us?" I waved my hands at him, nearly knocking over my iced tea. "Another human being down the crapper, and we don't even know who's responsible or why."

Dammit.

Tears pricked my eyes, and I fought them hard, pushed them back. I wasn't going to cry in front of Malone, despite how utterly frustrated I felt.

I picked up the menu, pretending to study it intently, but my mind was still miles away.

"Andy?"

When I didn't respond, Malone reached across the table and slid the menu from my grasp. He turned it right-side up before he handed it back.

"Maybe now it'll make more sense."

"Oh, God, I'm sorry." Molly's case was really getting to me. My chest even felt heavy, like someone was pressing a hand against my rib cage, making it hard to breathe deeply. What was next? An ulcer? Hypertension? Hives? "Can we talk about something else?" I pleaded. "Just for tonight?"

"No problem." Malone touched my hand, and I put down the menu and saw the worry in his face. "We could both use a break." He smiled sympathetically, his expression sweet and concerned.

I nodded, and his fingers tightened over mine. A ripple of electricity ran through me, lifting goose bumps on my skin. I only hoped my hair wasn't standing on end.

"Andy, I. . . ."

"Ah, are you ready to hear the specials?"

The waiter appeared out of nowhere to hover above us.

Brian's hand left mine to slip back across the table, and I felt my cheeks warm.

We listened to the specials, but neither of us ordered them.

Crab cakes for me. Ahi tuna steak for him.

The waiter gathered up our menus, then left us alone.

Malone drained his beer.

I pushed the lemon around in my tea with the straw.

"So," we said at the same time.

We both laughed and smiled awkwardly.

"Cissy tells me you went to Columbia," he started off, getting the "where'd you go to school" thing right out in the open. "I love New York City."

I sighed and pinched my fingers together. "Mother's fudging the truth just a smidge."

"So you didn't go to Columbia?"

"Columbia College, yes," I told him directly. "Columbia University, no."

Malone scrunched up his nose. "I don't believe I've heard of it."

"It's a small art school in Chicago." I fiddled with the straw again. "I studied graphics and computers, so web design seemed a natural evolution. It's what I love to do, though my mother thinks it's a hobby, something to keep me busy until I'm properly married off. Little does she know, I don't intend on walking down the aisle anytime soon. Though I have the perfect white dress hanging in the closet, never been worn."

"A wedding gown?"

I shook my head. "It was for my debut, which

never happened." He didn't ask why, and I didn't explain. "Just one more thing my mother holds against me."

Brian chuckled. "So you've been bucking the system your whole life, huh?"

I liked the way he put that. "Yeah, I guess I have." I figured it was his turn for the third degree and asked, "Tell me about your family. I mean, you must know everything else about me already, what with the firm practically having a dossier on my parents."

Abramawitz, Reynolds, Goldberg, and Hunt had been counsel of record for my father's pharmaceutical company before he'd died and, after, when Mother had sold it but remained on the board, they'd continued to manage her legal affairs. Only the staff at Elizabeth Arden's Red Door day spa knew her more intimately. So I wasn't stretching the truth by much.

"You're not originally from Texas, are you?" I asked him.

"What, did my Midwest twang give me away?" He pushed at his glasses in what I'd already come to learn was a nervous habit. "To make it short and sweet, I grew up in Chesterfield, which is a western suburb of St. Louis. Did my undergrad work at Washington University, so I didn't venture too far from home."

So I was right when I'd figured him for a "Show Me" kind of guy.

"How'd you get from there to Harvard Law?"

"By plane," he said and grinned.

"Very funny." I nudged him under the table with the toe of my pink high-top sneaker, and he wagged his eyebrows.

"Okay, I worked my ass off."

"So how did you get from Harvard to Texas? And be serious, would you?"

He shifted in his seat and made a show of putting on a straight face. "J. D. Abramawitz brought me to Dallas, and that's the truth. He recruited me after I'd been working for a few years in Boston. I'd always wanted to come down this way, ever since I was a kid and saw J.R. Ewing shot on Southfork." He ignored my groan and continued. "I had envisioned wearing a cowboy hat to the office." He lifted his hands to adjust an imaginary Stetson. "But I've only seen a few of 'em around. Nobody rides a horse to work, either. Mostly everyone's very friendly, and the weather's great."

"If you like it hot."

"I had more than my share of snow in April, so I'm not gonna knock blue skies and sun."

"What I wouldn't give for snow in April," I remarked, and he looked at me as if I was bonkers. "Hey, I grew up here. I've had my share of sun. When I was in Chicago, I got to see the four seasons, which is two more than we get in these parts. Don't you miss them?"

"If I want the four seasons, I'll listen to Vivaldi."

"Good to know, since Mother has tickets to the symphony for a Vivaldi tribute next month.

Should I have her call? I know she has your number." I tried not to sound snippy, but maybe I did, just a little.

He crooked a finger at me, and we bent nearer over the table, so near I breathed in the smell of him, the warmth of male mixed with lemony aftershave. "No offense," he whispered, "but I'd rather go with her daughter."

"No offense taken," I whispered back.

I marveled at the black of his eyelashes, the curl of chestnut brown on his brow, and I realized I'd stopped breathing for an instant.

Right on cue, the master of bad timing — our waiter — appeared, bearing a tray of steaming dishes.

Malone and I drew apart, settling back into our seats, barely glancing at each other until the clattering had stopped and our meals were presented. I inhaled deeply, thinking I'd died and gone to heaven.

The waiter mercifully disappeared.

And we grinned goofily across the table like a couple of teenagers out on a first date before we picked up our forks and dug in.

Chapter 23

The night was sultry, no other way to describe it. Or maybe I was just in a generous mood. The sky was dark as velvet with the twinkle of stars above and the shimmer of neon signs creating a glow over Addison, all the way up Belt Line as far as the eye could see. Restaurant Row seemed alive with color and motion, cars zipping to and fro.

At that moment, there wasn't anywhere on earth more lovely.

I didn't even mind the sweat slipping down my back, and I had no fear of oregano in my teeth as I'd done a quick inspection in the ladies' room mirror before we'd left. A Tic-Tac took care of the rest.

Brian walked me to my car, his hand brushing mine, our voices low, and our laughter a gentle ripple across the still air.

Made me sorry I'd found a spot to park the Jeep so near the entrance to the restaurant.

He held open the Wrangler's door as I climbed in, and he hung there a minute before he pushed it snugly closed. I rolled down the window and he leaned in.

"This was nice," he said.

I agreed. It was. Though I'd be damned if I'd tell Cissy.

"I'll see you in the morning."

"In the morning?"

"At Jugs," he reminded me. "The police should have their warrants in order to search the place. Lindstrom said they should be there by ten."

"Okay."

I didn't tell him about my conversation with Julie, the one where she'd claimed I was acting weird and should take a few days off. If she fired me before I'd found what I needed to clear Molly — and I wasn't even sure what that was — then all my efforts would be for naught. I had to move faster, dig deeper. Like where Julie and Jim Bob were concerned. If I didn't get to the bottom of their relationship, it might be too late to do Molly any good.

For nearly two hours, I'd barely thought about the case or what might happen beyond this evening. I felt the knot in my stomach return. My shoulders tensed. A second earlier, I'd been wishing Malone would kiss me. Now I had other more important things on my mind.

"Sleep tight," he said, brushing my cheek with his fingers.

"You, too."

I watched him walk across the lot. He gave a wave before getting into an Acura coupe, and I sighed with relief that he didn't drive anything more pretentious. Brian Malone was no show-off, and I liked that about him.

One of the reasons I didn't want to disappoint him.

I decided to drive for a bit before I went home. I was suddenly keyed up. Malone had gotten me thinking about Bud's murder again, and I needed to unwind.

There was something about a car ride that had always soothed me. Mother had told me stories about nights when I'd howled from the crib so that she and Daddy couldn't catch a wink even with pillows over their heads. They'd finally taken me out in the Cadillac, and Cissy had held me in the back seat while Daddy had made several slow trips through the Park Cities. It had put me out like a light. So, any time I didn't fall asleep like a good baby, into the car I went. Better than Sominex. I still had trouble staying awake on road trips if I were a passenger.

When I was driving, it was a different story. Instead of knocking me out, the rhythmic thunk of the tires on the pavement and gentle motion of the shock absorbers somehow relaxed me, made my thoughts more clear, convinced me that I could sort out any problems in my life between traffic signals.

So I drove west on Belt Line from Quorum, where Truluck's was located, heading slowly toward Midway. Checking out other cars at the light at Inwood/Addison and listening to Sheryl Crow croon while my fingers tapped a beat on the steering wheel.

I looked around me as I surged forward on green, traffic amazingly heavy at ten o'clock on a weekday evening. Countless cars moved around me, everyone in a hurry to get where they were going. Wherever that was.

I hit another red light at Beltway Drive and glanced to my right, over into the next lane.

A white Lincoln Town Car with tinted windows idled, the streetlamp picking out the pockmarks on the hood. I could see them even better from my elevated position in the Jeep Wrangler, and it took but an instant for recognition to dawn.

My heart accelerated, like I'd put my foot on the gas for my pulse. I slunk back against my seat hoping the driver couldn't see me.

The light flicked to green, and the Lincoln lurched ahead.

My delay in forward motion earned me a couple of rude honks, but allowed me to glimpse the license plate.

MCY 653.

Reverend Jim Bob's car.

It could be no other.

So what was he doing in Addison at this hour?

Shouldn't he be on the air, performing on his twenty-four-hour "live" ministry and spreading the gospel to bored cable viewers? Though I guess he taped the show or else he'd never have time to do anything else, such as preside over memorial services for people like Bud Hartman or attend board meetings and luncheons, much less spend time with Mrs. Jim Bob and the kids.

Or check into the Motel 6.

Because that's where the Town Car was headed, turning right into the motel parking lot just before the jammed Midway intersection.

I couldn't imagine the preacher having any reason to be there except for a tryst. And I had a feeling I knew who with. The lovably manic Julie Costello. Which would explain the tight purple dress she'd donned for her "prayer meeting."

Adrenaline gushed through my veins.

This could be my chance to kill the proverbial two birds with one stone. Or at least stun them with a well-aimed breath mint.

Heck, it was worth a shot.

I tried to veer into the right lane, but it was too late to get over without causing an accident. I managed to squeeze the Jeep into the left turn lane at Midway, though waiting for the light to change was a killer. My fingers tapped an impatient beat on the wheel so fast the Goo Goo Dolls couldn't begin to keep up. I switched off the radio and sighed until the green arrow appeared, and then I hightailed it back onto Belt Line, pulling another U-turn at Beltway.

It seemed an eternity had passed before I bumped the Wrangler into the motel's parking lot, trying to spot Jim Bob's white sedan to no avail.

I parked in front of the office doors and went inside, drumming up a story in my head as I approached the night clerk, a solid-looking Hispanic man who smiled politely.

"Can I help you, ma'am?"

"Oh, gosh, I certainly hope so," I told him, doing my best to appear frantic, turning my keys over in my hands and gulping in air like I couldn't catch my breath. "It's my father. I think he checked in just a few minutes ago. I *have* to see him. It's an emergency."

"Your father's name?"

"Uh, geez, I'm not sure if he used his real name." I was damned sure Jim Bob Barker had not registered as himself. Leaning over the counter, I whispered, "He's with his *tootsie*, you know? He and my mother aren't divorced yet, and he has to keep a low profile. Probably paid cash for the room."

The smile disappeared, and the clerk peered at me with dark eyes that had probably seen this act before, though the script doubtless changed with each performance. "I'm sorry, ma'am. I'm not allowed to give out information on guests. I wish I could help you, but I can't."

"Yes" — I looked at his nametag — "yes, Ronaldo, you can. Maybe this will help." I worked a folded twenty-dollar bill from my change purse and slipped it out onto the desk. Oh, man, I was gonna be broke before the end of the week at this rate. "Just to jog your memory." I winked at him, sly-like. "He drives a white Lincoln Town Car." I rattled off the plate number for him, having it memorized by now. "He's about six feet two, a hundred ninety pounds, salt-and-pepper hair."

"The man who was just here?" His palm casually covered the bill. "The guy with the beard and mustache?"

A beard and mustache, huh?

So I wasn't the only one playing dress-up.

"He has piercing blue eyes."

I could tell by Ronaldo's expression that he knew exactly who I was talking about.

"Sorry, ma'am, I still can't help you. It's against our policy." He artfully slipped the hand with the twenty into his pants pocket.

Had I just been conned by a con?

What was the world coming to?

It left me no choice but to pull out the big guns.

I reached in my purse, wrapped my fingers around my Tic-Tacs, and withdrew them. I shook them noisily at him without letting him see the container. "My father needs his nitroglycerin, Ronaldo, or he might go into cardiac arrest. He has a horrible, horrible heart condition. Please, just tell me the room number, and I'll take his pills to him." I quickly shoved the breath mints back inside my purse. "You don't want him going into heart failure after a night of passion with a woman who's half his age, now do you? How would it look for a man to die at your motel because you prevented his own daughter from delivering his medication?"

Ronaldo's eyes widened as I finished, and he glanced around the lobby. A couple who'd swept through the doors stopped and stared at us. I held my breath while Ronaldo glanced at some papers on the desk. "Larry Jones, room 145," he said under his breath.

Larry Jones?

Wasn't that the name of the guy in Pine Bluff, Arkansas, who'd been made the figurehead of ERA, Inc., the front for Jim Bob and Bud's partnership? If I remembered correctly, Jones also happened to be Jim Bob's brother-in-law.

Smooth, Rev.

"He wanted a room around the back." Ronaldo swallowed. "Should I call 911 or anything?"

"No need." I patted his hand. "I'll take care of my dear daddy. That's why I'm here."

He nodded and mopped at the sweat on his brow.

When I got outside, I hesitated before climbing into the Jeep. My hands shook as I reached into my bag and pulled out the Tic-Tacs, shaking a couple in my mouth, not liking the bitter taste left behind from so many lies.

It almost scared me how good I'd gotten at telling them.

If I didn't stop soon, I'd have to start wearing flame-retardant Levis.

My blood still buzzing, I climbed into the car

and slowly drove around to the rear of the building, counting room numbers as I went until I saw the white Lincoln parked in front of 145. Beside it — surprise, surprise — was a little red Corvette. Julie must've driven in while I'd been at the front desk, pleading my case to Ronaldo.

I pulled the Jeep into a spot across the way, backing in beside a Dumpster. After I cut the engine, I sat there for a few minutes, staring at the drawn curtains in the window of the room where Jim Bob and Julie were holding their late-night Bible study — reenacting the scene from the Garden of Eden where Eve does a strip tease with a snake, no doubt — and I tried to come up with a plan. Only, I couldn't think of anything. Nothing that made sense.

I just knew that I couldn't fail Molly and David, even if it meant embarrassing myself by confronting the preacher and the cheerleader without cue cards.

As though wearing hot pants in public hadn't killed any pride I had left.

For some reason, that made me feel calmer as I got out of my car and quietly closed the door. Before I approached their room, I made sure my cell phone was in my purse. Just in case I had to quickly dial 911.

I pounded with my fist until I heard Julie's high-pitched voice yell, "Who the hell is it, for Christ's sake?"

Now what kind of language was that for a prayer meeting?

"Room service!" I said the first thing that sprang to mind.

Did they even *have* room service at Motel 6?

I had no idea.

"We didn't order anything!" she shouted back. "So scram!"

Nuts.

I drew in a deep breath, failed to come up with any alternative, and decided to be honest. It was a stretch.

"All right, it's not room service, it's me. Andrea." I practically kissed the door, my mouth was so close to the wood. I tried to peer through the peephole, but it didn't work in reverse. "I know you're in there, Julie, and I know who you're with. So please, open up or I'll call Cinda Lou Mitchell on my cell and tell her to get her camera crew out here for an exclusive."

Swift thinking, Kendricks, I thought, and pressed my ear to the door, picking up on some mumbling and then the noise of the locks being undone.

The door flew open, and Julie stood there in her purple dress, although her hair was mightily disheveled, her lipstick smeared around her mouth. Before I could utter so much as a "howdy-do," she grabbed my arm and hauled me in.

"Hey. . . ."

She pushed me inside and slammed the door.

I nearly tripped over the bed, dropping my purse onto the already-rumpled spread. I rubbed my arm as Julie reset the locks, and I decided she was a lot stronger than she looked. Did cheerleaders lift weights? I was willing to bet she could bench press me over her head.

But I had pepper spray, I reminded myself, reaching for my bag and jamming my hand in to locate the bottle. I palmed it, my finger on the trigger, concealing it against my thigh.

Quickly, I took in the small room around me, finding no sign of Reverend Jim Bob. Well, except his jacket hanging over the back of a chair. Then I realized the bathroom door was shut tight. God, don't you love a man who hides in the toilet when trouble comes knocking?

Julie peered out the drapes, probably checking to see if I'd come alone.

Maybe I should've called Malone, caught him in his car before he'd gotten home.

Though he would've tried to talk me out of going there, wouldn't he?

Not that it was the first stupid thing I'd ever done.

Julie spun around, blond locks flying, though a wisp of hair caught in the corner of her mouth as she hissed, "Shit, Andrea, what the crap do you think you're doing? Did you follow us here from the church after the prayer meeting?"

Was she serious?

"What are you, like a stalker or something?"

I ignored her questions, posing one of my own. "Does Reverend Jim Bob check into the

Motel 6 after prayer sessions with all of his flock or just with you?"

"You're nuts," she protested, but I shook my head.

"Save it. I saw his Lincoln outside."

She crossed her arms forcefully and called over her shoulder. "You can come out of the bathroom, Jimmy."

The door slowly creaked open, and Jim Bob peered out. He still had on the mustache and beard that Ronaldo had mentioned, and I noted a slight resemblance to Robert Goulet.

His eyes widened when he saw me. I'm sure he had no clue what I was doing there. In fact, I wasn't so sure myself and was beginning to think this idea was more foolish by the minute.

"I told you she was acting pretty strange, Jimmy, and now she shows up at the motel." Julie prattled on breathily, not hiding her distress. She had her hands balled into fists. "I shouldn't have felt sorry for her. She was out to get us from the start. I should've known it."

"Hush, baby, hush." Jim Bob stepped to her side and set a hand on her shoulder. He looked at me, the fake mustache wiggling as he spoke. "You were at Bud's memorial service."

"Yes."

"You've been working at the restaurant since the murder."

"Yes." My heart was smacking so hard against my rib cage, it sounded like someone was hammering in my head. I wasn't sure where this was going, but I had a vague notion.

"Are you a reporter?"

"No." It was a relief to actually admit that.

Jim Bob studied me carefully, rubbing his chin, working the beard off in the process. I don't think he even noticed. He came toward the bed, his long legs closing the space between us in a few strides. He reached out his hand. "I'd like to see your identification."

"Good thinking, Jimmy," Julie cooed, clasping her hands together. "She might be undercover."

"Undercover? As in, police?" Peggy Martin had wondered the same thing, and it tickled me to even think I'd been mistaken for a cop. "C'mon, guys, get serious." But serious is exactly how they looked. I wet my lips. "Listen, why doesn't everyone have a seat so we can discuss this calmly," I suggested, though neither jumped at the invitation.

"Give me your handbag," the preacher demanded in that mesmerizing voice, the one that got little old ladies to mail him their Social Security checks without flinching.

"You want it? Come get it."

I still had the pepper spray clutched at my side; but it was two against one, and I didn't like the odds. Part of me was sure they wouldn't harm a hair on my head, but the other part wasn't convinced.

"Okay, take it." I held out my purse with my

free hand, and the Reverend Barker stepped forward and snatched it out of my grip. He ripped open the snap and fumbled inside its leather belly. He pulled out my cell phone first and tossed it on the dresser with a clunk that made me wince. Then he found my wallet, flipped it open, and began thumbing through its contents. He passed one of my business cards to Julie.

"Andrea Blevins Kendricks," she read aloud. "ABK Graphics." Her chin jerked up. "You film pornos?"

Yuck. "No, no. I'm a web designer."

"So you do porno web sites?"

Was that interest in her eyes?

"I don't do porn in any capacity," I assured her. "Though I do pro bono work sometimes." Which had her looking even more baffled. I half-expected her head to start spinning like Linda Blair in *The Exorcist.* "I design totally legitimate web sites," I explained. "Like for charities and small businesses. And that has nothing to do with the reason I've been working at Jugs."

"I don't get it." She pulled a few of my credit cards from their slots and tossed them at me. My Neiman Marcus, Saks Fifth Avenue, and the platinum MasterCard and Visa. "Well, it hardly looks like you're broke." Angry red blotches stained her face. "What else did you lie about, huh? I'll bet you're not even pregnant. Probably never been divorced. Have you even waited tables before? Because you suck at it, if you don't mind my sayin' so."

313

Geez, way to hurt my feelings.

"So I lied." I shrugged, hardly wanting to defend myself to her. "But it was for a good cause."

Molly, I nearly added, but didn't want to drag her into this. Or maybe I was just afraid of Julie's reaction.

"What cause? Like those Mothers Against Porn? Are you part of their operation . . . ?"

"No," I interjected.

She shook a finger at me. "You want to tell us what's really going on, or should we call the cops?"

"Go ahead," I told her. "That'll give me a chance to fill them in on you and Jim Bob."

She laughed. "We're not doing anything illegal, sugar. Immoral maybe, but that's a different story. Can't arrest us for what we do between the sheets."

"I'm sure Mrs. Barker would beg to differ."

Jim Bob frowned, obviously not finding that funny. "You're the one who came barging in. Why don't you tell us what you came for?"

He was right.

It was time to lay my cards on the table.

"I thought maybe we'd chat about ERA, Incorporated," I said, watching Jim Bob's eyes widen at the mention. "I'm sure the police would be interested in knowing why a TV preacher would own a restaurant like Jugs and have a jerk like Bud Hartman as his partner. I wouldn't mind hearing that story myself."

"How did you find out about ERA?" The preacher's voice took on a frightened tone. Perspiration had loosened the gum on the mustache, and it hung cock-eyed over his lips. Every time he breathed, it danced. Not an attractive look for him.

"A friend of mine checked it out. A lawyer," I said, figuring that would keep them in line. They wouldn't hurt me — would they? — if they believed someone else knew what I knew. "He dug up info about the partner's insurance, the ten million you'd get if anything happened to Bud. What I don't understand is how you got tied up with him in the first place. Was it blackmail?" I inclined my head at the two of them. "Did he have photos of you and Julie? Is that why he was killed?"

"No, it was nothing like that!" Julie blurted out. "Bud and Jim Bob go way back," she said, ignoring Jim Bob's attempts to silence her. "They're both from Magnolia, Arkansas. Jimmy used to own a bar called Hillbillies. Bud hung out a lot there after he got bounced from Texas Tech."

Hillbillies, huh?

"The theme of the restaurant," I voiced my thoughts aloud.

"It was years ago, before Jimmy got religion, sold the bar, left Arkansas, and made a new life for himself in Dallas."

"Julie, please. . . ."

But she didn't heed his warning. "Bud

tracked Jimmy down. His church was just starting up then, and Bud took advantage of that. He decided to settle in Dallas and open a restaurant. He got Jimmy to invest and called it 'Jugs' to remind Jimmy where they came from, of all the hell-raising they did together once. The drugs and the booze. All the women."

The preacher turned away, shaking his head.

"Bud had photographs from those days. Bad ones." She reached over to stroke Jim Bob's arm, but he pulled away like she'd burned him. "Bud showed me a couple of them one night. They were in bed with a girl. Bud said she was thirteen. He called it a 'hillbilly sandwich,' if you know what I mean."

"I get the picture."

And it wasn't pretty.

"Bud told me he had enough on Jim Bob to ruin his career. He had Jimmy running scared, thinking of his church and his TV show, everything he'd lose if word ever got out. All that money going down the tubes."

Glug, glug.

Now that wasn't hard to imagine.

It was mere embezzlement that had toppled Jim and Tammy Faye Bakker, and a single hooker had tarnished Jimmy Swaggert's once-shiny image. Allegations of fraud had scattered Robert Tilton's flock to the winds.

But a photo of Jim Bob and another man in bed with a teenaged girl?

He'd be lucky if his congregation stopped at tar and feathers.

"How much were you paying Bud?" I said to Jim Bob's back.

He slowly turned around. "A hundred grand."

"A year?"

Julie snorted, gazing at me as if I were an idiot. "No, silly. A hundred grand a month."

My mouth fell open.

Bud Hartman had been bleeding Jim Bob out of nearly a million and a quarter annually? That was hardly pigeon feed.

I couldn't believe it.

"Did you kill him?"

"No." Julie took her lover's hand and held on tightly. "Jimmy had nothing to do with that, and neither did I."

"Can you prove it?"

This time, the preacher responded. "We were together the night Bud was murdered. *All* night," he emphasized, not seeming embarrassed in the least at admitting the indiscretion. Well, what was the point? "Julie pretended to feel ill so she could get out of closing up with Bud. We met here, probably around the same time as tonight. Neither of us left 'til right before sun-up."

"Did you pay cash?"

"The night clerk will remember me," he said. "I registered under the name of Larry Jones, as usual. It'll be in their records."

How cozy, providing each other with alibis.

"We're in love," Julie declared, gazing up at Jim Bob with gooey eyes. "Sometimes it just happens, whether you want it to or not."

Gag me with a silver spoon.

I squirmed on the bedspread, still hiding the pepper spray. "The police might not be so quick to buy your story. Bud's death set Jim Bob free of his blackmailer, plus he'll get the money from the partner's insurance. Not to mention full ownership of the restaurant. I'd say he had more than enough reason to want Bud gone for good."

"No," Julie piped up. "That's not the whole story."

Oh, man, there was more?

"So fill me in."

"Bud left all his worldly goods to his mama in Arkansas. Though she hasn't been right in the head for years. Lives in a nursing home, and she couldn't care less about a restaurant in Dallas. Probably doesn't even know where Dallas is. Bud was her only child. He assumed her power of attorney when the Alzheimer's got bad." Julie paused to glance at Jim Bob, who sighed, chin sagging to his chest. She kept going. "He had his lawyer fix up a document that said I had first dibs on buying his half of Jugs from his mama if anything ever happened to him. He wanted to make sure there was money to pay for his mama's care, and he didn't want Jim Bob taking over. He knew Jimmy would shut the place down, and he wanted it to be a burr in Jimmy's hide forever and ever."

That certainly sounded like Bud Hartman.

Still, it didn't add up, not enough to satisfy me.

"How're you paying for Bud's half?"

She glanced up at Jim Bob. "I'm getting some help from Jimmy, and he's happy to do it, aren't you, sugar? I told him it was a small thing compared to his church finding out what a bad boy he's been."

Ah. So the blackmail continued.

I almost felt sorry for the Rev.

Almost.

Well, I'd heard enough for one night. I wanted to call Malone and spill the beans on Jim Bob and Julie, see what he wanted to do. I'm sure the police would definitely be interested in knowing what I'd just learned.

I wasn't entirely certain they weren't guilty of stabbing Bud to death, yet nothing they'd told me so far had convinced me they had.

My only hope was that the cops would find something on the surveillance tapes from the Jugs's locker room that would settle everything once and for all.

Because my detective skills seemed to be sorely lacking.

My watch showed quarter past eleven.

I was wiped out, and I wanted to get home.

Nancy Drew probably packed it in every night by ten.

"Wow," I said. "Look at the time. It's been fun, folks, but I've got to run."

319

Julie stood before me, hands on hips. "Sorry, sugar, but the party's not over till we say it's over."

Sugar.

The word set off a loud ping in my brain.

My heart did a nosedive into my belly as my pre-dinner discussion with Brian tumbled quickly through my head.

"He had acute hypoglycemia . . . low blood sugar . . . no prescriptions found in his belongings besides some arthritis medication . . . they also ran something called an insulin C-peptide level, which showed the combination of very low blood sugar and a normal C-peptide . . . someone likely administered insulin from an outside source, an IV or possibly a syringe . . . the police are investigating it as a suspicious death . . . Hicks didn't have a heart attack . . . someone tried to kill him."

Another conversation surfaced as well, remarks Julie had made after Bud's funeral that hadn't seemed to matter at the time.

"Have you ever seen Mrs. Jim Bob? She looks like somebody blew her up with a tire pump. That's probably how she got diabetes, from eating too much sugar."

I stared at the Reverend Barker.

His wife had diabetes, which meant he had access to her medication and supplies.

Jim Bob had killed Bud and then he'd gone after Fred Hicks, too, giving him an overdose of insulin via syringe.

320

Julie was his alibi for the night of Bud's murder. She was lying for him.

It all fit well enough that I believed it. Which scared me silly.

I tried to swallow, but my mouth was too dry.

Julie was wrong. The party *was* over.

For me, at least. I wanted out.

"You know what? I apologize for interrupting your, uh, prayer meeting." I couldn't look at Jim Bob so I switched my focus to Julie, who still blocked my way to the door. "Without further ado, I'll say goodnight and let you go back to your, um, praying." Calmly, I slid off the bed, forgetting that I clutched the pepper spray. Without thinking, I pointed it toward Jim Bob, who still held my purse. "Would you mind giving that back, Reverend?" My voice was barely audible, even to my own ears. But apparently what I said didn't matter.

"Jesus, she's got mace!" Julie cried.

You ever see your life flash before your eyes, and it looks like an awful B-movie? In slow motion?

Jim Bob lunged at me.

There wasn't time to move.

He tackled me, throwing my body onto the bed, flat on my back, and knocking the wind from my lungs.

I felt the mattress bounce as Julie threw herself into the mix, and four hands grabbed at mine, prying the pepper spray from my fingers. We were so tangled up, like three big kids caught in a wild game of Twister, that I didn't even know which body parts were mine.

"Stop struggling," I heard Julie growl, but I wasn't the one who struggled, pinned down as I was beneath her and Jim Bob, their combined weight making it impossible for me to draw in a deep breath, much less wrestle.

"Help," I gasped, which is when the blast of pepper spray hit me square in the face like a welder's torch, burning everything it touched. I wanted to scream, but no sound emerged, my throat paralyzed. They scrambled off of me, and I doubled over, rubbing at my eyes, which only made the pain worse. I coughed and retched at once, my chest tightening horribly, so that I thought I would die then and there.

Somebody yelped, "Now look what you've done," but I was in too much discomfort to care.

I was barely aware of being carried into the bathroom and thrown in the tub. Pipes screeched as the shower was turned on and cold water rushed at me. Voices churned around me, and hands splashed water at my face while I moaned and flopped around blindly, swallowing mucus and saliva, feeling dizziness sweep over me.

I must've passed out soon after — I have a very low pain threshold — because when I came to, Julie and Jim Bob were gone.

Chapter 24

It took a few minutes to rouse myself to a state anywhere near awake, and a few more to unfurl my body from a fetal position. The hands of my watch were too blurry to see, so I had no idea how long I'd been curled up in the tub, soaking wet and shivering.

The shower was no longer running, but a puddle had formed beneath me. I spit into the drain as I drew my head up from the damp plastic mat.

Using my fingers, I pried my eyes wider and surveyed my surroundings. The white of the bathroom made me wince, and things seemed fuzzy at the edges. But at least the burning pain was gone. My mouth and tongue felt raw, and there was a horribly bitter aftertaste, like I'd chugged a bottle of Tabasco or swallowed fire. Which I guess I had.

I turned on the tub and cupped my palms to catch the water. I sipped and spit each mouthful into the drain until most of the nastiness was gone. I found a damp washcloth draped over the tub's rim and blew my nose into it none too gracefully. It took several noisy attempts before I could breathe normally.

There. Better.

My legs shook as I gripped the handicapped bar and drew myself up. Water dripped off my clothes, and I could still smell the spray on the fabric.

I peeled off everything one piece at a time and turned the shower on, allowing a lukewarm drizzle to wash over me. Clumsily, I stripped off the wrapping on a tiny bar of soap and rinsed my skin thoroughly, wanting to get every bit of the chemicals off.

By the time I'd toweled off, I nearly felt human again. I cleared a circle free of condensation on the mirror and took in my reflection.

My eyes were puffy and red. My nose a shade closer to pink. My skin had a faint sunburned appearance, though basically it looked like I'd spent the night crying over a boyfriend who'd dumped me.

How the heck had this happened?

It all came back to me in a rush. My stupid attempt to confront Jim Bob and Julie, capped by a tussle on the bed and the blast of chemicals to my face.

My head hammered with a hangover I hadn't earned. When I'd bought the pepper spray, I'd never imagined being on the wrong end of the nozzle. The instructions said it would floor an assailant for a couple hours, but they'd mentioned nothing about knocking someone unconscious. Maybe I was more susceptible than most. Then again, as a kid, the mere sight of blood could make me pass out.

Still, it was good to know the stuff worked. I'd just have to be more careful who it was pointed at the next time.

I'd set my wristwatch on the counter while I'd showered. I picked it up and studied the face carefully, able to read the hands well enough.

Eight-thirty.

That couldn't be right, could it?

Had Jim Bob and Julie left me there overnight? In a pool of water in the bathtub, all by my lonesome? What if I'd croaked?

Or was that their intention?

Did they think I knew too much? Is that what had happened with Fred Hicks?

What if they came back for me?

I had to make like a banana and split.

But I didn't want to put back on my wet, pepper-sprayed clothes. Would I have to sneak out of the Motel 6 wearing only a towel?

Oh, God. I was going to have to call Mother, wasn't I? Then I'd have to tell her what had happened, how I'd put myself in grave danger by getting myself locked in a motel room with a couple of killers, or a killer and his mistress, anyway.

Another shot of pepper spray was almost more appealing, but there was no way around it.

I reached for the knob and turned. Pushed harder, finally getting my shoulder into the act, but the door wouldn't budge.

No, no, no!

They'd wedged something against the knob on the other side. Probably the desk chair.

If I were at the Ritz-Carlton, I could use the phone beside the toilet, an amenity that Motel 6 obviously didn't offer.

This couldn't be happening.

My voice didn't sound like much, more like a rasp than a howl, but I yelled as fervently as my lungs could bear and pounded on the door with my fists. When no one came to my aid, I began to bang on the walls. Surely someone would hear and call the front desk.

"Help, please . . . help!"

It was another fifteen minutes before I heard noises on the other side, and the door popped open to reveal a redheaded girl with a ponytail in a starched white shirt with a nametag that identified her as NANCY AMES, ASST. MANAGER. Alongside her stood a bemused older woman in a maid's uniform.

"Good Lord, chil'," the latter said, her drawl pure East Texas, "how in hell did ya get yourself stuck like this?"

"Bless you," I croaked and planted a kiss on her gray-frizzed head. Then I gripped the hand of the assistant manager and nearly pumped her arm off. "I was getting claustrophobic."

"Should we call someone for you? Maybe the police?" Ms. Ames tentatively asked. "Were you shut in on purpose? This room was registered to one of our regulars, Mr. Larry Jones, so if he did anything. . . ."

Maybe I should've told her to ring up the police, but instead, "It's just a small misunderstanding," came out raggedly through my lips. An understatement of the year if ever there was one.

She looked skeptical. "If you say so."

"I do." I would talk to the cops about Jim Bob myself.

"All right, we'll leave you alone then."

She shooed the housekeeper from the room, the older woman muttering again about "these crazy kids." I walked to the door, blinking at the piercing sunlight. I shielded my eyes with my hand and glanced across the parking lot to see my Jeep sitting a bit lower than it should have.

My gaze dropped to the tires, and I realized they were flat on the ground.

Son of a gun.

Someone — and I knew damned well who — had let the air out.

Did they think stranding me at the Motel 6 would keep me silent until they could get their stories straight for the police? Or worse, run off to Belize?

I bit my lip to keep from sobbing.

Slowly, I closed the door and retrieved my cell from the dresser where Jim Bob had flung it. I sighed with sheer joy when I heard the dial tone. Then I hit the button to speed-call Mother on her private line.

"Please, please, don't ask," I said the instant

my mother picked up on her end. "Just grab some clothes and shoes I can borrow, and come get me." To her credit, she made only a small noise of surprise when I told her my location. "Oh, and would you call AAA and tell them I have four flats?"

She didn't say a word other than to assure me she was on her way.

Not even to chastise me, and the mess I'd found myself mired in, or to bemoan how my life would have been so much easier if I'd gone to SMU and pledged Pi Phi.

Under any other circumstance, I would've assumed Cissy'd been lobotomized.

But, for now, I was grateful.

Mother wasn't nearly so quiet on the drive to the restaurant. I filled her in on the bare essentials of what I'd done: tracking down Julie and Jim Bob to the Motel 6 and accidentally getting doused with my own pepper spray. She didn't need to know that I thought Jim Bob was a cold-blooded killer. Since she saw for herself that I was shaken up, but alive, it opened the door for a genteel drubbing.

"You should've had Mr. Malone accompany you, at the very least. What in heaven's name were you thinking, going after those two alone?"

"Mo-ther." I dragged the word out into two long syllables.

"You must take after your uncle Darwin on

your father's side, because the Blevins certainly don't have any crazy people in our attics."

Ouch.

"You should've known better," she clucked. "I should ground you for a month."

"You can't ground me. I don't even live at home."

"Watch me."

I sighed and stared out the window of the Lexus, wishing she would cease and desist, but there was little hope of that.

Whatever she doled out, I had to take. She'd ridden to my rescue again, extricating me from a bind tighter than Grandmother's girdle. Not only had she taken care of my Jeep with a phone call to the mechanic who babied her Lexus — rather than AAA — but she'd brought me clothes from her own closet. The very back of her closet, I should say. I had on the navy blue short-sleeved silk sweat suit that I'd given her last Christmas, one she'd never worn. On my feet, a pair of her Ralph Lauren sneakers that were also brand new and half a size too small.

But I was hardly in a position to gripe. My wet clothes and shoes were rolled up and stowed in a plastic Motel 6 laundry bag in the trunk. My mother insisted on taking them to the dry cleaners for decontamination once I'd mentioned the pepper spray.

Before she'd let me into her car, she'd made me call Brian and relay the story to him via my cell phone. I felt like I'd been punished twice already.

"I told you to stay out of this from the beginning, didn't I?" She rubbed it in, her usually smooth drawl crisp around the edges. "Instead, you had to stick your nose where it didn't belong, and you nearly got yourself killed because of it."

"It was only pepper spray, Mother."

"Well, it didn't do a thing for your appearance. You look like something that Houston dentist ran over three times in her Mercedes."

"Thanks for the compliment."

I'd removed my contacts and added some eye drops before I'd donned my glasses, and my skin wasn't so red anymore. Whatever adverse effects I'd had from the chemicals had worn off, although the bad taste in my mouth remained. But it had little to do with the spray I'd swallowed.

Much as I hated to admit it, Cissy was right.

I'd screwed up.

I only hoped I hadn't done too much damage. I knew Jim Bob had enough money to disappear for parts unknown with his paramour, never to be heard from again. Was it too late to call his prayer line and put in a bid against that happening?

I guess I'd know soon enough if Julie had fled Dallas with him, since Jugs was fast approaching. I could already spot the huge billboard that towered over the Villa Mesa parking lot.

It wasn't yet ten o'clock, but at least one blue-and-white was already parked at the front of the building. Malone's blood-red Acura was there, too, and a dark sedan I didn't recognize.

Since it looked like the gang was all there, I asked Mother to slip the Lexus into a spot near the entrance.

She made a noise as she turned off the ignition. "Oh, pish, I nearly forgot."

"Forgot what?" I'd unhooked my seatbelt but remained in the seat.

"You asked me to dig into the Mothers Against Pornography, so that's what I did."

I sighed, about to tell her it didn't matter anymore, when she reached across me for the glove box, popped it open, and retrieved a black plastic box.

She dropped it into my lap. "I phoned that precious Cinda Lou Mitchell. . . ."

"Precious?" I muttered, prying the box open to reveal a cassette marked with a label that read MAP and last year's date.

". . . and I asked her if she could help me with a project I was doing, researching women's groups in the city that needed funding," she went on, hardly slowing down. "I inquired about footage her station might have on Mothers Against Porn and their protest targets, and she had this tape ready for me first thing this mornin'."

I wondered exactly what was on it, and if it

was even worth watching at this point, but I thanked her regardless.

She put her hand on my shoulder as I reached for the door handle.

"Andrea, darling, I'm not done."

I let go of the door and swiveled back around. "What else?" I whined, impatient to get inside.

"You wanted the story on the Women's Wellness Clinic and Peggy Martin, and I've got it, chapter and verse." She fiddled with a faceted rock on her finger that winked in the light spilling in through the windshield. "Peggy Martin used to be married to a prominent urologist at Medical City. Buffy Winspear's brother-in-law saw him for prostate problems, though he swears the surgery was botched because he ended up impotent."

I groaned. "Too much information."

She sniffed, ignoring me. "Peggy Martin and her husband were divorced some years ago, and she opened the clinic after she went back to school to get her nursing degree." She touched a pinky to her mouth, fixing her lipstick in the rearview. "Apparently, the money came from her settlement with Chet."

"So she got divorced from a urologist named Chet Martin? So what?"

I didn't see how this whiff of gossip would help Molly at all.

Mother reached for her Prada purse as she said, "No, honey, that's her name, not his. Buffy said she went back to Martin after the split. Her married name was Carter."

Carter?

My ears rang.

"Did you ask if they had a daughter?" I couldn't bear drawing this out any longer. "Is she named Sarah?"

"Of course, I asked," she snipped. "Buffy couldn't recall the girl's name specifically, but she did remember the Carters had tried to get the child into Hockaday. She was turned down, poor dear. You see, Donald Winspear was on the board and blamed Dr. Carter for the trouble with his, ah, equipment. . . ."

She kept on a while more, but I no longer listened.

I'd already heard enough.

My mother's girl talk with her pal Buffy Winspear had proven more fruitful than my trip to the Wellness Clinic. Now I knew that Sarah Carter wasn't just another Jugs waitress whom Bud had taken up with. She was Peggy Martin's daughter. Which made all the sense in the world. It explained Nurse Peggy's strong resistance to telling me where Sarah was and what had gone on between her and Hartman.

I couldn't wait to tell Malone.

Though I wasn't sure how important it was.

With Mother not far behind, I stuffed the videotape in my purse, scrambled out of the Lexus, and strode toward the building's entrance.

The double doors pushed open at my touch,

and I led Mother inside the hallowed walls of Jugs, only half-listening to her critique of the abominable décor as well as the dress and demeanor of the customers she'd seen when she'd barged in the other night.

The sound of raised voices led me straight to the locker rooms. As I entered, I spotted a hysterical Julie, a brown-suited Brian Malone, and a slender, balding fellow in a dark suit congregated with two uniformed cops and a jeans-clad guy with a ponytail and orange shirt that had HI-TECH printed in black letters across his shoulder blades.

"What the hell's going on?" Julie was ranting. "Just what do y'all think you're doing?"

All eyes were on her as the dark-suited man, whom I pegged as Assistant D.A. Lindstrom, calmly held out a baby-blue legal document to her, though she kept slapping it away.

Only Malone turned as I quietly slipped into the room with Mother on my heels. He raised his eyebrows, and I shrugged helplessly. I'd asked her to wait for me out in the dining room, but she'd politely declined. Apparently, she wanted to keep me in plain sight for the rest of my life.

Trying to remain unobtrusive, I stuck my hands in my trouser pockets and watched from the sidelines. I prayed Mother would do the same.

"You can't push me around like this!" Julie wailed. "I'll call my lawyer!"

"You can call an attorney if you want, Ms. Costello, but that won't change things," Lindstrom told her.

"What gives you the right to tear my place apart?"

"If you'd read the warrant, ma'am," he said and tried to present it again.

She smacked it away.

"Consider yourself served," he barked at her and stuck the document down the front of her open-necked T-shirt, where it wedged tightly in her cleavage. Since I'd seen Julie stash her tips there, it wasn't altogether a bad choice. "We've authority to search the premises for surveillance equipment that might yield evidence in the investigation of Bud Hartman's murder."

As Julie argued with him, I watched Malone make his way to my side.

He nodded at Mother before turning his attention on me. "Are you okay?"

"I'll survive."

If he noticed my eyes were still red behind my wire-rims, he didn't say a thing. And I liked him all the better for it.

"I've got news about Sarah Carter," I told him, and filled him in on what my mother had learned from her friend, that Sarah was Peggy Martin's kid, which would explain why Peggy acted so overprotective about the missing waitress.

When I'd finished, he said, "When we're through here, I want you to tell Lindstrom everything you know that relates to this investigation. And I mean *everything*."

I nodded.

Mother tapped my shoulder. "Is that the woman who paralyzed you with your own pepper spray?" she breathed in my ear.

"Hush," I warned her, turning back to Malone. He looked at me in the most extraordinary way, and I felt self-conscious and, worse, guilty. I hadn't exactly filled him in on my theory that Jim Bob was responsible for Bud's murder and Fred Hicks's insulin overdose, though I promised myself I'd tell him as soon as I could do it without whispering. I figured the surveillance tapes would prove Reverend Barker was guilty anyway, and I didn't want to distract him from the events at hand.

Which seemed to be getting interesting. "Did I miss much?" I asked.

"We're just getting started. Julie Costello hasn't exactly been cooperating."

Right on cue, she let out a hellacious scream.

"Stop, right there!" Julie shrieked as the Hi-Tech guy crouched atop the lockers and began to pry the ceiling fixture from its home, sending a shower of plaster down on those below.

"Careful, dammit! Do you have any clue what fixtures cost these days?"

Ignoring her cries, the ponytailed fellow kept working until he'd dislodged a small camera and transmitter. He disconnected the pieces and handed them down to one of the cops, before hopping to the floor. He pointed eagerly. "The rest of the stuff's in thirteen."

"Excuse me," Malone whispered, slipping away to join the circle of bodies that formed around lucky locker number 13. From where I stood, I could see it was bolted closed with a sturdy-looking Yale lock that seemed more apropos of a storage shed.

"Get it open," Lindstrom snapped to no one in particular, and one of the uniforms pulled his gun from his holster and took off the safety.

Julie flung herself in front of the locker, arms outspread. "You're not shooting anything, you got that?"

Lindstrom seemed to weigh his options for a moment before commanding, "Get the metal cutters from the trunk, would you? And, please, take Ms. Costello from the room, if you would. Perhaps she'd be more comfortable in the back of the squad car."

One of the boys in blue eagerly took Julie's arm and held on despite her attempts to shake him off. She caught sight of me as he futilely attempted to usher her toward the exit door.

"You! This is all your fault, you nosy bitch!" Julie glanced around her frantically, appealing to anyone who would listen. Her gaze stopped on Malone. She stabbed her finger at him. "Hey, I recognize you! You're the boyfriend who dumped her when she found out she was pregnant! Except none of it was real, was it?"

Mother's elbow bumped my ribs, but I didn't react.

"And you!" she turned her tirade upon Cissy. "You're the nutty Mother who stormed into the restaurant, aren't you?" Julie howled, "They were all spyin' on me, don't you get it?" Her voice spiraled higher, like an out-of-control soprano.

"Sweetie," my mother called to Julie in her best-honeyed drawl and pointed at her mouth. "You've got lipstick on your teeth, dear."

Julie instantly clammed up, and the cop was able to shepherd her from the locker room without further resistance.

"Mother," I scolded.

Cissy shrugged. "Well, she did."

The second cop returned with a tool that resembled oversized wire clippers. In the blink of an eye, he snapped the lock apart.

Lindstrom opened the locker to reveal what appeared to be a compact-sized VCR, even a tiny black-and-white monitor.

"It's got infrared digital surveillance capabilities with as high-powered a receiver as you can get anywhere," the Hi-Tech guy explained as he poked and prodded the thing until it spit out a videocassette, which he held out like a trophy. "Looks like this has the most recent images. It can print them out as individual frames, or you can view it like a video."

Malone's sideways glance met mine.

"The machine time and date stamps everything, so you'll know exactly when all the images were shot," the Hi-Techie went on.

"Thanks for your cooperation." Lindstrom took the cassette from him. "I'll copy the thing for you, Malone, after I've had a chance to look it over downtown."

I tugged on Brian's sleeve. "There's a VCR and TV in the office," I told him.

He turned to Lindstrom. "If you don't mind, Jed, I'd like to take a peek at the video now. Its contents could potentially vindicate my client, and I'd hate for her to stay locked up a minute longer than necessary. I'd also like for Ms. Kendricks here to take a look." The faint stammer kicked into gear, "S-she might be able to help us identify people on the tape. She has, er, an inside knowledge of the restaurant."

Lindstrom eyed me skeptically.

"C'mon, Jed," Malone turned persuasive. "Don't you want to make sure you've got the right person in jail?"

Lindstrom softened. "Okay, I'll give you this one, but you owe me."

"Lead the way, Andy," Malone said.

After begging my mother to wait for me in the dining room, I left the yellow lockers behind and marched up the hallway to Bud's office.

Malone and the assistant D.A. entered after me. Lindstrom closed the door.

It wasn't difficult for them to spot the electronics equipment behind Bud's desk. They made a beeline to it and switched on the TV so that a blue screen popped up. Then Lindstrom pushed the cassette in the VCR and pressed "play."

The television went from blue to fuzzy for a minute before the locker room came into focus from a bird's-eye view. The wide-angled image was a crisp black and white. For several long moments, the room stood empty, the time ticking off the seconds at half-past six in the morning. Lindstrom fast-forwarded it until people came into view.

The lunch shift, I realized, recognizing Rhonda, Christie, and Ginger, feeling almost queasy peering down at them while they undressed to don their uniforms.

I closed my eyes.

"Move it ahead, would you," Malone asked.

After forwarding and pausing half a dozen more times, Lindstrom finally paused the tape when the date stamp showed midnight on the eve of Bud's murder.

Girls went in and out, touching up makeup, fixing a ponytail, shedding clothing. I knew most of the names and reeled them off when I could. Then, at around eight o'clock, there was Julie, dragging Molly into the changing room, holding her by the arm as they had what appeared to be a heated conversation.

"Julie Costello and Molly O'Brien," I said, my mouth dry. "I'll bet that's when Julie asked Molly to close for her. I know Molly didn't want to. She never liked to be alone with Bud after that one . . . mistake."

"Thanks for the running commentary, Ms. Kendricks," Lindstrom remarked.

Malone squeezed my hand.

But I paid no attention to either of them. My eyes were glued to the screen.

Lindstrom forwarded the tape carefully, through long periods of nothing, stopping every now and again when someone came into view.

And then it was midnight, and the lights went out in the locker room, allowing the invisible infrared beams from the camera to take over. No wonder Bud had paid through the nose for the equipment. The images stayed crisp, the details virtually as vivid as before. There was Molly, tugging off her uniform and pulling on her street clothes. As she did, Bud appeared on the edge of the screen, lingering near the doorway and then moving closer.

I felt afraid, even then. The hair bristled on my arms. Because I knew what was coming, and I couldn't do a thing to stop it.

Molly pulled her shirt over her head, leaving the hem outside her blue jeans, and turned around, coming face to face with Hartman, his broad form blocking her escape.

She did a little two-step and slipped past him, though his hand reached for her as she went by, before he followed her and disappeared from the frame.

I could imagine the next few minutes as the time stamp slowly ticked them off on the screen.

Bud catching up to Molly and pushing her against the counter in the kitchen. Pinning her beneath him, giving her no choice but to reach behind her for the knife and to strike out at him.

I stared at the colorless locker room on the monitor.

It was deserted.

I ached for someone else to show up, to prove Molly wasn't the last one who'd seen Bud alive, but there was nothing there.

Nothing.

My heart sank.

"Well, looks like the show's over, folks," Lindstrom declared, and he moseyed over to the VCR.

"Wait," I said, seeing something in the corner of the screen.

Lindstrom hesitated.

The locker room was no longer empty.

A figure appeared, lurking at the edge of the room, keeping against the wall and inching toward the doorway. I squinted, as if that might help me detect a gait pattern, a distinct feature, anything more than a sturdy backside and the top of a baseball hat.

"Someone else was there," I said, though Malone and Lindstrom saw it, too. I felt Malone's fingers settle over mine.

Was it Jim Bob?

Or Sarah?

"Freeze it, Jed!" he hissed, and the assistant D.A. caught the VCR in time to pause the frame as the figure stepped into the doorway.

It was hard to make out much beyond a body clothed in dark-hued top and pants, maybe a sweat suit. The bill of the baseball cap hid the face so all I could delineate was a vague curve of a chin.

I couldn't tell who it was, but I knew what it meant.

Fresh hope bubbled inside me. I could hardly breathe; the realization was so overwhelming.

"This changes everything," Malone announced, voicing my thoughts exactly. "It proves Molly O'Brien was not alone with Hartman the night he was killed."

"Let's not be hasty, my friend. But it does bear looking into," Lindstrom agreed, albeit reluctantly. "Do you recognize our mystery man?"

"I can't see squat." Malone shook his head. "What about you, Andy?"

I took a step closer to the television screen, as if that would help my vision. The odd upper-deck view didn't help. Neither did my recent pepper-spray episode, which made things blur the more I stared. Something did strike me as odd, but it was hard to put into words. Maybe it was the shoes. I couldn't visualize them, couldn't see if they had laces or stripes. It was almost as if the person wore slippers. But I kept that to myself, preferring not to be laughed out of the room by a sarcastic assistant D.A.

Sighing, I gave up. "I can't tell anything from this."

Malone gently patted my back. "The police can analyze the tape, digitally enhance it. Maybe that'll make whoever it is more identifiable."

"I hope so."

Because it was the best shot Molly had.

After the viewing, I talked to Lindstrom for nearly forty-five minutes while one of the officers took notes. I didn't leave anything out, and my detailed description of the night before had Malone turning purple. I couldn't look at him without my voice cracking.

When I was done, Lindstrom told me they were taking Julie down to the station house for questioning. He also was sending a squad car to bring in Jim Bob Barker. Lindstrom seemed particularly interested in grilling the preacher after hearing about the man's diabetic wife, his affair with Julie Costello, and Bud's blackmailing him. The Reverend Barker certainly had some " 'splaining to do," as Desi used to say to Lucy.

The surveillance equipment and tapes from the restaurant were packed up for review downtown along with what they'd recovered from Bud's condominium. I suggested they have a chat with Peggy Martin at some point to find out where her daughter went and if she was okay.

Something about the elusive Sarah Carter still rattled me.

Malone volunteered to take me home after a cell phone call confirmed that Mother's mechanic had returned my Jeep to my condo, all four tires full of air. Cissy only let me go after fussing over me for a few long minutes, tucking my hair behind my ears, and adjusting the collar on the sweat-top. If it had been anyone but Brian, I doubt she would've let me go.

On the way to my place, Brian let me have it. He ranted on about my ill-advised involvement in the case and how I should never have trailed Jim Bob to the motel alone. I sat there and took it until he parked in front of my unit — right beside my resurrected Jeep — when he finally stopped to draw a breath.

At which point, I leaned over and pressed my finger to his lips.

"Zip it," I ordered.

He looked hard at me, ruffled hair falling onto his brow, his glasses slightly askew. "But, Andy," he tried to protest, only to find my entire palm over his mouth.

It was my turn.

"I'm going inside, where I'm taking off this dreadful outfit and these shoes that pinch my toes, then I'm soaking in a bathtub until the past week is a memory. Oh, and I'll watch a little TV when I'm done." I thought of the MAP videotape inside my purse that Cinda Lou Mitchell had kindly provided. "And I will not answer my phone, so don't even try calling me. I need peace and quiet."

That said, I turned to grab the door handle, but he caught my wrist.

"If Jim Bob really murdered two men, you got lucky last night, you know. He could've killed you, Andy."

Where had I heard that before? He was beginning to sound an awful lot like my mother.

My eyes slid back to his, and I did my best to smile, though it faltered more than I would've liked. "Hey, I'm okay. And Molly's going to be even better than that soon, right? Oh, geez, and David will be ecstatic."

He reached out to tuck a thumb beneath my chin, and I felt warm in all the right places. "Promise me that your detecting days are over. You took a lot of foolish risks in the name of friendship, and, while I admire your chutzpah, I hope you never do anything as ludicrous as that again."

I blinked, not feeling warm all over anymore.

Just hot under the collar.

I knew I'd think of something brilliant to say later, but, for now, I couldn't even form the smallest word on my tied tongue. Instead, I inched away from him, let myself out, and slammed the door with such force that the Acura rocked.

"Andy!"

"Stuff it," I shouted over my shoulder.

He opened his window and yelled after me as I hurried up the sidewalk to my condo, but I didn't turn around.

Once inside, I peered through the drapes to find Malone still sitting in the car, right where I'd left him, and frustration swept through me.

Your detecting days are over. Foolish. Ludicrous.

What had he expected me to do, for God's sake?

Stay home, eating bonbons and sipping tea, watching soap operas, and putting this silly murder investigation out of my pretty head while Molly was still locked up?

Not a chance.

Didn't he realize I was the girl who'd bucked the system (his own words)? Who'd given up her deb ball because her heart wasn't in it and who'd squashed her mother's dreams by going to art school in Chicago?

If he didn't understand that I'd never be the kind of woman who colored inside the lines, then he wasn't the man I'd hoped he was.

He finally drove away in a screech of tires, and I let the curtains drop.

Hey, my relationship with Malone had lasted longer than some of my blind dates, I mused, trying to cheer myself up.

But the thought didn't make me feel better.

Chapter 25

 A soak in the tub with my favorite Crabtree & Evelyn bath gel, Lily of the Valley, might've made me smell like something that bloomed in Mother's garden, but it didn't do much to improve my mood. I was still upset with Malone and had an unsettled feeling in my stomach about Bud's murder, Jim Bob Barker, and Sarah. Something still didn't fit, but I couldn't put my finger on it.

My hair wrapped in a towel, I plunked down on my sofa to watch the videotape Cissy had retrieved from Cinda Lou Mitchell. It was a compilation of Mothers Against Porn protests that Cinda's station had covered in the previous year or so, beginning with a parade of marches against strip clubs, anywhere from a dozen to fifty women holding placards and chanting things like, "Clean Up Our City, Sweep Up Smut!" Peggy Martin was always among them, leading the troops.

The tape was twenty minutes long, and I nearly turned it off halfway through. Until something I saw made me sit up. I turned the sound up and listened to Cinda Lou chatter about a protest outside a peep show near Love Field. She noted in a brief follow-up that the group was successful in getting the place closed down.

I stopped and played the tape again at least three times before I hit the pause and froze it on a single frame.

The Mothers Against Porn stood in front of a small building with a neon sign shaped like a pair of legs that shimmered pink. The name of the club flickered off and on.

NUDE 'N NAUGHTY.

Fred Hicks had been found in his car, parked at that very spot.

The synapses in my brain started firing off in rapid succession.

One question in particular I couldn't shake.

What if Jim Bob Barker didn't kill Bud or go after Fred Hicks? What if it was someone else? Someone who had a beef against Bud and who had access to insulin?

Oh, crap, had I pegged the wrong person?

Was it possible Jim Bob was innocent? Okay, not as in "pure as the driven snow," but at least not guilty of stabbing Bud Hartman.

My doubts nipping at my heels, I scrambled from the couch and into the bathroom to toss off the terrycloth turban. I grabbed my blow dryer and fixed my hair in two minutes flat. My eyes still sore from the pepper spray, I left my glasses on and didn't bother with makeup. I pulled on faded jeans and a multicolored Lycra Tee, grabbed the videotape and my handbag, and rushed out the door as my phone started ringing.

On the drive, my mind kept going over everything I'd seen and heard, looking for a telling moment that would assure me I was doing the right thing.

But I didn't have any proof, just my instincts.

I had to talk to Peggy Martin.

Once I arrived, I didn't do anything but try to remain unobtrusive. I sat in the Jeep outside the Women's Wellness Clinic for nearly half an hour in the shade of an oak tree. Though I had my windows rolled down, the afternoon heat was uncomfortable to say the least. Sweat dampened the hair at my neck and stuck my clothing to my skin.

I waited to make my move, until the time was right.

I watched people come and go through the front door, and I stayed put until the parking lot emptied out at noon and the security guard took a break, going off around the side of the building for a smoke.

Now.

Just as I was about to get out of the car, my cell phone chirped loudly.

I snatched it from my bag and snapped, "Mother, I can't talk. . . ."

"It's Malone . . . please, don't hang up."

I nearly did. "I'm busy, Brian, so don't. . . ."

"I'm at the D.A.'s office," he ran over my protest. "The crime lab techs are enhancing the tape from the locker room, and they're convinced the unidentified person is a woman, not a man. It's definitely not Jim Bob Barker, because he's over six feet, and they figure this person is five feet six at the most."

"I could've told you that," I snapped, still steamed.

"What do you mean?" he asked. "What aren't you telling me?"

No more games, I decided. So I stopped playing coy. "I'm at the Women's Wellness Clinic to see Peggy Martin one more time. I think she murdered Bud," I told him. "And tried to kill Hicks, too."

"What?" I held the phone away from my ear.

"She's a nurse, Brian. She has access to syringes and insulin, and even latex gloves and surgical garb. She could've done it all without leaving a clue."

"Andy, you need to go home. Let the police handle it from here on out."

"You'd still be twiddling your thumbs while Molly rotted away in Lew Sterrett if I hadn't been involved," I reminded him, wondering why I'd ever thought he'd see my side of things when he was so obviously nearsighted.

"Twiddling my thumbs? What I'm doing is working within the system, which is how it's got to be from this point forward. So let it go. I'll call Lindstrom and get someone down there. . . ."

I had too much on my mind to argue.

"Goodbye, Malone."

I pushed "end" and returned the cell to my purse.

Then I took a deep breath, hopped down from the Jeep, squared my shoulders, and strode across the parking lot.

"Can I help you?" The receptionist glanced up from her desk as I entered. She was not the same woman I'd seen the day before.

"It's all right, Jackie. I'll take care of her."

Peggy Martin appeared in the doorway behind the front desk.

"Go get a cup of coffee," she urged the young woman. "It's a slow afternoon."

The receptionist eagerly took her up on her offer and scurried off.

I didn't see another soul. The waiting room was deserted.

"I know why you're here," Peggy said, the face framed by the gray cap of hair wearing a resigned expression. She didn't look menacing, merely sad, and I couldn't imagine she'd ever hurt me.

Without another word, she motioned that I follow her, and I went. She led me back to the same empty examination room where we'd chatted the day before. Very deliberately this time, she closed the door.

I heard the soft click of the lock and the noisy shuffle of her feet on the floor as she took a couple steps toward me.

"You've found out, haven't you?" she said before I'd opened my mouth. "You've learned that Sarah is my daughter."

"I'm not the only one who's aware of that, Peggy." I set my purse on the countertop, beside the boxes of disposable supplies — tongue depressors, thermometer covers, latex gloves, and plastic syringes. I saw something else I hadn't noticed before in the corner. A locked cabinet filled with medicine. "The police found videotapes and recording equipment at Bud's condo," I informed her. "They have computer files he kept with names and dates. Sarah's on the list."

"But those tapes . . . they were destroyed." Peggy's skin appeared so white against her navy blue scrubs. "He turned them over to her, and she burned them."

So Peggy had known about the tapes? Why hadn't she told the police from the start?

Now I was confused. "Why would he do that? He wasn't the kind of man who did good deeds."

"Because I" — her chin trembled — "I threatened to destroy him, if he didn't. I swore I'd kill, burn the restaurant down, whatever it took. He was ruining her life. God knows how many other lives he wrecked as well."

She'd trusted Bud to do right by Sarah?

I wanted to laugh. She couldn't possibly be that naïve. I'd never met Bud Hartman, but I already knew he was a habitual liar and a blackmailing cheat.

"They've collected the surveillance equipment from the bedroom at Bud's home and from the locker room at Jugs."

"The locker room?"

That threw her for a loop. She wavered, but caught the edge of the countertop to steady herself.

So she hadn't known, not about the camera at the restaurant.

I didn't want to do this, but I had no choice.

"They're going over the evidence now," I told her. "Especially the tape from the night of the murder. There's someone on it . . . someone besides Molly, which proves she wasn't the last one who saw Bud. They know it was a woman." I forced myself to look in her panicked eyes. "Molly didn't kill him, Ms. Martin. But that's no surprise to you."

"A tape . . . from that night?" she echoed.

"Made by a digital camera with infrared lighting so even darkness is as clear as day."

She swayed again. "They've seen . . . everything?"

I didn't answer. I wanted her to believe it.

Faking a calm I didn't feel, I asked, "Why don't you tell me about Sarah and Bud? If I understand what happened, maybe I can help you."

"Oh, God," Peggy said, voice cracking, a rush of tears skidding down her cheeks. "You can't imagine what she went through, you can't begin to know. It crushed her when she found out what he'd done. That he'd filmed them together

354

and was selling tapes of them on the web. She begged him not to, and he just laughed at her. Told her it was all in fun. Can you imagine? All in fun." She spat out the words, hatred filling her eyes, brighter than tears.

We stood barely five feet apart in the tiny exam room, the smell of disinfectant surrounding us. A small shiver tickled my spine, but I refused to be afraid of Peggy Martin. I honestly didn't believe I was in danger. She looked so benign, standing there in her dark scrubs, nametag pinned to her breast, tears in her eyes, devastated.

She started to pace, and the rustle of her steps on the floor drew my gaze down to her feet.

Oh, man.

I flashed back to the freeze frame on the TV, the figure in a baseball cap and dark clothes, and those odd-looking shoes, like slippers.

She paused suddenly and saw what I was staring at.

"We had in-patient surgeries this morning. I'd forgotten to remove them. Do they bother you?" She gestured down at the protective booties covering her sneakers.

Did they bother me?

I shook my head numbly.

It was all there, right in front of me: the booties, gloves, scrubs, and syringes. The easy access to drugs, like insulin.

I had no doubt anymore.

It was Peggy.

She'd killed Bud and put Fred Hicks into a coma.

Instead of fear, I felt depressed.

"Where is Sarah?" I asked, because I wanted to be sure she was somewhere safe and not alone.

"At her grandmother's in Omaha," Peggy said, chin trembling. "She's afraid everyone will find out, that someone will see the tape and recognize her. She can't hold her head up anymore. She might never be the same again." The front of her smock was blotched with her tears, and the hands she clutched at her breasts shook like palsy. She was this close to shattering to pieces. "He was the first man she'd ever been with. The first one, don't you get it? She believed she was in love with him, and he robbed her of her innocence completely." She shook her head. "Sarah was never the same after I divorced her father. She was like a lost little girl. We fought all the time, and I *know* she went to work at Jugs to spite me. I arranged the protests there to watch over her, but it wasn't enough, was it?"

I wanted to reach out to her, to reassure her with a touch, to tell her things would be all right. But that was too big a lie, one I couldn't even bring myself to tell.

Besides, what she'd done had put my friend in jail.

I couldn't forget that, no matter how hard I tried.

"You stabbed Bud Hartman."

It seemed to take a minute for her to digest what I'd said.

Then, abruptly, she laughed. The sound made me jump, it was so unexpected.

"I only wish I'd done something sooner. Then my baby would never have been hurt. She'd still be whole. She'd be home." She hung her head, adding hoarsely, "I should have stopped him long ago."

"You went to see him that night." The scenario played in my head, how it must have gone down. "You had on dark scrubs and a baseball hat, and you wore booties to cover your shoes and latex gloves so you wouldn't leave prints. You hid until after the restaurant closed and everyone left. But Molly was still there. She'd stayed to help Bud."

She didn't interrupt to tell me I was wrong, so I kept going.

"You saw what happened between them. You watched him attack her . . . watched her grab the knife and cut him in the face. And then you picked up the knife after she ran out, and you plunged it deep into his back."

Peggy shook all over, and she hugged herself as if that would steady her.

It didn't.

"I wanted to make him suffer for what he did to my baby. I wanted him to hurt the way that he'd hurt her." Mucus ran from her nose, wetting her lips. "I'd brought along a syringe filled with insulin. I wanted to scare him, to make him sick and afraid of me, scared enough to leave the girls alone." Her eyes flickered, moving, reliving it all over again. "If he hadn't forced himself on your friend, he might still be alive. If he had only let her go."

"I'm sorry," I said, because I couldn't think of anything else. "I'm sorry for what happened to Sarah. I'm sorry for you." But there was more I had to know. "What about Fred Hicks? Why'd you go after him, too?"

She wiped a hand beneath her nose. "He saw me leave the restaurant before he found the body. He knew who I was, because of the protests. He'd learned I was divorced from a doctor and that I'd opened the clinic, so he figured I had money. He called me here and demanded I pay him or he'd go to the police and tell them I was the one who murdered Hartman."

"How much did he want?"

"Fifty thousand."

My mouth formed an *O*, and I realized it might as well have been fifty million to someone like Peggy Martin. Hicks had been wrong in assuming Peggy had cash to spare, if my mother's sources at the Junior League had gotten it right about her pouring her divorce settlement into funding the clinic. No wonder she'd felt so backed against the wall.

"I didn't have that much, and there was no way I could get it." She paced the room once more before she slumped against the exam room door. "Hicks was heading to the airport and wanted the cash before he took off, so I arranged to meet him behind the closed-up peep show. I wore clean scrubs and booties, and I had on gloves, but it was too dark for him to notice until it was too late. I shot him up with the insulin, and he reacted to it quickly. I waited until he was unconscious, then I checked his pockets. He had nearly five thousand in cash in an envelope inside his jacket."

The missing money from the bank deposit bag. Hicks had stolen it.

"I figured he wouldn't be needing it, so I took it." Her eyes begged me to understand. "The clinic is always running in the red, and I put it to good use, thinking it would help make up for what . . . what I'd done." She flung her arms in the air, and then wrapped them around her middle. "It's all his fault. All . . . his . . . fault."

I blamed Bud Hartman, too, for all the trouble he'd caused.

"You'll have to talk to the police," I said softly, taking a cautious step toward her. "You can't let another woman — another mother — pay for a crime she didn't commit."

"I know," she sobbed, sliding down against the door, sinking to the floor, and burying her head in her knees. "I know, I know, I know."

I thought I'd feel different when I found the truth, when I'd proved Molly's innocence. Like I'd won the lottery.

But I didn't.

"Kendricks, are you in there?"

A fist pounded the door.

Malone.

"Is everything all right? Can you hear me?"

He banged again.

"Andy?"

"I'm okay," I called back, quickly lifting my glasses to rub the damp from my eyes, while across the room, Peggy Martin moaned and rocked herself, wounded beyond repair. "It's going to be all right," I told him.

Another lie.

One too many.

Chapter 26

 "Would you like more tea, Andy?"

I glanced up into Sandy's smiling face and shook my head. "No, thanks. I'm fine." My glass of iced tea was still more than half full.

"How about you, Cissy?"

"Just a little would be lovely."

Sandy topped off her glass, set down the pitcher, then descended the stone steps toward the lawn below where David rolled around on the grass with the new puppy Mother had given him. At least it was a cocker spaniel and not a Great Dane, so maybe Molly wouldn't have a heart attack when she saw the pair when Malone arrived with her — I checked my wristwatch — any minute.

I looked over to the chaise longue where Mother had settled herself. She'd donned a hat and sunglasses to protect herself from the sun streaming on the back terrace. All she needed was a cigarette in one of those long holders, and she'd have been a dead ringer for Gloria Swanson in *Sunset Boulevard*.

Okay, maybe not a dead ringer, but close enough.

She caught me grinning at her and said, "You certainly look like the cat who swallowed the canary."

I didn't let on to her what I'd actually been thinking. I doubt she would've found the comparison to Norma Desmond flattering.

Instead, I tipped my chin toward the lawn, where David and Sandy alternated tossing a ball to the puppy. "I do believe you're going to miss him."

"Oh, for heaven's sake," she said and sniffed, closing her *Town & Country* with a snap and setting it down in her lap. But I saw the twitch of emotion at her mouth, and I knew I was right.

"Mother?"

"Well, he is well behaved."

"Molly's a good mom," I quietly commented.

Though Cissy didn't agree with me, neither did she disagree. Which I figured boded well for Molly. Mother could have just as easily made a snide comment about "that scholarship girl" who'd been arrested for murder.

But she didn't.

"Maybe you could help her out," I dared to suggest. "You know everyone who's anyone in Dallas. She can't go back to Jugs, and she has to support herself and David. She always did love fashion, so maybe Terry Costa or the Gazebo?"

"I might be able to arrange something," she

362

murmured from beneath the wide brim of her hat, and I knew it was as good as done.

"I want to tell you how, um, great you've been through all of this, Mother, and how much I, uh, appreciate your, er, assistance," I stammered, sounding like Malone when he got riled up. My family didn't do emotions well. They were awkward. Like hugs. Neither the Blevins nor the Kendricks had ever embraced sentimentality. Believe it or not, I was the sappiest of the bunch.

She turned to me, pulling her 1930s-style Donna Karan shades down to the tip of her powdered nose to reveal the twinkle in her pale blue gaze. "You might not feel so grateful when you find out what it'll cost you."

I sank back against the cushions and groaned. "I'll accept whatever punishment you dish out. Just *please* don't recruit me to walk the runway at one of your charity fashion shows. You know how I hate to play dress up."

"Really? So those purple shorts and tight T-shirt were, what, a new look for you?"

Oh, hell.

I turned to glare at her, and she winked.

The second time she'd done that in a week. What was going on?

"I think you'll rather enjoy what I've got planned for you, Andrea, dear. I certainly will," she added with a laugh as disconcerting as breaking crystal.

"Mother." I didn't like the sound of this. In

fact, it frightened me. "Maybe we should talk about whatever you. . . ."

My plea was drowned out by a joyful squeal. "Mommy!"

David dropped the red ball he'd been about to toss to the cocker and rushed across the lawn as Molly and Malone appeared around the corner of the house.

Getting to my feet, I scurried over to the low stone wall and waited, a shiver dashing up my spine as I watched Molly lift her son into her arms. She held on to him, burying her face in his shoulder, turning round and round until I thought she might fall down, dizzy.

"Baby, my baby," I heard her saying over and over as she planted kisses on his face.

"I wanted to make him suffer for what he did to my baby."

For an instant, Peggy Martin's sobs rang in my ears.

I had to remind myself that life wasn't always fair.

Molly let David down, and they both fell to the grass, giggling.

Her gaze came to rest on me, and I grinned.

The smile she gave me in return made me feel like I floated on air.

Okay, maybe life *was* fair on occasion.

Malone loped up the stone steps and stood beside me.

"So it's over," I said as he tried to smooth down wavy hair ruffled by the wind.

"It's definitely over," he assured me. "All charges against Molly have been dropped. They couldn't hold her, not after they had Peggy Martin's confession and the digitally enhanced tape."

"Poor Peggy," I whispered, turning so that my hip touched the low wall. "It's all so horrible."

"Poor Peggy stabbed a man to death and put another man in a coma," Malone said, as if I needed reminding. He loosened the paisley-print tie at his throat and unbuttoned the top buttons of his starched yellow shirt.

"Bud had violated her daughter, or have you forgotten?" I nudged him with my foot. "And Fred Hicks tried to blackmail her. They weren't exactly shining examples of human nature."

"Point taken, but that doesn't justify double murder, which is what the D.A.'s going to charge her with since Hicks won't make it off life support." He crossed his arms and looked at me in that earnest way of his that reminded me of Jimmy Stewart. "Ms. Martin can plead temporary insanity and take her chances in court. If she gets a sympathetic jury, maybe she'll get off with a stay at a mental health facility. A *long* stay, if you get my drift."

As in the rest of her life. I got it.

"It's one of those cases where no one comes out a winner," he remarked, and, for once, I didn't argue with him.

"I still don't understand why no one ever pressed charges against Hartman. If just one waitress he'd harassed had spoken up, had actually gone to the authorities, maybe none of this would ever have happened."

"Most people tend to avoid conflict if they can," Malone said and pressed a finger to the bridge of his glasses to hike them up. "Sometimes it's easier to ignore a bad situation, pretend it doesn't exist."

He was probably right.

Still, if there was one thing my father had taught me — and my mother, too, mostly by example — it was never to take crap from anyone.

If you didn't stand up for yourself, no one would.

The puppy barked, and I turned to see David on his knees, arms around the wiggling creature. Molly knelt at his side, a hand on his arm as if she were afraid to let him go.

"She's lucky to have you, Andy," Malone remarked, and his fingers brushed mine so that I thought he'd take hold.

But he didn't.

"If it weren't for you, she'd still be in jail with a pretty bleak road ahead of her. I don't know too many people who'd go to the lengths you did in order to bail out a friend you hadn't spoken to in years."

"You don't understand." I sighed, still watching David and Molly.

"Try me."

I took a deep breath and hoped I wouldn't sound like a fool. "If you're lucky in life, you'll meet at least one person who's true-blue," I started gingerly, not sure how to explain the bond Molly and I had forged or if it could even be explained at all. "Molly was like that. She didn't care how I looked or what I wore or if my daddy was rich. She liked me for myself, or maybe in spite of myself." I shrugged. "You don't forget friends like that."

His mouth curved upward, a silly grin that made me wonder if he were mocking me.

"Maybe that sounds silly." I couldn't look at him.

"No," he said. "It doesn't sound silly at all."

"Oh." I stared down at my hands, embarrassed regardless.

He toed me with his loafer. "Hey, you're not the only one who's loyal to a fault."

I squinted up at him.

"Seems the cops couldn't get Reverend Jim Bob to 'fess up to being blackmailed by Hartman or anyone else. He wouldn't even admit to having an affair with Julie Costello. Just claimed they were good friends who prayed together now and then."

"Oh, God." I couldn't believe it. "So that means Julie's still got Jim Bob by his, um, collection plate?" I actually felt sorry for the guy. "So who was it who said crime doesn't pay?"

"Well, I know that it wasn't a lawyer."

Epilogue

 I climbed the staircase leading to the foyer at the Morton Meyerson Symphony Center, listening to the click-clack of my footsteps on the peach marble as I carefully ascended in the high-heeled Manolo Blahnik sandals that Mother had insisted I wear that evening.

"Come now, Andrea, quit dawdling," Cissy scolded from behind.

I sighed, picking up the pace as much as I could without falling on my face. Above us, the tinkle of piano keys resonated, floating above the hum of voices.

I emerged into the foyer and hesitated, surveying the crowd in black tie and gowns that milled about with champagne flutes in hand.

Mother came up beside me and hooked an arm through my elbow. "Please, Andrea, try to look happy to be here. It's a benefit, not a funeral. No one died."

Oh, yes. Someone had.

Me.

Or, at least, I wished I were dead. Better than to be here amongst a host of Mother's friends who would no doubt chat about me behind my back, reminding each other that I was the debutante dropout. The daughter of a Blevins and a Kendricks who was a no-show at her own coming out.

I started to cringe, until I caught myself.

So what?

Who cares if they did yap about me?

At least I'd give them something more interesting to discuss than which Thomas, Richard, or Harriet had faces lifted, tummies tucked, or noses bobbed since the last Symphony gala.

I held my head high, relieved to find my sense of humor intact. I'd need it for the next several hours, because there was no backing out.

This was my repayment to Mother for her allowing David to stay at her house and for keeping him out of the hands of social services. Oh, and for the snooping she'd done, for which she seemed inordinately pleased with herself.

One night, I told myself.

"An Evening at the Symphony" to benefit Children's Medical Center. One thousand smackeroos per ticket. With Cristal and dancing in the foyer prior to the night's performance of Handel and Beethoven.

I had survived blind dates far worse than this.

"Oh, look, Andrea, there's a friend of yours." Cissy nudged me, and I scanned the gaggle of glitterati to find the familiar face.

"Mother," I said under my breath.

Brian Malone walked toward us.

"Go on," she hissed in my ear, giving me a less-than-gentle shove.

I stumbled forward, nearly falling from the heights of my unsensible shoes, though I steadied myself and smoothed down the front of my blue raw silk dress. Another item Mother had insisted on. It clung to my skin in a way that made me feel more naked than the hot pants at Jugs.

Malone tugged at the cuffs of his tuxedo as he approached, looking strangely grateful to see me. But not at all surprised.

"Wow, Kendricks," he said and took me in with wide eyes. "Is it really you?"

Mother had made me go with her to José Eber's in the afternoon to have my hair and makeup done, and I felt like a complete fraud, certainly not like the Andrea Kendricks who'd defied her mother and Dallas society in one fell swoop.

"You look great, too," I told him, and he blushed.

He bent closer so I could hear him over the pianist and the schmoozing. "You want to dance?"

I stared at him. "Do you?"

"As a matter of fact, I do." He took my hand in his and led me over to the area where couples gracefully swirled, twirled, and dipped. I only hoped I wouldn't step on his toes. I doubtless could maim him pretty good with my spiked heels.

He pulled me close, and I inhaled the smell of him, the scent of soap on his skin beneath his lime-tinged aftershave.

"What a coincidence that you're here," I got out.

"It's no coincidence, Andy."

I wrinkled my brow. "Oh?"

"Cissy invited me," he said.

"She did?"

"I'm surprised you didn't know."

"Mother's full of surprises."

My eyes narrowed, I peered over his shoulder and spied her across the foyer.

She was watching us.

Beaming.

I hadn't seen her look that pleased in years, since she'd found the pear-shaped gold Judith Leiber bag at Neimans. On sale.

"Is everything all right, Andy?"

"Never better," I snapped.

"I thought it was pretty generous of her," Malone remarked. "She picked up my tab."

"For the ticket?"

"Yes, that, too. And for Molly's defense."

My feet stopped moving, and Malone bumped into me. "I told you I'd handle your fee," I said, caught between disbelief that Cissy would've helped out "that scholarship girl" and miffed that she'd done it without telling me.

"Well, don't worry, your mother took care of everything."

She certainly had, I thought, amazed at how

371

quickly Mother worked. I swear, if she'd been as good at science as she was at manipulation, she would've been making nuclear weapons with her Little Miss Chemistry set while the other kids were concocting stink bombs.

"Cissy arranged for us to sit together during the program," he said, his breath tickling my ear. He held me so near I could feel his heart beat against mine. "And then, afterward, she suggested drinks at the Mansion in the Library."

"Mother is too thoughtful," I replied, dripping sarcasm, but he seemed oblivious.

I gazed up at his smiling face and wondered if he had the slightest idea what he'd gotten himself into.

He bent over to whisper, "I say we lose your mom at intermission and go find a burger joint that'll serve a gorgeous brunette and a lawyer in a monkey suit."

Then again, maybe he did.

About the Author

SUSAN McBRIDE was born in Kansas City, Missouri, and earned a B.S. in journalism at the University of Kansas, graduating with Distinction. Vowing that nothing would get in the way of her "novel" ambitions, she moved to Dallas and worked a variety of odd jobs in order to support her writing endeavors. Ms. McBride is the author of three novels in her Maggie Ryan series and is founder of The Deadly Divas, a group of four "sassy scribes" who tour the country. She currently lives in St. Louis, Missouri, and you can visit her Web site at *www.susanmcbride.com*.